MIDNIGHT SKIES

"After you left Zimbabwe, I could think of nothing but you. I came here thinking, perhaps I could scoop you up, take you back with me."

Sela leaned away from Jonathan. "What exactly do you mean?"

His gaze stayed on her and he spoke softly, barely moving his lips. "I could see us together in the camp."

"And?"

He looked away, his profile firm yet gentled by the warmth of the moment. "Together always."

Arranging her coat around her, she managed to put distance between them. Was he talking marriage? Then she turned toward him and found his arms waiting to receive her.

Jonathan's lips teased hers again, his hands under her wrap molding her waist, rubbing her back.

"We're right together," he murmured.

She agreed.

LOOK FOR THESE ARABESQUE ROMANCES

WHISPERED PROMISES   (0-7860-0307-3, $4.99)
by Brenda Jackson

AGAINST ALL ODDS   (0-7860-0308-1, $4.99)
by Gwynn Forster

ALL FOR LOVE   (0-7860-0309-X, $4.99)
by Raynetta Manees

ONLY HERS   (0-7860-0255-7, $4.99)
by Francis Ray

HOME SWEET HOME   (0-7860-0276-X, $4.99)
by Rochelle Alers

Available wherever paperbacks are sold, or order direct from the Publisher. Send cover price plus 50¢ per copy for mailing and handling to Penguin USA, P.O. Box 999, c/o Dept. 17109, Bergenfield, NJ 07621. Residents of New York and Tennessee must include sales tax. DO NOT SEND CASH.

Midnight Skies

Crystal Barouche

Pinnacle Books
Kensington Publishing Corp.
http://www.pinnaclebooks.com

MIDNIGHT SKIES is dedicated to the author's husband, who encouraged her to write this story, and to all her writing buddies in Sacramento and Seattle.

PINNACLE BOOKS are published by

Kensington Publishing Corp.
850 Third Avenue
New York, NY 10022

Copyright 1997 by Cleo Fellers Kocol

All rights reserved. No part of this book may be reproduced in any form or by any means without the prior written consent of the Publisher, excepting brief quotes used in reviews.

If you purchased this book without a cover, you should be aware that this book is stolen property. It was reported as "unsold and destroyed" to the Publisher and neither the Author nor the Publisher has received any payment for this "stripped book."

Pinnacle, the P logo, and Arabesque are Reg. U.S. Pat. & TM Off.

First Printing: December, 1997
10 9 8 7 6 5 4 3 2 1

Printed in the United States of America

One

As the cameras came in for a close-up, Sela Clay flashed her warmest smile toward the audience. She looked expensively attractive, her hair straightened as the network liked, flowing waves touching her shoulders, her dusky-brown skin showing rose overtones. As the monitors flashed the logo for her television show, *The Natural World,* she thanked the woman she had been interviewing. A representative of the Sierra Club had talked about the encroachment of civilization on wildlife. It was a good lead-in for the following weekly segment, *Getting Acquainted With Animals.*

Every Friday, handlers from the National Zoo brought in one or more animals for Sela to spotlight. The producers assumed she would like animals, and gradually her affection for them deepened. Yet, snakes were where she drew the line. No holding, no petting.

As the cameras cut away, Sela stood and stretched. During the commercial break she liked to review the schedule, and get her thoughts in line. An hour show five days a week, with up to six guests per show, left little time to daydream. She prided herself on being prepared. Today the handlers would bring a coyote, a very shy and intelligent animal found in every part of the United States. She must remember to ask if any had been sighted in the Washington, D.C., area where KDCA had their studios.

Returning to her swivel chair, she chatted with the makeup girl who powdered down the film of perspiration on Sela's forehead. Under the bright lights, the cameras left little to the imagination. But Sela's early days had prepared her. Teenage years studying ballet had given her grace, and on-the-job training as a weather girl had prepared her for the unforeseen. "In a bad spot, never let people know what you're thinking," her mother had told her. But complete silence was not the way of television. As Doppler radar whizzed by, Sela lost her place, shrugged her shoulders and said, "Well, someplace it's going to storm." Now, she prided herself on her professionalism and laughed when her compatriots ran the old film. She had learned a lot during her seven years working local shows and was grateful that a fleshy man telling jokes had replaced her doing the weather.

Automatically, she took the note the producer, Jennifer Strong, handed her. Jennifer, fortyish, blond, and determinedly liberal, had worked with Sela for the last three years. Reading, no zoo segment today, Sela nodded. Last-minute cancellations were part of the job and, although upsetting, were never disastrous. Usually old standbys, freshmen senators or representatives, filled the gap. Sela asked them about the first time they visited a zoo or went to a National Park. Today the substitute was a complete stranger.

She had time only to skim the top layer of information before the audience was reading the applause sign and, encouraged by Jennifer, were clapping enthusiastically. Sela tried not to frown. A foreigner from some African country that had forged its independence when she was still in school was taking the chair next to her. No time to practice pronouncing his name.

She smiled into the camera. "Sorry, our animal handler is unable to be with us today to show you Wily E. Coyote and all his pranks and praiseworthy attributes. But, I assure you, you won't be disappointed. Her professional smile grew in intensity, and she paused a half second before glancing at the TelePrompTer to continue smoothly, "Today we have Jonathan MO-ka-ne."

"Mo-KA-ne," came the rich, deep voice from the guest's upholstered chair to her right.

"Mo-KA-ne," she repeated, noting with a shock that the man who lounged near her had his long legs stretched out in front of him and they were bare. Nothing but skin showed between Jonathan Mokane's tan twill shorts and his ankle-high hiking boots. His plum-black color made her skin appear pale in contrast.

"Jonathan Mokane," Sela continued, her heartbeat increasing, "is a man who comes to us all the way from Zimbabwe . . ."

"It's situated just north of South Africa," he finished for her.

"What brings you to our part of the country, Mr. Mokane? You don't happen to have . . ." She spoke rapidly and put a smile into her voice before glancing at him again, feeling the import of his presence like a touch of the hand. His safari shirt had epaulets and short sleeves; his muscles were casually relaxed but evident. She had been going to say, "a coyote up your sleeve," but ended lamely, the laugh in her voice almost going off key, "a coyote in a box back stage?" She smiled into the camera. "I suppose there's something noble about an animal who proliferates like the coyote."

Mokane's voice with its British accent boomed at her. "To clarify the subject, we don't have coyotes in Zimbabwe."

He sounded bored, which always made for a poor

interview. Her gaze scooted off his shoulder. "But I was sure you had wild dogs or something remotely like the coyote. Or am I misinformed?" She smiled, realizing she was half flirting with him, her eyes doing tricks of their own accord. He was so close that the clean smell of his bath soap and his newly shampooed hair carried to her, fresh as the outdoors. Her own fragrance, splashed on with a lavish hand, seemed as overdone as a rose in full bloom.

"In Africa we have the coyote's cousin, the jackal. Although I doubt I'd call it a *noble* animal." Jonathan Mokane shrugged, a touch of scorn in his voice. "The jackal is a scavenger." He shook his head.

Relieved that he hadn't responded to her flirtatious manner, and yet let down that he hadn't, she continued. "No, I suppose not." She glanced at the TelePrompTer, looking for clues about Mokane, but the electronic script was only now showing the proper pronunciation of his name. Having only superficial knowledge of Zimbabwe, she felt a moment of panic. A dreaded silence followed, and heat rose through her body, flooding her cheeks. She registered Mokane's slightly mocking smile even as her mind raced. All her life her grandmother had maintained that Africa was Sela's spiritual home. Now, she had a chance to shine, and important questions eluded her. She let her professional smile take over. "So what animals will I see if I visit your country?" No matter how he affected her, she determined not to show it again.

His look skimmed her face. "What do you want to see?"

She grinned and shook her head, telling herself he was only an interview, not a romantic prospect. "No contest. Lions and tigers." Appealing to the audience, a ploy that had helped her in the past, she said, "Isn't that the first choice of all of us, the predators?"

MIDNIGHT SKIES

The cameras scanned the five rows of people recruited from the SPCA, the kennel clubs, veterinary schools, and wild animals farms, and recorded for posterity their nods and smiles.

Mokane shook his head. "You have to go to India for tigers."

Sela's flush deepened, bringing a rosier tinge to her skin. As the camera came in for a close-up, showing his mahogany-colored face in profile, she wet her lips, took a deep breath, and told herself to relax. Like her Grandma Minnie said, "All men are the same under their clothes. Just some a little better."

Mokane said, "As for lions, last year a pride adopted a spot near my camp." His voice carried the timbred sounds of Africa and made her American television voice sound pallid, meager. A shiver of pleasure ran up her spine.

His gaze went to her and held. "Aren't you going to ask me what I'm doing in America?"

How could she forget to ask the obvious questions? She was letting his wide mouth and sculpted features sweep her away like a juvenile. Relieved to find the TelePrompTer script beginning to funnel information, she said, "I understand you have an engagement at the Smithsonian."

He nodded as she gave times and location, and she relaxed now that the TelePrompTer had caught up with her. Most men with that kind of powerful jutting jawline must be used to adulation. His thick dark brows framed intelligent eyes that gleamed brightly, now that she had almost made a giddy fool of herself. He had seemed amused, half-laughing, when she'd been uncertain where Zimbabwe was located. It made her instantly recall the first time she'd applied for a job.

"Where you from, girl?" the network man in personnel had asked.

"I'm from here, D.C."

"No one's from here. They *come* here from Ohio, Montana, Florida, Georgia, and all points in between."

But she had been born in the District of Columbia. So had her father, and her grandfather, who worked the New York Central Railroad. Only the women had come from other places, her grandmother from Georgia, her mother from Pennsylvania.

She realized she had been chatting with Mokane while her mind took that step into the past. Maybe it was his voice, sounding so cultured with its British accent, that lulled her. He gestured at the end of a sentence, bringing his hands into play. His fingers looked strong, and his short nails had a pearly translucent luster that pointed up even more the dark satin of his skin.

"Perhaps you'd elucidate for all of us some of your country's history." Smiling sweetly, she knew she looked as if she'd tasted a honeycomb, but she felt silly for speaking in such a stilted way.

His eyebrows rose slightly, and he shrugged before saying, "Zimbabwe used to be called Southern Rhodesia. We got our independence in 1980." Once more his penetrating gaze found hers and held it.

"So tell us about your wild game camp."

"It's called the Lobengula Safari Camp, and it's situated in the Zambesi Valley. A wild area. No television, no roads, no McDonald's. Just me and the animals." He grinned and, as a map of Africa appeared on the monitor, he explained, "My camp is along the Northern border, near the River." He moved slightly to point out the exact location of the camp.

As he went on about it, she wondered if he was using her show as a commercial for his business. It wouldn't be the first time a guest had done so. When he turned her way again, she lifted her head and half faced him. On screen it would appear that she was gazing into his eyes, but she was purposefully avoiding them, now. His skin seemed oiled and polished, and her desire to touch it hadn't abated, but her suspicious nature had risen. "So you're here in the Capital area to show slides of your camp and give seminars about the wild animals," she read from the TelePrompTer.

"Yes, people who come to Lobengula during your summer months, which is our dry season, can see most of the big game, as well as the antelope types—the waterbucks, kudu, impala."

She kept her voice even. "But for the next few weeks you will be at the Smithsonian."

"Starting tonight when I give a slide lecture at the Museum of Natural History." He leaned toward the audience less than ten feet away. "Be sure to come. I promise you won't be disappointed. The pictures and history of the camp are spectacular. I hacked the camp out of the jungle with my bare hands, made it a small paradise."

As he gave the information without waiting for her to prompt him, Sela began to feel irritated. He even got into a discussion with a woman in the audience, and Sela had to have a mike taken down so the woman could be heard.

All the while he smiled, laughed, and stretched like a black panther, Sela seethed inwardly. Before she could mention his book, he did. "Zambesi Camp," he said, "I wrote it in longband, on lined note paper, and I typed it when I got back to town the next summer." He smiled into the camera and at the audience; *he took over her show.*

"Mr. Mokane's book is now available in area bookstores," Sela said quickly. His composure had to come from extreme arrogance, and this irritated her immensely.

He gave the name of the publisher.

"Fascinating," she muttered when he paused, her smile iced in place. Smoothly, she told an anecdote about the Smithsonian and its founding, ended by asking the audience to thank her guest for coming, and the segment was over. She managed not to look his way again.

While assistants unhooked his microphone, she stretched and prepared for the next segment, telling herself to put him and the whole sequence out of her mind. But technicians and audience surrounded him as if he were a minor god ready to perform miracles.

Jennifer Strong hurried over to Sela. "Message from the big brass."

"Andrew Carrington Bowles?" He was the head of the studio.

Jennifer nodded. "Said he was surprised you didn't know more about Zimbabwe." She shrugged. "His subtle way of saying 'bone up.' "

And of reminding me I'm not indispensable, Sela thought, a snippet of fear racing through her. She sipped water while she glanced through her notes in preparation for the next guest and a discussion about the commercialization of America's National Parks. When Jonathan Mokane left without looking her way, she wondered why she felt cheated.

The feeling stayed with her through the final minutes of the show and the drive home to the Anacostia section of D.C., where she lived with her parents. Her father, Samuel Clay, had worked as a janitor during her early childhood, before he got a job delivering mail. In her estimation, he was the smartest person she knew, leading family discussions and dispensing wisdom. Her mother, Miriam, a practical nurse, came a close second. She loved them both very much.

"Yes, twenty-eight and still at home," she always said before anyone could ask. The thought of living apart from her parents and Grandma Minnie seemed ridiculous. They let her lead her own life, but when she needed them, they were there. Anyway, she liked home-cooked meals and friendly talk. Until the right man came along, her address would be the same as theirs. Her family meant a lot to her.

"They'll try to tell you different," her father had said once. "Try to say black people know nothing about family."

She parked the Buick in the garage and, as she entered the red brick row house, she thought, not for the first time, that it had a comfortable, settled look. The living room furniture still had the shine of new, even though it had known that room for twenty years. Mostly, the family congregated around the dining-room table. The oak still bore a high luster. The older of her two brothers, Louis, was a military officer at the Pentagon, married to a full-time homemaker. They lived in Loudoun County, Virginia, with three children and a fancy mortgage. The other brother, Lawrence, worked for the IRS and had an apartment near Dupont Circle. Her little sister, Nefari, who affected Egyptian clothes to go with her name, was still in high school and, along with Sela, lived at home.

Now the sounds of Charlie Parker, her grandmother's favorite musician, carried from a radio playing in the back of the house.

"Grandma Minnie, are you hiding from me?" Sela cried, putting her purse on the hall table and setting her briefcase on the floor nearby.

Her grandmother, a tiny, spry lady whose smile made everyone forget her wrinkles of age, came to the doorway. "Girl, you the one been hidin' your talents. Where you get that man you had on your show today?" She wiped her hands on her apron and beamed at Sela. "He was mighty fine."

"Who you talking about?" Sela teased, kissing her grandmother on the cheek as she passed, and sniffing the air of the kitchen. Chicken for supper.

"You know who I mean. That man from Zimbabwe."

"Oh, that one." Sela opened the refrigerator. "Any cake left?" She stared inside.

"Go on with you. You gain a pound, they toss you out faster you can say Fats Domino. Anyways, your folks be home soon. Chicken and dumplings. Greens cooked with bacon and cornbread with honey and butter."

"Just a little piece isn't going to hurt, Grandma."

"Well . . ."

"You and me. Coffee and cream. Cake. Lots of talk, like when I was little." She grinned at her grandmother.

"You sweet-talking me. Think I'll forget about that man. He's no jive talking, slow moving street corner bum. He a real man, that Africaner."

"Grandma . . ."

"Listen to me." She poured two cups of coffee and took them to the table. The room was big, with two windows, cupboards to the ceiling, and a china closet for the good dishes. "I wanna see that man. I need to ask him about the big waterfall your great-grannies talked about." A far away look came over her face. "I was no higher than your brother's babies when they talked about the Big Water. It roared like ten lions and it sprayed high as ten elephants. They feel that mist but they don't see no river, no falls, till they walk and walk. For days. I remember when they told me, they had that African look in their eyes." She shook her head. "I gotta talk to that Mokane man."

Sela had heard the story often, but it never ceased to intrigue her. How had people from the inland—if her ancestors had lived near Victoria Falls—ended up on the West Coast of Africa where most of the slaves had been shipped from? Once, when much younger,

MIDNIGHT SKIES 15

she had argued with Grandma Minnie, saying the story was most likely a myth, distorted by years of telling. Her grandmother's mouth had become a grim line. Sela had never mentioned such a thing again, and once her grandmother had told her more of the story. Sela felt she would remember forever the fervor in Grandma Minnie's voice as she related the sad tale of Sela's great, great, great grandmother, a woman kidnapped from her home and eventually taken by slave dealers to America.

She sliced two pieces of chocolate cake and slid one plate across the table. "I'll eat less at dinner."

Grandma Minnie laughed, but she sat down and began eating. "You gonna take me to see Mister Mokane?" she asked between bites. "Or you expect your old granny to go in a taxi like a common woman? Course no cabs around at night. But I can take the bus and walk from the corner. Everybody talking about exercise today."

Sela sighed, knowing her grandmother would put a guilt trip on her, remind her of her own daily stints at the health club or running through the neighborhood. In school she'd excelled at track until she'd sprained her ankle before an important meet. "You don't have to take a bus. Or cab. Or walk."

"I don't want to give you no trouble," Grandma Minnie said, her voice all brown sugar again.

"Grandma, I'll take you to the slide lecture." Next to her father and mother, Grandma Minnie was her favorite person. Anyway, it might be nice to let Jonathan Mokane know that using her show to promote his business was pretty low, no matter how beautiful his skin and pretty his speech. Telling him off would be cathartic, and she'd never have to see him again.

But four hours later Sela felt like shaking her grandmother. Jonathan Mokane had successfully charmed

Grandma Minnie. First with his pictures and talk, and then by his smiles and attention. He said he wasn't sure about Grandma Minnie's ancestors, but the Big Water had to be Victoria Falls—higher, broader and with a larger volume of water than Niagara.

They stood in front of the room, near the screen where elephants and cape buffalo had thundered, where lions had roared, and baboons had come down from trees, almost on cue, like a circus act. Sela had no opportunity to tell him off, or tell him anything, for Grandma Minnie invited him to the Clay family reunion picnic the next day, and he accepted.

Sela's mouth opened, but no words came.

Grandma Minnie put a hand to her gray hair. "You just tell me your hotel and Sela here will pick you up."

"I'm at the Sheraton," he said, his gaze touching Sela's fully for the first time that evening.

While he had talked about his remote camp and answered questions from the audience, she had watched him unobserved, thinking that his dark eyes changed color as he moved. Or was it her imagination? Now he was looking straight at her, but something else was flashing. Interest? Yes. Challenge? Yes, again.

She felt as if she were in a competition with him, and whoever won would call the next move. It was almost sexual, the feeling rising between them, continuing even as Grandma Minnie talked, her own gaze easy and kind.

That's it, Sela thought. Sex. She also felt a remoteness in him, as well as a need to show her he was boss. Well, she'd show him. Neither confirming or denying that she would pick him up, she turned aside and knew relief when the audience surrounded him, and she could break away.

"Grandma, how could you invite him?" she asked later as she maneuvered the car through half-dark streets. "Our reunion is a family picnic, not open to everyone who happens to be African."

Grandma Minnie shrugged. "He might be family. He's Shona. Maybe we are, too. He knew the Big Water."

"That doesn't prove anything. Maybe your ancestors lived near a river in flood, or lived in the desert and saw a river for the first time," Sela said then wished she had kept quiet.

Grandma frowned and, turning her head away, looked out the side passenger window. "Make fun if you want."

After a while, Sela said. "I'm sorry." Growing up, her brothers had made a joke of the Big Water. Although she had never joined them in their fun-making, she had not taken the story seriously, only been impressed by her grandmother's emotions.

"It's okay," Grandma Minnie muttered, but her mouth was grim.

They rode in uneasy silence the rest of the way.

At the house, Grandma Minnie said, "You going to pick Mr. Mokane up or you gonna make your Daddy drive all that way?"

Sela didn't hesitate. "Of course I'll pick him up. It's on the way to Rock Creek anyway. Woodley Road, west of Connecticut Avenue." As the words came out a warmth stole over her, and she remembered once more the glint in Jonathan Mokane's eyes and the long, long length of his thickly muscled legs.

Two

Jonathan Mokane had been waiting thirty minutes. He was just about to go back into the hotel when a long, red car pulled up and stopped next to him. He watched with guarded interest as Sela nodded from the driver's seat, reached across and unlocked the door. "Good morning," he said, getting in, and was barely seated when she eased into traffic.

"I had to stop by the studio on my way. Sorry to be late." She glanced toward him. "How are you, Mr. Mokane?"

Her words were polite but perfunctory, and he felt the chill of things unsaid. Did she resent giving him a ride? Her perfume, subtle but unmistakable, wafted pleasantly, and as he usually did with standoffish people, he proceeded as if she had smiled broadly at him. "Very fine, thank you, Miss Clay. And you?"

"I'm well."

So abrupt, the words clipped, no soft edges. Yet in that moment his gaze met hers, he saw a fleeting something that told him that underneath that brisk exterior lived a warm woman. Turning away, he watched through the windshield, seeing Sunday traffic that would make Zimbabwe's capital city's rush hour seem like nothing, but the stream of cars didn't irritate him as much as Sela's continued indifference to him. No matter what he said, she remained remote. "And your grandmother, she is well today?"

"She's just fine."

"She is a most remarkable woman." He smiled, darted a look at her.

"We think so." As she waited for the light to change, she tapped her hand lightly on the wheel.

So impatient, he thought, deciding it was an American trait, everybody rushing everywhere. When she looked in his direction, she blinked as if she were surprised he was sitting there. Or maybe not sure she wanted him with her? But her eyelashes fluttered lightly and made him even more aware of her big eyes and high cheekbones.

"Every day I fight this stupid traffic," she muttered.

He waited, but she said no more. Sun was sparkling in a show of late summer, tree leaves only beginning to change, the grass still crisp. After a while he said, "It's a beautiful day."

She nodded without emphasis.

Five minutes passed while cars became a steady stream. He wanted to ask, where are they all going, but instead he said, "I trust your parents are also well."

"Yes, thank you."

Another silence followed. Deliberately, he kept his eyes on the road. She drove fast, slowing down only when she reached the single lane road where a line of cars stretched ahead of her, slowing down her progress. Again she tapped on the steering wheel with the heel of her hand. Finally, she signaled a lane change, sped around a slow car and made it back in line just before a truck whizzed by in the opposite direction.

"Do the rest of your family drive this fast?" The words came out in a growl he hadn't intended.

She darted a glance at him, a surprised look in her eyes. He felt her gaze take in his long, bare legs.

Grandma Minnie had told him not to dress up, so he'd worn his safari shorts. Had he misunderstood, he wondered, seeing a slight frown on Sela's face. Last night for the slide show he'd worn long pants and a white scarf, and at one point had slapped a pith helmet on his head. Everyone had applauded. "If you'd rather not make conversation, say so. I was merely trying to be polite."

"Sorry, when I drive, I concentrate on the mechanics. As for the family, I imagine they're all well, and as for driving, my brothers make me look like I never got away from the starting gate." She almost smiled. "You'll meet them soon."

"Why don't you like me, Ms. Clay?" He had been through too much in his life to let a slip of an American treat him like he wasn't there. Anyway, he'd never have to see her again.

Her glance raked him. "I don't dislike you."

"But you don't like me."

"I don't know you."

"That's true."

"I could say the same for you."

"You think I don't like you?"

"Do you?"

"I don't know you."

"See what I mean?"

He laughed, and to his relief heard her own laughter, like a tinkling bell, join his.

He leaned back. "That's better. At least your family won't think I've violated you enroute."

"My, you do talk fancy," she said. This time her glance was friendly.

"You didn't get your job talking *un-*fancy," he retorted. Her clothes were expensive, her car filled with extras—automatic this, automatic that, music purring softly in the background. She probably got a large salary and bonuses. He'd had to scrape to make this trip, even though the publishers were putting him up while he was in the United States.

She shrugged.

He said, making sure he sounded his most British, "Aren't you suppose to say 'touché?' "

Again came that quick, disturbing look, her eyes seeming to probe his. Her face was shaped like a heart, the eyes large, well-spaced, the mouth sensuous, the nose straight, and the skin so dusky he wanted the taste of it in his mouth. As even more exciting thoughts made inroads on his mind, he looked out the window.

"You sound as if you know all the American *clichés*, Mr. Mokane."

"As kids we watched American movies and tried to decide what was real—the movies we watched in a tin warehouse or the war that raged in and out of our town. We fought for independence. Like Americans. But the Americans I saw in the movies didn't seem like those I read about in the history books." He said the words easily, but something inside tightened, and his early years became a kaleidoscope of memories, stretching out to today. He'd taken up a gun and joined the guerrillas when he was sixteen.

"As a little kid I used to wonder why all the Africans in the movies were villains or oafs. That's not what I heard at home. Then I started school." That tinkling laugh came again.

He felt the following silence grow more comfortable. Again he looked toward her. "For appearance's sake anyway, call me Jonathan. Isn't that the American way?"

Her smile reached her eyes and held. "Okay, Jonathan."

Sunshine seemed to fill the car, illuminate it, drive out the cold. He relaxed the rest of the way to where the extended family had gathered in Rock Creek Park.

"Hey, Sela!" a man called as she and Jonathan got out of her car.

"That's my brother, Louis," she explained, and then in a louder voice said, "Hey, Louis, this is Jonathan Mokane."

The family had taken over three tables. Coolers, picnic baskets, boxes, and bags of provisions were lined up on one. Grandma Minnie and a woman he imagined was Sela's mother—for she had the same heart-shaped face—were guiding the setting up. Louis and a group of men fussed over charcoal briquettes. Other men were busy setting up horseshoe stakes and a badminton net.

"Mister Mokane," Grandma Minnie cried, "come here and meet the folks. I told them all about you."

The children running in and out paused as he went to Grandma Minnie and took her hand. Although there was no physical resemblance, something about her manner, her friendly demeanor, reminded him of his own mother.

"This is my son, Sela's father, Samuel. He the one sees the mail stays on time."

"Glad to meet you." Jonathan shook hands, took measure of the man. Darker than Sela, same height, with gray coming into his hair, direct.

"And I'm Sela's mother, Miriam. Glad you could join us." The plump, pretty woman smiled and drew him into the circle of people beginning to congregate near lawn chairs.

Jonathan spoke softly. "I hope I'm not intruding on a family party."

"Not in the least. We always welcome extras," Miriam said.

Grandma Minnie chuckled. "Some of the folks who work with Sela come out here every year."

"They'll be here later." The tall man who had called

MIDNIGHT SKIES 23

out to Sela earlier shook Jonathan's hand. "As Sela told you, I'm her brother, Louis."

His face was rounder and his body stouter than his father's, and his instant friendly attitude was probably generational, Jonathan surmised.

"And I'm Lawrence." From two tables away a handsome man wearing aviator sunglasses, white pants, and a pale blue pullover held his hand up. "How you doin', brother?" he called.

Grandma Minnie continued, "That's Sarah sitting by the tree, Sela's aunt, and that boy pretending to be a man is her son, Willie."

"What's up?" Willie said, hooking his thumbs in pants which rode low on his hips. He wore a T-shirt so big it hung like a nightgown. He moved with a self-conscious strut to the table where Louis's wife was setting up large thermoses of lemonade and iced tea.

She smiled. "I'm Brenda Mae, and Louis and I've lived almost everywhere except Zimbabwe. Let me pour you a drink while you tell us about it. You can meet the rest of the family later."

"The Army got Louis early," Grandma Minnie said, taking Jonathan by the arm. "They been all over Europe and even California."

Everyone laughed, and Jonathan accepted a lawn chair. Soon he was the center of a smiling group who wanted to know about Africa. Leaning back so that the sun warmed the top of his head, he told the things tourists routinely liked to hear—tales about the animals, the flora, the size of the falls.

"Maybe you knows our people," Grandma Minnie said and told the story of the Big Water again. This time she added, "One of them chased that rainbow to the bottom. Or maybe climbed it to the top."

"They could have been talking about Victoria Falls," Jonathan explained, giving the tourist descriptions that said it was wider than Niagara and at peak flow the mist could be felt at the Victoria Falls Hotel a mile away.

"Lordy me," Grandma Minnie said shaking her head.

Everyone smiled, and soon the talk became general, with much laughter and many family anecdotes.

Jonathan watched Sela spread a blanket in the shade. She walked like a cat, softly and easily, he thought, but warily as if she knew she was being observed. Stretching out on her stomach, she pillowed her head on her folded arms. If the family wasn't present, would she allow him to stretch out beside her? He wanted to think so. Even though she had given him little encouragement, something in her told him she'd like it. He knew he would. He made himself look away, pretend she hadn't filled his thoughts since he'd appeared on her show.

After a while the men, led by Sela's father, began to barbecue ribs, and one by one the women drifted off to dish up the other foods that had been brought in abundance. When Sela got up to lend a hand, Jonathan was left with Willie and the children.

He gave the little boys each a polished crocodile tooth and the girl a plastic container of lion's hair. All three leaned against his knee and looked up at him with worshipful eyes while he recited tales his grandmother had told him—about the medicine man and the lost bones, about the healing woman and the talking birds. And always somewhere in the telling, he found himself gazing toward Sela.

Once she lifted her head and, her gaze, gliding by his, caught for a second, and he held his breath, communing with her silently, knowing something was happening, but not sure what. She gave no clue. He didn't know whether to back off or proceed with caution. As he was working up indignation—he liked to know where he stood—her younger sister arrived just as Grandma Minnie announced it was time to eat.

In a flurry of skirts and words, an Egyptian bracelet hugging her arm, and long dangling earrings jingling from her ears, Nefari got in the serving line behind Jonathan. "You really from Zimbabwe? We're studying Africa in school."

He smiled at this much younger version of Sela. "What grade are you in?" he asked, holding out his plate toward her father.

Samuel placed a large rib in the center. "There's more where that came from."

Everyone laughed.

As Nefari tossed her braids, the few plaited with conch shells jiggled musically. "I'm a Junior. Next year, twelfth and graduation."

"Then university?"

"I may travel first." She followed him closely, talking rapidly. "That's if I could go someplace like your camp. Grandma Minnie told me about it. Do you have an apprentice program, or something like that?"

"Not exactly, but we could probably work something out if you cook or do laundry," he said as potato salad and beans were piled next to the ribs.

"You're kidding me, huh? I couldn't learn to guide?"

"Afraid not." He tried not to smile. To be a guide took rigorous training and grueling tests. Some men who had grown up in the bush had trouble passing the final exam.

"She no good for laundry," Grandma Minnie said putting a piece of cornbread on Jonathan's plate. "Can't even wash her own socks."

Everyone laughed and, rolling her eyes, Nefari took a place at one of the picnic tables. The others followed suit and, during the general quiet as they concentrated on food, they questioned Jonathan. Everyone wanted details about his camp, his life, and he answered carefully, wanting them to understand at least in a small way.

He was taking a second helping of sweet potato pie when the producer and a cameraman from Sela's television program arrived. "They're crazy for soul food," Nefari said in a stage whisper.

Jonathan looked at her blankly.

"He doesn't understand what that means," Sela said moving around the tables with a pitcher of iced tea. Her long-legged, bouncy stride made it impossible for him to look away.

For a time his gaze met hers again, and a strange emotional tide washed through him, shaking him with its fury. He wanted to kiss her and then shake her, take that superior smile off her face. So he didn't always understand American idioms, that didn't mean he didn't understand her. She had ignored him all through the talk, and now that her bread and butter friends were here, she was moving around with animation, introducing them to those who hadn't met them before. Their white skin was so pale in comparison, he thought, not sure how they fit into Sela's life. Only a fraction of Zimbabwe's whites remained after the revolution, the rest moving to England, South Africa, Australia. Those who had stayed on cooperated in making the country a viable presence in the world. Finishing his meal, he moved away from Sela and her friends to throw horseshoes with Louis.

But he could not entirely avoid Sela. Later in the afternoon, as the sun slanted toward the far horizon, he decided that someday, somewhere, he wanted to make love to her and with her, disregarding the voice that said she was only a spoiled American. He'd crush her body beneath his, touching her with all his senses, making her feel. Simply seeing her sent currents of excitement coursing through him, and he knew by her body's signals, and the light in her eyes, she wouldn't mind boisterous, unashamed love, and he wanted to give it to her, wake her from her surface wariness, her animosity, and vanity. But did she even know her own desires? If she did, would she stand, breasts thrust out, legs apart, head tilted to the side, her mouth petulant but appealing, the lower lip slightly distended? He doubted she knew the full impact she had upon others. Also, before he could bed her, feel those satiny limbs entwined with his, before he could even think of love, he must settle the anger in his own mind, not only at her, but at some of the aspects of his own life. But first he must best her in whatever way would work. This time when her glance crossed his, he didn't let hers escape, but held it until it was his turn to throw his horseshoes.

People were leaning back, patting their stomachs, refusing third helpings, when Jennifer Strong wiped her mouth on a paper napkin and said, "Sela, I think we should take the show to Africa. Really. The ratings would be terrific."

Sela shrugged. Ray Charles's pleasing sounds were coming from a tape deck in her car; around her the sights and sounds of Rock Creek Park wrapped her in familiarity. People jogged along the trail. Family groups congregated near the picnic tables, and a local sculptor was showing his works at the Art Barn. Why Africa? As a child she'd listened to talk about Martin Luther King, memorized his "Free at Last" speech for a school program and knew all about "black pride." She supported black films and attempted to get noted actors on her program. She wasn't always successful. Black faces still weren't that visible on television, and the thought of being a token periodically rankled her. She also listened to rap stars her mother hated, and routinely had lunch with her white fellow workers. Africa was remote, a place that had little relevance in her daily life. Only her grandmother talked about Africa as if it were the promised land. "You paying for the trip?" Sela asked.

"If you are, take me," said Art Biggs, the cameraman, a red-headed irreverent Irishman.

Jennifer gestured expansively. "It's a natural. We tape the show in Jonathan's camp. My god, I can see it—a lion in the bush, the show's logo coming up over it." She grabbed another rib, waved with it. "I think I'll talk to the brass about it. Seriously."

"But maybe I don't want to go to Africa," Sela said, softly, her gaze going to Jonathan Mokane, sitting there looking so smug because he had won at horseshoes, beating Louis two games out of three. All day her mother had fawned over Mokane and her father, who routinely ignored celebrities, had sat nodding and asking questions as if Mokane was the last word on everything. Grandma Minnie had acted as if he were the best thing since Louis Armstrong and Joe Louis—icons of her day. Even Willie had loosened up enough to ask Mokane a few questions, and the kids were absolutely smitten.

As the talk zipped around and then came back again to Africa, she got up. "I feel like I've been wed to this chair. I think I'll get some exercise."

"You gonna run?" Nefari asked.

Sela nodded. "Want to come with me?"

"In these?" Nefari indicated her gold colored, laced sandals.

"She thinks she's some kinda Egyptian," Grandma Minnie said to Jonathan.

"And her older sister?" His gaze went to Sela.

"Sometimes she think she a track star."

"Hardly. I just like to run." Did they have to tell him everything?

"She won a medal in school," her father said, sounding proud.

"Not just one," her mother added.

"She coulda been in the Olympics if she hadn't hurt her ankle."

"Television isn't so bad," her mother said.

The two smiled at one another, and the rest of the family laughed, clearly in accord.

Sela knew they were proud of her. She tied a red sweat band around her forehead. "How about you, Brenda Mae? Want to go with me?"

"I think I'm glued to this chair. But take Louis." She grinned kindly. "He needs to lose a couple pounds."

Louis shook his head. "Cost too much to put it on."

"You just resting on your laurels," Grandma Minnie said, but she looked proud. He'd been the first in the family to earn a college degree.

"Where do you run?" Jonathan asked, standing up.

"There's a trail over there." Sela pointed.

"I used to do a little running."

"Really."

"I carried messages."

Sela tightened her shoelaces, pulled up her socks.

"You deliver telegrams?" Grandma Minnie asked. "Sela had a cousin who delivered messages in New York. Rode a bicycle."

Jonathan Mokane shook his head, and his voice grew quiet, and the words seemed to come from some place deep within him. "This was during the war. Between lines." He looked toward the ground. "Sometimes I ran . . . barefoot."

Sela cocked her head to one side and regarded him. "I wear my shoes."

"You *have* shoes."

How dare he throw out a fact like that? As if blaming her for having advantages and asking her and her family to feel sorry for him for not having the same. Each member of her family had worked hard to get where they were. If it hadn't been for affirmative action, would she have her present position? Sure, she was good, but often it took more than that, knowing the right person, going to the right schools, having a certain look. Grandpa Clay's job on the railroad had come with perks—free passes, a steady wage, knowledge of distant places—but that didn't mean it had been easy. Silver forks whose tines were bent, marked Southern Pacific—or whatever line he worked at the time—appeared on their table along with heavy, chipped plates with the railroad stamp. Louis had gone into the army as an enlisted man and worked himself up, taking college courses at night. Go back far enough her family could talk slavery. Why should she bleed for him?

"If you'll excuse me, I'm going now." She turned away, not wanting to hear about Jonathan Mokane's war, or his animals, or his camp. Not that she didn't sympathize, didn't care, but in some way his stories took away from her family's achievements, and this was a day when they should parade their accomplishments, really shine.

She was almost to the trail when he stopped her, his words winging after her, hawk-like, dipping and soaring, his voice signaling his anger. "I'll race you. Impartial and equal. Timed. Judges. The entire article."

Whirling, she faced him, saw the lights in his eyes daring her, the thrust of his jaw. Saw the family staring, surprised, not understanding. She hardly understood either. Something was happening between her and Jonathan Mokane, good or bad, she wasn't sure. "What for?"

"What for?" His look said he wanted to best her, but his look said much more, too.

She used her on-air voice, smiled sweetly. "A race is a competition, either against the clock or an opponent. During the war, as you so kindly informed us, you undoubtedly raced bullets. If we run, what is it for, Mr. Mokane?"

"Jonathan." He forced a smile. "You forgot my name already?"

"How could I . . . Jonathan?"

Uneasy laughter spun through those watching. She knew her parents were puzzled, and Grandma Minnie looked in a lecturing mood.

Mokane lifted his head higher. "If I win, you come to Zimbabwe."

"Great," Jennifer cried, her blond hair flying as she jumped up. "It's just the kind of angle the sponsors will go for!"

Sela felt her blood rise dangerously. How had this happened, this disintegration of the family reunion? Had she set the tone by letting some of her television friends join in, and now this man—who interested her so much she would never admit it to anyone—was taking over in a way that made her want to cry out in frustration. Instead, she said in an even tone, "And when I win?"

Jonathan shrugged. "You don't have to go."

Jennifer shook her head. "No, you need to extract some clever forfeit from him." She went toward them, her Eddie Bauer clothes looking properly subdued, her body brimming with expression.

"I'm sure she will think of something fitting," Jonathan said, as Jennifer tied a blue ribbon on his arm and a red one on Sela's. "So we can tell you apart."

Everyone laughed, and Grandma Minnie shook her head.

While Jennifer talked about camera angles, Jonathan exchanged looks with Sela. She felt the blood rise in a tide to her cheeks, her breasts swell, her body grow warm, but she couldn't look away.

Jennifer waved. "Art, you have to film the finish. It will be the start of the show, 'The Natural World in Zimbabwe.'"

"Gotcha." Art ran toward the KDCA truck.

Sela's father said. "No disrespect, Mr. Mokane, but you're six, seven inches taller than Sela."

Louis nodded. "A handicap will fix that."

"Give her a head start," Lawrence said.

Everyone had their ideas, and soon Willie and Lawrence were marking out a two-mile route, and Grandma Minnie was setting up chairs at the finish line.

"I call the start," Grandma Minnie said. "You listen good, cause I ain't breathin' the same words twice."

Sela and Jonathan walked the twenty-five feet to the start.

"You sure you want to do this?" she asked mockingly before she moved ahead the eighth of a mile the family figured would be a fair handicap.

He raised his eyebrows but said nothing as she took her place, her behind wiggling in her bright red shorts, her legs looking strong and capable, as if they could wrap themselves around a man and never let go. He watched until she was out of sight, and then he took his stance, Willie there to see he didn't start ahead of time, Louis with her to see she got off when Grandma Minnie called and not sooner.

Late afternoon sun was freckling the path. All seemed serene. Jonathan took a deep breath.

"On your mark!" He bent down.

"Get set." His fingers touched the dirt.

"Go!"

Jonathan watched Sela sprint off, moving easily, her body an oiled machine shifting precisely. He burst forward but paced himself, staying with her, reserving his strength for later. Challenging her had been a foolhardy thing, he saw that now. She probably ran every day and, despite what he'd told her, he was out of shape. Guiding tourists, traveling to America, touting his book hadn't left much time for exercise. For days on end he'd done nothing but sit in offices, talk on radio shows, and haunt television studios.

For five minutes he maintained the pace. Then she turned a corner, went around a tree, and, suddenly, she was out of sight. The path curved, up and down slightly, through foliage that encroached upon the trail, and he lost track of her soft footfalls. Afraid she had increased her speed, he pushed himself harder, his eyes on the ground, seeing the leaves, the damp spots, the places to avoid. He was feeling the run now, his muscles protesting, his breath coming fast.

Glimpsing her again, running faster now, he realized he had passed the mile marker, the red ribbon Jennifer had hung in a tree. He ran faster. The land curved away now, slightly downhill, and he used it to force a swift pace. When his second wind came—he remembered it from years ago—how it let him run for miles. His muscles were loose and easy now; the harsh air in his lungs had become like ambrosia, spurring him on; and he felt as if he were flying, his feet barely touching the ground.

As he passed the blue ribbon that signified another half mile, he saw her, going full speed, her legs stretched like rubber bands, bending in sheer beauty, arms pumping in a graceful rhythm. He sought for and found, that extra spurt of energy that would send him neck and neck with her.

But then the trail twisted, the trees growing close to the edge, their gnarled roots twisting into the path. He lost her again.

When he came out into the straightaway, he saw she had stopped and was standing, rubbing her ankle.

She's been hurt, he thought, and a sudden keen sharpness slapped him in the chest, made his eyes smart, made him want to cry out, "You all right?" She'd stumbled, maybe bruised her ankle—or worse.

The look she sent him made him slow his stride, made him admit he wanted to stop for her, see if she was all right. He imagined his hands on her leg, rubbing, soothing. If her ankle were sprained or broken, he'd swoop her up, carry her in, take her for treatment. Why else would she look so injured, so hurt? He imagined running with her in his arms. She would be light, but soft and firm, and the taste in his mouth felt better than ever, told him he and she would come together, sometime, somewhere.

He was almost upon her, close enough to see the way her breath forced her breasts against the thin cotton of her T-shirt, saw the down-turned look of her mouth, as if she wanted to cry but wouldn't. She had guts, and he admired this so much, he wanted to shout out, "I'm coming for you. I'll take care of you, it'll be all right."

Then before he could reach her, she was off, her legs stretching out, her feet pounding the trail without a sign of trouble.

"What the hell?" he called, his eyebrows flying together. Then, as his feet touched the place where she had stood rubbing her ankle, a stream of children suddenly erupted from the trees. Little children of four, five, and six, a slew of them, filling the trail, stopping him in his tracks.

She knew they were coming, he thought as he waited while they spilled out like frolicking fawns, their leader following. "Don't forget: the first one spots a maple tree gets a prize," the woman guiding the group called.

It was two minutes before Jonathan could get through

the milling, laughing group, two minutes which meant she could be thundering down the homestretch ahead of him.

He forced himself to sprint again, breathing through his mouth, gulping at the air as if it were rationed. His feet flew over the ground, the foliage blurred by, and then he saw her ahead, caught up with her, ran neck and neck. Sweat was pouring from him, and as he passed her he saw she was slick and wet. He touched Grandma Minnie's hand a second before Sela crossed the finish line.

"Got it!" Art shouted, video camera riding his shoulder, his hair sticking out in all directions.

"If the old man goes for it, you're on your way!" Jennifer cried to Sela.

The family milled around, laughing, talking.

Sela wiped her face with a towel, and moved a little away to set it down on a table.

Jonathan followed her, pitched his words low, for her ears alone. "So that's how races are run here."

"Not really," she said, turning to face him. "Depends upon the race and the people running."

"And I'm one of those people?" He resisted the impulse to reach out and touch the line where perspiration ran down her cheek.

"Obviously. But you won, anyway. I'm not disputing that." She looked past him. "This is a dog-eat-dog world, I was just giving myself an edge, but you're trying to make me feel like the wicked witch of the west."

He needed to force her gaze back. "I'm going to make you live up to every bit of the bargain," he said in a low, urgent voice.

Her glance flew back to him, and she regarded him silently for some time before she smiled. "Let you in on a secret," she said. "No matter how Jennifer talks, my lily-white conservative boss isn't about to send this little old brown girl to Africa. I'm no Oprah Winfrey—merely a local girl trying to make good. So you just dream on, because you're going to do it without me. And no, I didn't cheat as you seem to think. I merely was waiting for you, giving you a chance." She turned away abruptly.

As he stood with an open mouth, he heard her say, "Lawrence, when you leave, will you drop Mr. Mokane off at his hotel? I have an appointment I have to keep."

"No problem. I go right by there." Lawrence hugged her.

A flurry of good-byes followed: Jennifer and Art leaving, the family gathering things together.

While Grandma Minnie and the others talked about how hard Sela worked—did you catch that show of hers with Jesse Jackson?—she drove off, her red car blurring as fast as her red shorts had earlier. Jonathan Mokane wasn't sure he'd won the race after all.

Three

Six weeks later, Sela was seated in the top-floor executive offices of KDCA in Arlington, Virginia, across from Andrew Carrington Bowles, Chief Executive Officer. Beyond the gleaming surface of his desk, a wall of windows overlooked the Memorial Bridge, with views to the Lincoln Memorial, the Washington Monument, and the Capitol. Sela waited for Bowles to look up from the papers and photographs spread out on his desk. His back was to the scene, as if he had seen it so often he could dismiss it.

Even though he had called her to his office and she was not coming as a supplicant, he made her feel like one. She leaned back and tried to relax, her gaze taking in the ficus tree, the high-powered telescope, the deep pile carpet. No matter how good she was, she had the feeling that she was the token black at the station, and the token woman doing animal shows. As for advancement, the glass ceiling was firmly in place.

Bowles, a tall man with heavy shoulders and an oval face, looked up and almost smiled. His eyebrows were as light as his skin, his hair slight, combed across his balding pate. "Ms. Clay." His mouth barely moved. "Jennifer Strong offered some convincing evidence why 'The Natural World' should go to Africa." He sifted through the photographs, held up one showing elephants, another featuring lions. "She seems to think Jonathan Mokane is charismatic. She thinks that you and he together on screen, wild animals in the background, would shoot our ratings through the ceiling." He shrugged, scooped the material together, and closed it into a file. "I'm not so sure. You have any thoughts about this?" He pushed his chair away from the desk, crossed his legs, and leaned back.

The memory of Jonathan Mokane had dimmed in the weeks since Sela had last seen him. Her conversations with him no longer repeated in her mind every night. Neither did she remember, as if marked forever, the times their hands had touched. But she remembered. Now Mr. Bowles had brought Mokane's image back fully, and it rose like fireworks on the Fourth of July. She hadn't wanted to admit to herself that she was deeply attracted. When he had burst into her life, she had been sure she was past the stage of instant infatuation. Now she found herself losing the edge of steel in her spine, becoming like soft solder. As the memory of his face shimmered in the air around her, and the cadence of his voice rumbled in her ears, she shook her head, forcing out words. "No, Mr. Bowles, I don't think Mokane and I mean instant ratings success."

"Don't play modest, Ms. Clay. We happen to think Jennifer might have a point." Bowles leaned closer. "What do you really think?"

He was merely looking at her, not scowling, but Sela knew that, despite his bland appearance, the man held power. She'd expected him to tell her what he had in mind, not ask her questions.

"The show has a good rating," she said, knowing she mustn't goof now. She had been in his office only one time before. That time she'd been sure he had seen the spunk and drive she had fostered all her life.

MIDNIGHT SKIES

He shook his head, his pale eyebrows scooting together. "Your show's plateaued, leveled out."

Your show. Her fault. "Last week we beat out Federal Geographic and Outdoor Scene."

"Two weeks before that you lost out to telethons for carpal tunnel syndrome or some such thing." He leaned back in his chair, unbuttoned his jacket. Beneath the camouflage of good tailoring a roll of fat hung over his belt.

She attempted a smile. "I think one was tennis elbow." Her smile faded. "But I get your point."

He looked out the window, turned back, looked at her directly. "You happy with us?"

"Oh, yes."

"Like your job?"

"It's great, Mr. Bowles."

"We need to stay current. When NBC got Willard Scott, we got Harvey Bannister. Pure corn—but it sells. So does Oprah. But she can't stay up there forever. Donahue tumbled. So will she. I see you as a potential contender."

"I'm flattered." The station's token African-American, she thought.

"Of course, you may not be able to translate to national."

"National?"

"If we pull off this Africa thing, it will catapult us. Mokane's book has climbed the lists. A month on top and holding. We need to grab him before someone else does. If you and Mokane don't fly, we'll rethink the whole show." He tented his fingers. "Some people were a little nervous when I signed you. They wanted more glitz, glamour, someone talking relationships, sex, music."

Carefully, she kept her gaze level and didn't move an inch.

He rocked forward, pressed a switch, and blackout curtains moved across the windows. He punched a button, and the giant television monitor on the wall opposite the windows lit up.

" 'The Natural World' in Africa," Sela heard. The film Art had shot of Jonathan and her flashed by, spliced with shots of wild animals and photos of Jonathan Mokane. Adding a few slick touches, Jennifer had come up with a five minute demo that made the whole concept seem possible.

"These were the clinchers," Bowles said, as he flicked another switch and Mokane's slides showed on the screen.

Sela saw again the pictures she and Grandma Minnie had viewed at the Smithsonian, heard Jonathan's voice narrating. She watched his handsome face, his lean, hard body and felt a lightning-like jolt race through her.

As the screen went black, Bowles said, "The forest primeval." His voice had a dreamy quality, and he seemed lost in thought for a moment, before he opened the draperies.

Not letting him see the irritation she felt for his superficial statement, she waited quietly for him to continue.

"KDCA wants you to go to Mokane's camp with Jennifer and Art." As the monuments and Capitol came into view again, he added, "While you're there, if we have time to set it up, we'll run the show live. Direct from Zimbabwe. If not, Jennifer can get tapes to us. Either way, we'll sweep the competition. We'll pay Mokane enough so that we'll take over the camp, no tourists to get in the way. And when you come back, maybe you'll be able to write your own ticket. Or . . ." He placed his hands palm down on the desk, his fingers splayed. He shrugged. "I never thought Oprah would last, either."

With a sinking feeling, Sela pictured herself in the unemployment line. "I don't have much choice, do I?"

"Your plane leaves Monday midnight and returns two weeks later." He punched a key and the computer behind him sprang to life.

It was equipped with a fax, a CD-ROM, and a Pentium Chip. She felt as if she were equipped with apprehension and a low-grade anger. Maybe it, as well as her knowledge and know-how, would carry her through the weeks in Africa when she'd have to be with Jonathan Mokane. Every time she looked at him she'd remember how he'd bested her at her family reunion. But what bothered her more was the way he made her heart beat. Years ago her love for another man, Frankie, had flared every bit as fast and then expired one day in flames twice as bright. She didn't like to think about that. No, she'd just remember how much Jonathan Mokane irritated her and also how much she'd love to show KDCA's Bowles she'd make a success out of anything she did.

On the plane, Sela felt isolated, stripped for a time from obligations, able to drift and dream. Until she'd begun to make money, she'd never traveled out of the country. Family visits, a pilgrimage to Harlem to see addresses famous from the Renaissance, and finally Europe with a friend.

Now, since there were no direct flights from the U.S. to Zimbabwe, she and the KDCA crew flew into London for the connection to Harare. In Britain, a six-hour layover was followed by an all-night flight to Zimbabwe's capital. The European trip she'd taken with awe began to seem like small potatoes. From Harare, where Mokane would greet her, she'd take another flight to

Kariba. From there small planes would fly them over the jungle to his camp.

Jennifer had said, "We'll wing it from there."

Sela felt as if she had been winging it all her life. The first African-American girl from her school to win regional debating honors. The first to star in the drama club. The first to fall in love.

Frankie. From Mississippi. He'd played the piano, jazz and classical music that shook the keyboard or purred gently, sending tremors of pleasure up her back. He had consistently garnered more praise than money. She had just graduated from high school and was starting college that fall, and she'd been deeply smitten.

Her mind floated back to those months. Soothed by the hum of the plane, she recalled again Frankie's presence, saw his beautiful dark face.

Flabbergasted by his presence, mesmerized by his talent, every fiber of her being had responded to his words, his voice, his ideas, his tenderness and passion. She'd held back nothing.

They were planning a wedding when he got his big break. A tour of South America, replacing a soloist who had gotten ill. Somewhere over the Amazon jungle his plane had crashed. There hadn't been enough of him left to bury.

Sela had immersed herself in studies and in the solace of her family. No one had ever interested her as much as Frankie. Until Mokane. Thoughts of him brought sweet licorice tastes to her mouth, spun colors as bright as the sun spiraling through her mind, and set her body to throbbing with desire. Exasperated at herself for letting such things happen, she hardened her resolve and told herself that in no way would she tumble into his arms.

* * *

Now daylight pressed against the plane as it landed, taxied up a field and came to a halt. Her first thoughts, like tiny birds insistently fluttering against the bars of a cage, winged toward Jonathan Mokane. Remembering the last time she'd seen him, Sela wondered if he'd be glacially polite, retaliating for her coolness at the picnic. As stairs were wheeled up, and Jennifer and the cameramen hurried out, Sela reminded herself that Jonathan Mokane was only a man she would be working with, not a man she loved. Slinging her carry-on luggage over her shoulder, she got up, excitement carrying her forward.

As she stepped through the plane's door, she talked into the microphone hooked to her jacket. "That's one small step for myself and a giant one for my Grandma Minnie, who couldn't be here, but who, like so many African-Americans calls Africa her spiritual home. It's a cloudy day, and colder than I'd expected, but it's good to be on firm ground again," she narrated as she moved across the tarmac to the waiting room. "Beyond us waits Harare, Zimbabwe's capital city."

And then everything became a jumble of impressions—of crowds of people, mostly black faces, straining to see, of Jonathan Mokane, a head taller than anyone else, moving like some king of old toward her. She smiled automatically and said the appropriate things into the microphone.

He was greeting her, shaking hands, taking her carry-on luggage, and she was answering, but she remembered nothing of what either of them said. When he stood so close, her hand in his, she wanted to reach up and touch his firm jaw, let her fingers trace the lines of his wide mouth. Years in front of the camera let her talk, glance around, say the proper thing while her mind seethed with inner dialogue and action. Jonathan's lips tucked into a half-smiling line, the wide ends rising and then the bow coming down in a quick pursing action so fleeting only she caught it. A warm, affectionate look, she thought, moving with him through crowds of jostling travelers standing on benches, jamming the aisles, bucking lines at ticket windows—all in order to glimpse her, the American. His hand on her arm, Jonathan Mokane guided her through the mob. Finally, she burst with him out the front door, but he didn't let go as he directed her to a van.

"So this is Zimbabwe," she said, thrilled at actually being in Africa.

"One part of it," Mokane said, tightening the knot in his striped tie.

In a suit and white shirt he looked like a businessman anywhere in the world. "I gather you don't think it's the best part."

"I was never partial to cities."

He directed her to a waiting automobile, the driver in uniform and white gloves. "For show," Mokane said in an aside.

A few minutes later, Sela, conscious of her responsibility, narrated, "Harare could be any big city in the United States, except that they drive on the opposite side of the street. And here, most all the faces one sees are black. Before I left home my Grandma Minnie insisted that if I looked hard enough I might find our family roots. But this show isn't about roots, but about Mr. Mokane and his safari camp." Expertly, she asked him the questions the audience at home would demand, and he answered easily, as he had done on her show in Washington.

Soon the sleek, modern surroundings of a hotel wrapped her in comfort no different from in similar hotels anywhere in the world. Lunch on a terrace at tables with umbrellas. Meeting city officials, asking environmental questions, not coming down too hard, feeling her way, and, halfway through, noticing that Jonathan Mokane got up and quietly left. Dinner with local celebrities: a group who based their music on the Temptations, a designer who hoped to take her dresses to Paris, a teacher who wanted Americans to send books to the villages, and a rap group who shouted Sucker, Sucker, Sucker. In between lots of laughter and talk, Sela looked for Jonathan Mokane. Jennifer said he had left a message; he'd see her in the morning.

Back in her room, Sela fell asleep while the television blared CNN News. Six hours later, the phone was screeching. She fumbled for it, and heard a British-sounding voice tell her it was her wake-up call. An hour and a half later, she was on a plane again, Jonathan Mokane sitting next to her.

"How are you this morning?" he said, his eyes veiled, not doing those things she had definitely seen in Washington.

"More tired than I thought I'd be," she answered truthfully. On the long flight to London, the layover at Gatwick Airport, and then during the all-night flight to Harare she'd been too excited to get much sleep. She'd boned up on the history and the culture of Zimbabwe before she left home, but wanted all the inside information she could get. "Tell me about the language."

"We have two main ethnic groups in Zimbabwe: Shona and N'debele, but English is spoken everywhere," he explained.

Coming from London, she had heard the soft murmur of voices speaking their native tongues. Now when the flight was delayed for the Prime Minister of Swaziland she didn't feel annoyed, but thrilled. Last night she'd met a woman who looked like Natalie Cole and other sleek, sophisticated American clones. When the Prime Minister entered, wearing colorful robes, she felt a renewed sense of being somewhere vividly different. "My grandmother should be here."

Mokane said, "How are your parents and grandmother?"

"They're fine. They send their regards."

"Many times I've remembered their generosity, inviting a lonesome stranger to share their family reunion." His eyes met hers.

For a moment she thought she saw something more than polite interest. But what if she was reading more than was there? She said carefully, as if he were just anyone, "They like to share."

"Does this family trait extend to everyone?" His gaze did not allow hers to wander. "I had the distinct impression you would rather I had stayed away that day at Rock Creek Park."

She shook her head. "Maybe I was mistaken."

"So if it happened again, you'd add your voice, invite me to your family picnic?"

She laughed. "I didn't say that! I said maybe I should have been more gracious at the reunion."

"Are you reserving judgment about Jonathan Mokane?"

His manner of distancing himself made her smile inwardly. "Yes."

"But I'm taking you into my camp. Showing you what means the most to me of any spot in the world. From nothing, I made it a success." His eyes blazed at her.

"Taking me there is good business. Hardly the same thing as a family reunion."

"The first round is yours."

She chuckled as his deep laugh joined hers. It was easy to joust verbally with him. It was something she did off and on the air always. Impulsively, she let her hand rest a second on his.

His gaze told her he liked the fleeting touch.

Careful, she reminded herself and drew back, saying she had work to do. After all, she wasn't here because she had these warm but confused feelings about Mokane. Opening the briefcase on her lap, she took out papers and immersed herself, keeping busy until the plane landed in Kariba an hour later.

The chill of the plateau country was gone. Sun glittered everywhere, glancing off the small building that was the terminal and shining along the wings of the two small planes that waited. As soon as the American's luggage and equipment came from the Boeing 737, it was stowed in the back of two four-seater Cesna 180's.

Sela followed Jonathan across the tarmac and a patch of yellowing grass to where the planes waited. He helped her into the back of one, got in beside her and in minutes she was in the air again.

Sitting beside Jonathan, her shoulder and hip touching his, the trip began to have a dreamlike quality. America, Britain, and then the endless night, the gracious service of Air Zimbabwe, the hum of the plane, nothing but dark outside the window, and finally Harare. And way too little sleep before the glitzy night in Harare. Now the small planes swooped across an escarpment, skimming just above rugged mountain ranges thrusting skyward. Wind tossed them like kites, and once Sela caught a glimpse of the second plane bouncing on the horizon.

But then, quickly, a calm followed. The sky was a bowl of blue, the jungle a solid mass of winter brown below. Over dense trees, winding rivers, the plane flew low enough for Sela to see hippos lumbering from the river and elephants coming to a water hole to drink.

Jennifer, sitting in the front seat next to the pilot, grinned over her shoulder and mouthed, "Okay," and brought her thumb to her forefinger making a circle.

Sela nodded, smiling. Her eyes felt gritty from sleep deprivation, her muscles weak, needing movement, but she felt overwhelmingly alive, awareness in every fiber of her being. No matter what happened, this was going to be all right, an adventure worth filming, a trip worth taking, a time she'd always remember.

Jonathan Mokane shouted in her ear: "There's no road down there, just a trail we travel by Landrovers. Each spring we take supplies in and we bring out what's necessary each fall. During the winter everything comes in by plane."

"Don't you stay there in the summer?"

"Can't. It's too wet and too dangerous—rivers raging, grass as high as elephants. Impossible to spot the animals until they're on top of you." His gaze swept her face.

She felt the warmth of his breath, smelled the musky scent of him. "How did you happen to come out here the first time?" she shouted into his ear. They sat so close together that his arm grazed hers. The forced intimacy kept losing its impersonal elements, and delight raced through her.

"I needed to get away, so one year I set out with a gun, a backpack, and a head full of ideas. When I returned to civilization, I knew I had to return to the bush. So, the next year, I made sure the land was mine, and then hacked a camp out of the jungle."

"How many people in your camp?" she asked as the plane routed a herd of buffalo, sent a flock of birds into flight, spooked a lone lion from its nap under a small tree. She leaned across him to watch the large cat disappear into the brush.

He smiled. "Fourteen tourists maximum. Besides myself, I have three guides, two cooks, a laundress, two maids, a dishwasher, and a handyman. We give the personal touch." His smile grew as she turned her head to look back.

She ignored the innuendo, intended or not, in what

he'd said. "I've heard that once you see Africa you're never the same again."

"Outsiders usually return. Some stay permanently. No tourists will be there during your stay, however. We couldn't accommodate all of you." He drew her attention to a scar among the trees. "That's the landing strip."

"That tiny place?"

He grinned, nodded. "Yes, but big enough for small planes, and that ribbon of water over there is the Zambesi River."

Sela barely had time to nod. The jungle was rising quickly, the plane landing into the wind, and the brown-and-yellowed brush was rushing at her. Twenty feet from the end of the runway, the plane stopped.

The pilot got out, Jennifer followed, and then Jonathan Mokane got down. Sela stood in the doorway and looked out.

As far as she could see, nothing but trees and brush met her gaze. A gentle wind stirred the grass, but, aside from that, she heard nothing except Mokane's breathing and the sound of his footsteps as he moved closer to her. No sounds of traffic, no sirens, nothing, just that grand, awesome quiet. Above it she heard the faint sound of the second plane approaching, and then the rustling, musical, soft sounds of the jungle came to her. Birds singing, animals moving, water gurgling.

She let Jonathan Mokane lift her down, his touch fleeting, his arms strong. She wouldn't have minded melting into him, letting his strength hold her up.

He gestured beyond her to a Landrover parked on a faint trail, with a driver getting out.

Mokane asked, *"Makadini,* Matui?"

Makadini: how are you in Shona. She had studied the book on the way to London.

"These are Sela Clay and Jennifer Strong from America."

The gray-haired little man bobbed his head, his smile sure and quick. "It is my pleasure."

"Matui is my right-hand man, does a little bit of everything about camp. If you need something, just ask him. He knows more than I do."

Laughing, Matui shook his head.

And then the other plane landed, and Art, the head cameraman and his two assistants, Ezra and Jim, got out and began unloading supplies and stowing them in the Landrover. Ezra and Jim, came from the poorer neighborhoods of Washington, D.C., and Sela determined to get their impressions soon. But now everyone was getting ready for the ride to camp. Art was taking pictures, Jennifer was taking notes and giving suggestions.

"Tell me again, how far is it?" Sela asked, not wanting to admit how tired she was feeling. Pushing herself, she turned on the microphone, said the proper things.

"A few miles." Jonathan helped her into the Landrover. "It won't be long before you can relax."

Matui shook his head in mock denial. "When I left, Sheba and her babies were eating the mahogany trees in camp."

"Sheba?" Sela looked from one man to the other.

"A big mama elephant. Thinks our camp belongs to her." Jonathan chuckled and leaned closer to Sela.

For a moment she thought he was going to kiss her, and her own lips grew lax. His eyes skimmed her face, a smile in their depths. He merely secured the door next to her, yet his voice purred in her ears as he said with a powerful sense of ownership, "Welcome to my home."

Four

As they left the airstrip, Jonathan Mokane pressed on the gas, and the open Landrover spurted ahead, past scrub mopane trees and olive green bushes that he supposed looked foreign and unfriendly to the Americans. The ground had an acidic quality that gave away to a red sand and looked nothing like what he'd seen in America. Of course he hadn't seen it all. He sneaked a look at Sela, expecting her to ask about snakes or maybe tigers. "Snakes are fairly scarce during the dry season, and tigers are indigent to India," was his stock reply. But she said nothing. He felt a burgeoning admiration.

Ahead, a gigantic tree loomed on the horizon. Its exotic appearance brought reactions from most tourists. Slowing the vehicle, he glanced at her again.

She did not disappoint him. Shaking her head, she whispered, "It's impressive. I assume it's the baobab tree?" She'd read about it before leaving home, but the pictures she'd seen had shown it in full leaf. It was hard to talk above the feelings that were gripping her so hard. Here, where time had stood still she felt closer to the past and the dream that had figured so prominently in her grandmother's life and to a lesser degree in her parents'.

Smiling, Jonathan braked to a stop. "Yes, that's the baobab."

The sturdy, substantial trunk, big around as a house, hugged the ground as if wedded to the spot. But ten feet or so above the top of the Landrover a maze of branches shot from the trunk in a tangle leading in all directions.

"It looks like it's an upside down tree," Sela said, sliding forward on the seat, her hair bouncing lightly. Jonathan wanted to reach out and touch her hair, feel that soft, glistening mass.

From the seat directly behind, Art swung the camera into play, and Jennifer leaned forward. "Is there a Baobab story?" she asked. Behind her the two helpers shrugged and old Matui smiled.

Jonathan tried to remember. There had been tales, but Sela's proximity wiped them instantly from his mind. "An old man told me the gods tore it from the ground to remind people not to become rooted in mundane, everyday things, but to reach for the stars, be everything you can."

Jennifer switched on her tape recorder. "Sounds like good philosophy. How about telling it again. For posterity."

Jonathan grinned. "Actually, I just made it up. Matui's the story teller."

Leaning forward so all could hear, Matui said, "The gods stuck the baobabs back in the ground upside down to remind the people, do not anger the gods." He shivered, as if in fear, and then grinned.

"Tonight at camp he'll relate a few tales."

Matui shook his grizzled head. "Thanks, boss." He smiled at the others. "He's always giving me new jobs."

Everyone laughed.

Jonathan put the vehicle in gear, and headed away from the clearing. The jungle moved in to surround the Landrover, trees meeting overhead, bushes brushing against the vehicle. Quiet descended, with only the birds singing and bushes brushing against the vehicle interrupting the silence. Occasionally he heard an "Awesome," from Art's helpers but Sela, saying nothing, kept her gaze on the jungle, and Jonathan found his gaze going to her often.

There was something about this woman that both intrigued and irritated him. Now, she wore a safari outfit that shouted Hollywood, sturdy enough not to tear to pieces in the bush but fitting like a second skin. With it she wore boots with high heels. The hat perched rakishly on her head had a long dangling feather that tickled his nose when she turned in his direction.

He sneezed.

"Allergy?" she asked.

"Only to feathers in the face. Your hat," he said pointedly.

"Wearing it wasn't my idea, believe me. My boss back in Washington has some pretty definite ideas about this whole show, including what I wear." No reason to go along with his dictates now. As soon as she arrived in camp she'd shuck the whole silly outfit, and wear her own clothes. She turned the hat so that the feather rode the other side. It was always a juggling act trying to please the "brass" and maintain a sense of autonomy.

Jonathan nodded to show his appreciation and understanding.

She smiled in return. He wanted to dwell on that smile, but driving demanded his attention.

Along the straightest stretch of trail, where a stand of sausage trees sometimes drew the almost extinct rhinos, wind gusting from the Zambesi River grabbed her hat and sent it flying.

"Oh," Sela cried, rising in her seat. "Maybe I should say good riddance."

Jonathan stopped the Landrover and, without grinding his teeth, bit back words about frou-frou clothing in the wilds. After all, she'd said it wasn't her fault.

"I'll get it." Sela started to get out. "My hat, after all."

Jonathan grabbed her arm, held her suspended, half in, half out of her seat. "No one gets out."

"But . . ." Sela sputtered, her gaze tangling with his. He read obstinacy and indecision as she tried to pull away from him.

"It's not safe," he said, yanking her back in.

Her eyes went soft. His proximity had made her forget momentarily all she'd learned in late night cramming as she read about Africa and Zimbabwe.

He didn't want to look away. Something warm, intelligent, but vulnerable shone from the depths of Sela's iris, something he wanted to investigate. But not here. Not now.

He reached across her, fastened the door. "Everyone stay seated. I'll be right back."

As Jennifer questioned, and Art panned with the camera, Matui spoke softly, explaining about rhino attacks, while Jonathan slipped the rifle from its case, hung it over his shoulder by the sling and got out. No one said anything, but he was aware of everyone watching him. He heard their breathing and the thick, rustling sounds of the jungle. His gaze swept the area, and he moved down the track. Before the bend leading back to the baobab tree, Sela's hat rested comfortably in a bush.

"Thanks," she said when he handed it to her.

"Better tie it on."

"Of course." Her look said, don't put me down by explaining what I should understand. She had clipped the words, and no matter that she might think he was patronizing her, he supposed he better give the wildlife lecture. He'd never met a group from America who was really knowledgeable about Africa, no matter how they postured. "This is wild animal country. You're safe as long as you're in this vehicle because the animals are used to it. They're not used to people wandering off in the bush." He paused and let his gaze go to Sela, but her eyes went blank and unreadable, as if she were affronted; but that, her pride would keep her from letting him know.

He sighed inwardly. Just like an American woman to take a lecture personally. Sighting a leopard's cache in a tree ahead, he pointed toward it and explained that the animal was probably stretched out on one of the branches overhead, near the impala it had dragged up into the tree. "They hunt at night, sleep during the day." His words bridged the unease he felt about Sela, and the unpredictable feelings bombarding him.

Sela, busy tying her hat down with a scarf, let her gaze sweep upward periodically. Jonathan waited for the moments when her eyes contacted his and wished he could spot a leopard so he could point it out to her, but none showed. Neither did the cape buffalo who usually trotted into the rough road sometime during the ride from the airfield to the camp. Except for the bird cries and the rustling of the underbrush, no sounds carried, and no animals ambled into view.

He pointed to the left, where a roof peeked through the foliage. "That's my headquarters."

"Your house?"

"Yes. I built it the first year I stayed here. The camp is less than a quarter mile from here, actually, but by road it's at least a mile and a half."

"Wouldn't it be better to park at your place and walk the fourth of a mile to camp?"

Art said, "And carry all our stuff in? No thank you."

"Don't look at me. My fetching and carrying days are over," Ezra drawled.

"Hey man, you better believe it," Jim added.

Jonathan watched Jim and Ezra slap hands gleefully. Jonathan looked away, not quite following their shared humor, his gaze finally resting on Sela, where it had wanted to be from the beginning.

"No matter what anyone says, I'm for taking the long way." She smiled at him, as if including him in the camaraderie.

Her open friendly look made him forget the rest of his orientation speech. "I usually drive back and forth, myself, and I always drive when I have guests." He grinned. "To state the obvious, it's safer."

Sela nodded. "I won't argue with safety, no matter how tired I am of sitting." She wiggled around and glanced over her shoulder at Jennifer.

"I know what you mean," Jennifer said. "One plane after the other, and all that food. I feel like I've gained ten pounds."

Art winked. "I hate to admit it, but you look pretty good to me."

As Jennifer and the three-man crew bantered with Sela again, the talk drifted to places in America where they'd seen wild animals, and Jonathan suppressed a smile. As if any of those places could compare with Africa.

"Safari parks are a big attraction in the U.S.," Sela said to Jonathan.

"They have any kind of animal you'd want to see, and you can drive through in your car," Jennifer added.

Jonathan imagined Matui smiling inwardly.

"All the animals of Africa in one place," Sela said. "We taped them for one of my shows. Art photographed lions, elephants, you name it. It was really something, and of course the ratings were great."

Art leaned forward. "I thought we'd see some game by now."

Jonathan cleared his throat. "Much of the time you

MIDNIGHT SKIES 57

don't see animals, but they see you." Still he wished the usual crowd would appear, do something spectacular to compete with the safari parks in America. He didn't like taking second place to a zoo-like setting that mocked the real thing. He cleared his throat. "We're almost to the camp. You can see it through that opening in the trees."

Sela leaned forward. "Where?"

Matui pointed. "See that roof up ahead."

"Oh," Jennifer muttered.

Jonathan wondered if the disappointment apparent in the single word was what the others were also thinking. Sela, too? He cleared his throat. "If you're looking for a resort, you'll be disappointed. We have no amenities like your American hotels or safari camps." He gunned the Landrover around a stand of acacia trees, and a thatched roof hut came into full view. Farther on, he passed another, turned a bend, and three more trees, facing the river, popped into sight, another turn, and the dry creek bed became visible in all its hot and stony magnificence. The view warmed him, took away the chill he'd allowed himself to feel. America had at times been puzzling, and these Americans were part of that feeling.

He stopped the Landrover, turned off the key. Home. Back where he belonged. The hum of insects, the drowsy look of day rushed at him, welcoming him. He glanced at Sela, wondering what she personally thought, wanting her to like the camp.

From the shadows of mahogany trees, staff members appeared to unload the truck, usher in the newcomers with smiles, and take luggage to the huts Jonathan had allotted them.

Jonathan felt a tightening in his groin as Sela got out and stretched, the thin stuff of her blouse tightening across her breasts. What was there about this American woman that so intrigued him?

"I thought you said Sheba was in camp." Her voice was light, interested.

Matui said, "That Mama elephant was here earlier. She'll be back."

Jonathan's gaze lingered on Sela, pleased that she hadn't forgotten what Matui had said earlier. He felt pleasantly surprised with her and looked away, his mind doing another turn as he wondered what it would be like to touch her. Dangerous thoughts for a man in his position. She was untouchable, an American, a person from another place and maybe another time. In many ways he supposed he belonged to the past, when life was slower and nature was appreciated, animals loose, not penned in safari camps. He said, "I'm sure you'll see Sheba before you leave." He glanced at the others, motioned them close. "This afternoon you'll have time to nap, walk around the camp, whatever, before dinner. Ms. Clay, I've placed you closest to the dining room, but all of you will hear the bell, and after dark you will be escorted back and forth to your chalets by guides with guns. I assure you nothing has ever happened, but we can't take any chances."

"Begins to sound serious," Art said, panning the scene with his camera.

"It is. I've put you and your helpers in those two chalets over there. Even though it's not the Sheraton, you'll all be very comfortable."

"Chalet has a classy ring," Jennifer said, adjusting the pink top that made her fair skin seem even fairer.

"You're in the one next to Sela."

"Great. Lead me to it."

Sela said, "Not me, I'm ready for some exercise after all that sitting."

Jonathan hesitated before saying, "I'd advise you two

ladies to put on high-top tennis shoes or heavy boots before you explore the camp."

Sela inspected a high-heeled boot. "I certainly wouldn't think of wearing these except for arrival. They're camera costuming," she explained, irritated that he had brought attention to the very thing that bothered her. Deliberately she let her gaze mock him as she struck a pose.

Jonathan said nothing as she leaned back, her eyes daring him to say something more. From the moment they'd arrived in Kariba she'd posed for the camera, unself-consciously. Now, she stretched out her legs, tossed her head. Her boots had tassels coming from the zippers, glittery rhinestones embedded in the heels. He supposed they'd look great on film.

Art filmed her leaning against the Landrover, sitting on the hood, standing near the door. "Great," he cried. "Give me some more near that hut. You, too, Jennifer. Better yet, let's go back to that stand of trees."

"Anything more than a few meters from the camp is off-limits," Jonathan said, his voice gruff, conscious that Sela looked like a movie star, not real, and he wanted both to rip the clothes off her body and to take her gently into his arms, at the same time. The contradiction made the pulses in his temples throb. Now she was frowning at him, as if she had been hurt by his curt manner, and he wanted to kiss the sulky look from her lips . . . and all those thoughts were foreign to him, more American than African, he thought. Bare-breasted women had not been a rarity in his youth. Neither were foreign women—the British always present.

Jennifer said, "Really, it's dangerous to leave camp?"

"Really." His voice had the bumpy sound of genuine annoyance, but he couldn't do anything about it.

"You're the boss," Sela said, her eyes tangling with his again in an exploratory way. Would she challenge his authority later? Some high-powered tourists chafed at what they called his authoritarian manner, the regimented life of the camp, but he knew it was necessary. Suddenly, he had the feeling he had forgotten to tell them something. But what?

He looked away. Soon everyone had been assigned to their quarters and were settling in. With deep anticipation, Jonathan drove back to his house. He'd been gone two weeks, and was anxious to touch base again.

Sela had a humming in her head playing over and over like a bad television commercial. *I'm in Africa, the Africa of Grandma Minnie's stories,* the words went. Grandma Minnie who had dreamed. Probably embellished. But had started from a real base, her ancestor's tales. Sela looked around her chalet. The bed had a mosquito net, the attached bathroom had no roof, and a termite mound rose like a sentinel in front of the hut. Everything seemed unreal, too wonderful to be true. She unpacked in a hurry, threw off the offending silk shirt, and the boots she'd fought against wearing, and was soon stripped to the buff. Jennifer had said the boots upheld an image the studio wanted her to maintain. Well, let them maintain it later, she'd be damned if she'd wear those clothes again while in camp. Jonathan Mokane had looked at her as if she were stupid, or maybe the appetizer at a feast. No way was she going to add to that illusion.

She felt sleepy, but excitement propelled her. She was really in the land of her ancestry, no matter whether her grandmother was confused about locations or not. How could she sleep? Anyway, a nap would only make her feel more logy. She needed to move, stretch her body, let the sounds and sights permeate her thinking until they were a part of her. Activity was needed, not sleeping away her time in Africa. She'd sleep when she got back home.

She dug out a pair of shorts, a pair of high-top Air-Jordans, and a T-shirt she'd bought in Georgetown for Martin Luther King Day. *We shall overcome* was printed in small letters left front. *King* was splashed in red and black across the back.

Stepping out from her chalet, she almost felt as if she were stepping back to another time. Thoughts of Grandma Minnie's talk of the rainbow and the great water rushed through her mind. "I'm in Africa, Grandma," Sela whispered, hugging herself ecstatically. Ahead of her, the bank fell away and, beyond a few meters of hummocky ground the Zambesi River flowed. She'd hardly noticed it before with Jonathan assigning them rooms and speaking in that disdainful way about her clothes. A wide river, she realized, a formidable deterrent to crossing back and forth easily. Beyond the green water lay Zambia, another country. She glimpsed the escarpment on the horizon but, close to camp, in the gray-green shallows, hippopotami swam, their lumbering bodies graceful in the water; their ugly mouths opening wide to become gaping pink holes—pink like Jennifer's outfit.

Forget it and Jonathan's disdain. Afternoon was cumulus clouds riding a blue, blue sky. Also the soft hum of insects, the sound of the doves calling, "work harder, work harder," and the gentle murmur of the breeze through the trees.

She started off slowly, barely trotting past the other chalets, the muscles in her legs responding, loosening like she wanted. Art, Ezra, and Jim were sleeping, their snores coming from the sides of the huts. She increased her speed, stopped a short way beyond the last tent and started back. Beyond her own chalet she found the dining room, tables and benches set up beneath the mahogany trees, their canopy forming a roof, their trunks and spreading branches the walls. Beyond them, at a thatched complex, she glimpsed the staff doing laundry, and preparing dinner. Their voices were like music, the words unclear. They didn't see her.

Shona, she thought, wishing she'd had time to study the language beyond the few words she'd learned. Looking out from the dining area, beyond the trees, the dry creek bed opened, with pink and salmon and tan undergrowth, sand and silt, spectacular through her rose-colored sunglasses, beautiful without.

To the left she glimpsed a path leading from the dining area.

She began running again, trotting slowly, easily. The way led a little downhill, and then along the edge of a drop-off to the dry creek bed. Sun flamed in the top branches of the trees, and a small whirlwind tiptoed along the dry riverbed and spiraled sand to a stop like a ballerina doing a pirouette.

Sela felt tired but good. The amazing scenes, more and more termite mounds rising along the edge of the bluff, the clouds foaming like water in the sky, reminded her of where she was. Pure heaven.

She glimpsed a roof among the trees. Jonathan's house? If so she was beyond the camp. But it was hard to figure out the boundaries. He'd never made it quite clear.

Something big moved at the edge of her vision, and a strange acrid smell assaulted her nose. Her scalp tingled and, slowing her pace slightly, she glanced out beyond the screen of vegetation. In the scrub before the sandy silt of the riverbed proper, a lion kept pace with her, gliding in and out of the brush so swiftly and quietly that she lost sight of it for spaces at a time. The hair on her arms rose and she stopped jogging. He doesn't see me, she thought, hesitating. No, not he, but she, a lioness. Males have manes. She froze, her gaze sweeping the area where she'd last seen the animal. It reappeared farther away. Then the sound came—a low, guttural purring and a throaty growl behind her.

She whirled. A lioness padded down the trail behind her—proud, sleek, and lethal. A blur of tawny color flashed as the lioness sprang. From the corner of her eyes, Sela saw the other one burst from the brush roaring, its fangs showing like ivory in the bright sun. She jumped. Backed into a tree, the rough bark scraped against her, the trunk held her in. A rare dizziness slammed into her. The world blurred as a gun went off and a torrent of sound blasted her eardrums. The charging animal crumpled at her feet, and the other veered, took off across the dry riverbed and was lost to sight.

Sela's knees felt like water that would spill onto the trail, onto the dying lion. She felt like she would crumple like a brown leaf blown by the wind. But no wind blew. Nothing marred the serenity and the horror of the scene.

The lion stretched, its limbs trembling, blood gurgling, while it opened its mouth for a last terrifying roar that shattered the air. Heart slamming against her rib cage, Sela pressed tightly against the tree. The taste of fear flooded her mouth while the animal stiffened, arched its back and slumped over dead. In its final throes, its paw touched her shoe.

She pulled her foot back, and looking up met Jonathan Mokane's concerned gaze.

"You stupid woman." The words were all growly, but warm and nurturing, too, soft at the edges. "You could have been killed."

She found herself wanting to huddle against his bare chest, cling to him, feel the comfort of his arms, his lips. He looked strong and sturdy, capable of fending off a pride of lions if necessary, and she wanted to cry her relief and terror into his chest, wipe her tears on his shirt, feel his strength and feed on it before she lifted her lips for his kiss. But he was going on and on, his voice rough as he spit out words that said she had put them all in danger.

"Tell me something I don't know," she snapped, the fright and fear hitting her like whips. As Jonathan's eyes grew flint hard, embroidering what could have happened, she moved away from the tree, lifted her head, and with a loathing she concealed, she pushed at the dead lion with her foot. There, that would show Jonathan Mokane: she didn't need his shoulder to cry on, even though she wanted to, very much. Too much, she decided, and she wasn't about to let him know.

Five

From somewhere in camp, Sela heard Matui call out, heard others answer before several people, exclaiming excitedly, converged on her and Jonathan.

The musical sounds of Shona rode the air currents for long moments, and then Jonathan said, in English, as if dismissing more comment, "Take care of the lion." Turning to Sela, he said crisply, "I'll escort you back to your chalet." Without waiting for an answer, he set off up the trail.

Feeling like a child about to be scolded by a parent, she trotted along behind him, the quivering inside her continuing unabated. His stride long and assured, the gun slung over his shoulder, his gaze swept the area.

Matui and the others surrounded the dead lion.

"The other beast?" she asked, coming down heavy on the last word, aware now of each movement of brush, each sound she couldn't identify. The air that had stood still before seemed electric with possibilities. Above her Jonathan's stilt house overlooked the spot where the predator had jumped her. Jonathan must have been on the deck that hung over the forest, watching as she came down the trail—came jogging down the trail. He would have spotted the lion following her before she did. She knew she should thank him, but shame and embarrassment kept the words from forming properly, no matter how hard she tried. Her mind had become blank, empty as a sieve.

"The beast?" he repeated, raising his eyebrows. "I expect she's back with the pride. They usually stay over on the other bank, but during the day they sun themselves in the dry riverbed." He glanced over his shoulder. "Don't worry, she won't be hanging around now."

"I didn't think she would," she muttered, forcing words from her lips. "How big is the pride? Mothers, cubs, siblings?" She had to make him see she wasn't entirely ignorant. When he muttered an answer, she added, "Look, I'm sorry about what happened." Obviously he hadn't been prepared for he was half dressed, his feet thrust into sandals, his chest bare. Had he run inside to get his gun, or was it always near at hand, like the big game hunters' guns of old had been?

"I don't ordinarily kill wild life," he said shortly. "That's not why I'm here."

"Me either," she said, shaking her head. *Damn him.* She wanted to rush up, grab his arm, make him listen to her apology. Now that she had managed to make it, he at least could act as if he'd heard. She glared at his back, and then, in amazement and with a fascination she wanted to deny, she watched the muscles of his back constrict as he walked along in front of her. They rippled like a mirage, now here, then gone, but the memory lingered.

He and she were approaching the eating area where Jonathan's staff prepared for dinner, knives flashing, dishes clinking. A moon-faced woman looked up and, suddenly, Sela felt conspicuous, on display. Although the sun was setting, casting long shadows, she and Jonathan were catching the full benefit of its still-simmering rays. Under the trees the cook and his helpers were cool, shadowy shapes, not saying anything, but thinking—judiciously?

An aberrant ray of sun caught the edge of a glass, and sent light spinning off in an oblique direction like a beacon flashing at night, almost blinding her.

"What you shooting at?" the cook called, his white apron setting him off.

"*Shumba*," Jonathan answered, his firm tread never slackening.

Heads shook. Voices clucked sympathetically.

As they neared her hut, Sela's awareness built to a fever pitch. *Shumba* meant lion in Shona. On the plane to London, she'd memorized words and phrases from her travel book.

Again Jonathan's muscles tightened and his jaw seemed like a slab of granite when he whirled to face her. He towered over her, a taut figure, faded jeans riding his hips. Like a giant ready to explode, he spoke so softly she had to lean toward him to hear. "You ever go jogging again, I'll send you and your crew packing so fast you won't know what hit you."

She felt her own jaw go firm and, taking a deep breath, she replied. "Mr. Mokane, I hardly set myself up as a tasty dinner for a lion on purpose." For a time she let her gaze meet his directly. His was hard, impenetrable. Except for something deep in the iris, something soft, but as she tried to fathom what it was, he lowered his eyelids and looked aside.

Wanting to blow up, scream at him, she rounded the corner of her chalet. Beyond it hippos were grazing along the shore, wading the shallows, their stubby legs barely visible. She turned back toward Jonathan. "Say what you want to say and get it over with." Why was she letting this man get to her so? A slight sheen of perspiration showed above his upper lip, and she wanted to reach up, wipe it off and then let her fingers explore his face—those firm lips, that jaw.

"Any idiot should know better than to run along an animal trail."

"Idiot! There were no signs. How should I know? You didn't exactly make the limits to the camp clear."

He shook his head. "The bottom line, you were on an animal trail."

"I had no idea it was an animal trail." She swept her arm around in a gesture encompassing the camp. "I took this path that leads from one sleeping hut to the next. That's all. If I spooked a lion, it wasn't my fault. I wasn't out there calling here, kitty, kitty."

A frown knit his brows together. "Say what you mean."

"I thought that trail was merely an extension of this path. Only when I was on it did I see it led to your place." She paused a second, saw his eyes waver slightly, as if considering and finding plausible what she said. "I was halfway down it when the lions . . . I had no choice. As for you, for some stupid reason I thought we could be friends. Maybe I was mistaken." For a second his eyes met hers directly and, again, she thought she detected gentleness and interest, but the look disappeared so fast she was sure she had been mistaken. She glanced away, heard him sigh.

"Lady, you make this difficult. I was sure I said I usually drive back and forth between my place and camp because of the animals."

His voice was more than matter-of-fact. The gentleness she had seen in his eyes came into his voice. She wanted to reach out, touch his arm, say she realized it was a misunderstanding. Instead she looked out toward the dry riverbed. A yellowish tan mound appeared halfway across. Vultures wheeled in the sky above, marking the spot where the dead lion lay. After a while, a sly animal sneaked from the brush, then another and another.

"Hyenas," Jonathan said, his voice hushed.

"How can you tell?" At this distance they were small dots surrounding the larger mound.

"They're always the first."

He handed her the binoculars that hung around his neck.

Lifting the glasses to her eyes, she swept them over the horizon until the shaggy creatures chewing at the dead predator came into view. "They look like ugly dogs," she whispered, her voice hushed, the burrs of confusion beginning to leave.

"With spots."

"I don't see any spots."

"You probably need to adjust the lens."

His hands touched hers, showing her.

A kid-like pleasure swept up her spine. His touch was fleeting and gentle, but suddenly she imagined the strength in those fingers, thought about how he must have steadied the gun before he fired, his body calm, prepared. Damn, she was acting like a teenager. She moved slightly away.

"I'm glad you're a good shot," she said quietly, smiling at him, much as her Grandmother Minnie might have done when she edged up on a problem knowing that she almost had it licked. His chest looked sculpted, like Michelangelo's statue of David. Only dark, dark and warm, and shining. A medal on a chain hung around his neck, the gold almost white against his black skin.

His half smile warmed her, took the last wormy feel from her belly, restored her equilibrium. He settled the binoculars in her hands and stood quietly while she peered through them. "You can tell hyenas from dogs, the way their shoulders slope down to skinny hindquarters."

She looked through the glasses for a long time, watching the flat-headed hyenas ripping and tearing at the dead lion with their jaws of iron. Survival, she thought, sweeping the jungle nearby, seeing the birds in the trees, hearing the hum of insects, smelling Jonathan's musky scent. Again, she wanted to lay her head on his shoulders, to relax. She knew about survival. Everyone in her family did. "Is *Shumba* a generic name?"

"Shumba is the matriarch of the pride. Then there's Feisty, and Baby. We try to name the animals that come into camp. But it's hard sometimes to distinguish one lion from another. Shumba was getting old, so she had some gray. Feisty has a round black mark on his shoulder where his mane begins, and Baby has a dot on her face."

"You're making me feel guilty as hell," she said handing him the binoculars.

He put them back around his neck. "You asked."

"I know."

For a time, they stood just looking out, not saying anything. When he inadvertently brushed against her, the casual touch raced through her like wine warming the blood.

After a time he said, musingly, "So you wanted to be friends."

She nodded. "I suppose it was a crazy idea."

"Really? I thought it was a great idea. I guess that will excuse you for this time." He smiled, held out his hand.

She put hers in it. The touch was formal, no matter the words.

"Well," he said, as the moment threatened to grow, to expand, become more than it should too soon. "See you at dinner."

She nodded. "I'll listen for the bell."

"Right." He hesitated a moment and then left.

It was a pleasurable time: the flickering light, continental food, Sela describing the setting and company, playing the part of M.C. for the cameras, knowing she was in her element, good at her job, and perhaps better than usual because Jonathan was there. She drew him out as well as the other guides, until they told animal stories that would play like gold on prime time television in the U.S. Afterward, with the cameras coordinating the move, everyone sat in captain's chairs around a camp fire and watched the brush for telltale eyes.

"Sure a far cry from my grandma's fat back and sow's belly." Ezra, the older of the two men from Washington, D.C., had a voice thick with a Southern accent.

The Americans laughed. The Shonas shrugged.

"That fat back thing anything like sadza?" Matui asked, his eyes crinkling.

"What's sadza?" the Americans asked as one.

"I get the cook to make some before you leave. Make Africans out of you yet."

Everyone looked thoughtful. Jonathan said, "Our clients come from all over, so we usually stick to continental cuisine."

"Cuisine?" Ezra parroted.

"I ain't et no cuisine," Jim said, rolling his eyes.

The Americans grinned, and Matui said, "That boy's a clown for sure," but Jonathan's face remained smooth, no smile, no frown betraying his feelings. What does he really think, Sela wondered, reminding herself she shouldn't care. She was here to do a television series, not to worry about Jonathan Mokane's reactions to things American.

A gentle breeze had been blowing, rustling the trees. When it stopped, the night grew so still that the biting, chewing, lapping sounds of the hyenas finishing off the lioness carried to camp. Their snuffling barks and yips as they licked the meat off the bones of the kill sent shivers of excitement up Sela's spine. She felt no fear, just a thrill that she was in Africa and safe and that thoughts of Jonathan spun like sugar through her mind. "If we could show the kill and the hyenas for the folks back home . . ." She looked around the circle, her own face eager, the others thoughtful as they slowly nodded.

"Let's see what we can do," Jonathan said, getting up and nodding to Matui, who rose slowly as if favoring old bones. "We'll take two Landrovers," Jonathan continued. "A flood light working off the cigarette lighters in each should spotlight whatever you want to film."

Sela climbed into the vehicle after him, Jennifer and Jim following. Art and Ezra rode with Matui. "Ten meters, no closer," Jonathan said as he led off, blazing a trail through the brush.

Beyond the camp, the night closed in, dark and impenetrable. Over the bank, through the scrub, out onto the dry riverbed, the Rovers purred, the sound of the motor drowning out all other sounds of the night. When the drivers stopped and turned the keys off, the silence moved in, and then the sound of the hyenas entered. One light spotlighted the remaining flesh and bones and cast the surrounding territory into shadows. The second light caught the animals squarely. For a while the scavengers looked fiercely into the cameras before they went back to tearing at the almost denuded animal. "So we end our first night in the African wilderness," Sela said into her microphone as the floodlights moved away, catching a pair of eyes here, a startled, towering shape there.

"Giraffes," Jonathan said. "Not many of them in this area. Count yourself lucky for the glimpse."

"I feel lucky," Sela whispered, in awe of something fleeting and elusive, but real, a return to a place her grandmother had hinted at: her ancestral home. Clicking on her mike, she recorded, "Tomorrow we'll take everyone on a game drive and show and tell you more about life on safari in this land where all life began."

She was shaking with emotion and grateful when the segment was over.

Putting his hand briefly over hers, Jonathan asked, "You okay?"

"Fine," she said. She wasn't sure. An elemental something had happened. She had seen life and then death, and she had felt a basic elemental attraction for a man with whom she had little in common. What did he know of mailmen and Pullman porters and women who worked two jobs in upwardly mobile America? And yet she felt elated, high.

When they were back at the camp again, Jonathan stirred the fire until the ghosts of the logs glowed, silvery red. Sparks floated up into the suddenly dark sky, the moon hidden behind a bank of clouds.

"It's beautiful," Sela murmured, sipping the brandy Matui passed on a teakwood tray, crystal snifters in the wilderness. Jonathan's shoulder touched hers as he pointed out a shooting star. She felt the heat of him, his breath like warm licorice tinged with mint.

"I'm glad you like it."

Such simple words, but it felt as if they had exchanged monumental disclosures. Was it because her heart was doing strange things whenever he was near? Or was it this wild primitive feeling that the world had stopped, returned to a more peaceful, if elemental, time? As the glowing logs slowly died, the smell of dead ash rose, and she reluctantly said good night to the others.

Jonathan walked with her to her chalet, the rifle cradled in his arm.

"Aside from the lion getting familiar with me, it was a great first day," she said when they stood at the entrance to her room.

"Just don't go wandering around at night. Wait until daylight."

"I promise."

"I'm going to wait until you go in."

"Okay, boss."

They both laughed.

She latched the door and chuckled at the senseless action. Between the thatch roof and the walls the gap was large enough for a grown man to enter. Or an animal. But no animal would want to get at her with all that luscious grass and meat out there for the taking. She undressed and got ready for bed quickly. As soon as she settled in under the mosquito netting, she was asleep.

A half hour later a munching, chewing, pulling sound woke her. She lay for a long time, listening. Then she pushed back the mosquito netting, tiptoed to the window and looked out. In the moonlight, a baby elephant, no taller than she was at the shoulders, stood ripping with its trunk at the acacia tree next to her door. He seemed playful, as well as hungry, and she watched delightedly for a while. The only sound he made was when he chewed or ripped at the foliage. His other movements were soft, soundless. Smiling, she went back to bed and to dreamless sleep.

An hour before dawn, the fiendish laughter of the hyenas and the growling of hippos woke her with a start. Looking out, she could just make out the big lumbering beasts everywhere. The hyenas weren't in sight. "The hippos are returning to the river," she said into her tape recorder. "My research tells me that the unwieldy animals are really very fast and forage up to five kilometers from the river at night."

And then the drums began to sound, Matui's wake-up call reverberating like a tribal beat through the forest. Sela lit her way by flashlight to the shower and stung herself fully awake with cold water, washing the night and the fatigue from her shoulders, and clearing the cobwebs from her mind. As she dressed, a flaring, blood red dawn lit the sky, making dark tongues of trees, and backlighting the camp. She hurried, aware that Jonathan and the others would be waiting for her in the eating area.

Like the day he'd appeared on her program, he wore shorts and a safari shirt and boots, and for a moment she stared, even as he stared at her. She was fully covered, slacks, shirt, pith helmet.

"I thought I should play the part for the television audience," she said shrugging.

He smiled.

She glanced around. There was no sign of the hippopotami, or the hyenas, or a trace of the dead lioness, but a line of elephants were moving down the game trail and through the bush along the way into camp.

"Come meet Sheba," Jonathan said, motioning Sela to his side, signaling her to move quietly, softly.

Jennifer was sitting with Art and Jim at the first picnic table, a cup of coffee cradled in her hands. Ezra wasn't in sight.

"Good morning, all," Sela called.

Jennifer jumped up, clipped a mike to Sela's blouse and turned on recording equipment. "Whenever you're ready," she whispered. "Unless you want to wait for Ezra."

Art and Jim moved to the periphery, and Sela said, "Maybe we should send someone for him."

Jonathan shook his head. "The elephants won't wait for you. By the time he arrives, they may be gone. He knew about wake up time."

"So we'll begin." Sela stepped closer to Jonathan. "Mr. Mokane, tell me about Sheba," she directed, as the matriarch elephant soft-footed up the trail where the lion had stalked her yesterday. The large pachyderm, her gray skin drooping, her trunk testing a leaf now and then, moved majestically.

As Jonathan talked, telling how he and Sheba accommodated one another, Sela moved closer to him, seeing on the monitor that Art was shooting so that they appeared in the picture with Sheba, the fringe of trees along the bank and the dry creek beyond as background. "You must remember these are wild elephants, and this is their territory," Jonathan said. "We try never to infringe on their needs. They won't hurt you if you stay out of their way."

"But they're coming right toward us," Sela said, backing closer to the tables where the grinning Shona workers continued setting up a quick breakfast of juice and rolls.

"They use the trail a lot. It cuts through on the other side of the dining area, behind your chalet. Sheba's the boss," Jonathan said, as the huge elephant walked with a rocking gait between the captain's chairs and the table, a scant six feet from where Sela and the others stood. "Grandmother, if you will, and that's Madonna, her eldest daughter. Being a bit precocious, she's already a mother. That's her son, wandering off toward the sausage tree. We call him Sting. He's still too young to go off on his own, so he stays with the ladies, but he likes to wander. Next year we might not see him with the herd."

"Do the others have names?" Sela asked, as Art followed Sheba with his camera, showing the dining area, now, as backdrop.

Jonathan grinned. "That's Sassy, and Bump. One Ear is following along behind Madonna."

Sela smiled broadly. "Bump was the baby elephant that was eating my tree this morning!" It had to be; Bump was the only one the right size. "Why One Ear?"

"One Ear is bigger than the other. And I suppose it *was* Bump you saw earlier." Jonathan gestured. "Although we sometimes get strange elephants in here, this is pretty much Sheba's territory."

The matriarch hesitated and looked back. Madonna, who had gone down into the brush to hurry Sting along, rushed to catch up. The others continued on, slowly, sedately, but they made way for Madonna when she returned, Sting at her side.

"They're eating the walls of our dining room again," Matui said, his eyes gleaming.

Sela said smoothly, "It's apparent that the people of Lobengula Safari Camp love their elephants and, unfortunately, it's apparent that it's time for a commercial break and for us to have our breakfast. More later from the heart of Africa."

"Yeah!" Jennifer cried and slapped her hand against Sela's. "Our ratings should go through the sky."

"How can we miss with a built-in elephant herd?" Sela asked, taking the cup of coffee Jonathan handed her. She smiled at him. He didn't smile back.

"High ratings seem to be extraordinarily important," he said.

Although there was no curl to his lip, Sela imagined one.

"Sure; they can make or break a show," Jennifer said, while the other Americans grinned.

"The all-important bottom line," Jonathan said.

Again Sela imagined his lip curling with disdain. She wanted to suggest that he lighten up, but diplomacy seemed the better approach. She merely shrugged. It was clear he didn't understand how things worked in the USA.

"Ten minutes," he said, glancing at his watch. "Everyone be at the Landrover in ten minutes, and incidentally if Ezra, or anyone, isn't there, we leave without them."

Jennifer rolled her eyes, and after he left she said,

"He's a bit stodgy, isn't he?" She wrapped a Danish in a napkin. "For the road. I wouldn't want to keep Jonathan waiting. He'd probably leave us."

"I think you exaggerate," Sela said, but she wasn't sure. And that was the thing: nothing about him was abundantly clear. She sent Jim to hurry Ezra along.

Six

Time in camp went by so fast that Sela had trouble remembering all the details without referring to her notes. But the highlights stood out—like the lush fringe of trees casting shadows on the Zambesi River. One morning a leopard moved with feline grace along the side of the trail, head down, tail high, returning from a night of hunting. Until then, Jonathan had been extremely polite, sharing his knowledge about the bush without encroaching upon her personal space, but, that morning, she sensed a subtle change. They had been rattling along in the Landrover, seeing nothing spectacular, the day dry, the grass rustling as the wind played with it, making her look for animals that didn't appear. She was beginning to notice the pangs of early-morning hunger that hadn't been assuaged by the rolls and coffee earlier, and she began to think about the eggs and bacon that awaited her in camp. Then she became aware of a blur at the edge of her vision. With a clamoring heart and renewed excitement, she sighted the cat. It glided a few steps before streaking off into the jungle, becoming invisible, its color and spots blending with the dying vegetation. The glimpse had been enough to impress its beauty upon her mind. She gulped a deep breath and turned her startled gaze toward Jonathan.

He was smiling and for a long moment, without speaking, she shared with him the thrill of witnessing something few people ever saw. The unexpected experience became extra special.

At first the exchange of glances appeared no different than sharing such a moment with anyone, silent communication between two people. But after a moment she became aware of the smile lines at the corners of Jonathan's eyes and the light glowing from deep in the iris. She looked away.

She saw his hand on the steering wheel tighten and he reported by radio to camp. "Leopard. Going into the brush adjacent to the boat launch."

He said to her, "It's been out hunting."

She nodded, knowing that there had been more to the exchange than the few simple words. Every day she woke thinking, today I'll see him again, sit next to him, feel his fleeting touch, but taking his cue, she tried hard not to show her burgeoning interest.

That afternoon, before boarding the boats for a lazy cruise downriver, she glimpsed the leopard sleeping on a branch, appearing as one with the kigelia tree.

Jonathan put his finger to his lips, and everyone tiptoed to the boats.

As quiet as they were, the leopard's ears went up, and his eyes opened, tracking them as they made a wide circle around the tree. That night, sitting in the circle of captain's chairs and watching the fire, when Sela heard a leopard hacking from the dense forest, her gaze flew to Jonathan's. Again he smiled at her, and she felt a special moment of sharing, even as he sent Art and Matui out in one of the Landrovers to spot the cat, though they never did. Jonathan's gaze made the nonevent important. It was as if he needed to share with her his love of the camp and the wildlife, and she dared in the deepest night to think it meant something beyond the moment, something that seemed utterly impossible in the daytime.

Another morning, a small herd of cape buffalo burst from under a grove of albida trees, their hooves digging in as they came to a stop a few feet from the Landrover. Their backs were crusted with mud from a wallow, and for a while Sela wanted to laugh, since they looked so comical, but Jonathan put a hand on her arm as he rocked the Landrover to a quick stop. "They're one of the most dangerous animals in the bush. Unpredictable. They charge with little or no provocation, and I don't look forward to their bashing in the side of the truck. If we're lucky, they'll consider it a stand-off and walk away." His voice was a whisper in her ear, his hand firm but comforting. She heard Jennifer's rapid breathing, the brushing sound of Ezra taking his still camera from its leather case.

One bull's polished black horns stretched wide, and its slanting eyes seemed to fix on her. Her own gaze shifted. "I'm wondering how much pounding this open vehicle will take," she whispered, making a rueful face for the camera. Again, Jonathan squeezed her arm. Smoothly, Art and Jim ground out videotape while Ezra clicked candids which the studio would use for publicity. Sela held her breath, hearing only the doves, "work harder, work harder" cry. The bull's horns looked like curved blades impaling the brightening sky. She whispered the words into her mike and then, without thinking, took a quick, ragged breath. Everyone smiled, and she knew the whole thing would look great on screen.

At last, the buffalo turned and trotted across the trail.

"Punks!" Ezra called after the animals.

Jennifer giggled.

Jonathan and Matui put the Landrovers into gear again, and Sela laughed out loud with relief.

A routine had developed, following the one Jonathan

used for tourists. Early-morning game drives by Landrover were spent photographing and watching from an open vehicle. Afternoons, they drifted along the Zambesi River in a boat or crouched in a camouflaged hide close to where the animals congregated. Nights game drives were to spot nocturnal movement. Daytime, escorted and guided nature walks elephant guns at the ready.

One dusk, Jonathan drove the Landrover into a natural park setting. As far as Sela could see, acacia trees towered above yellowing grass, cropped low, the trees spaced as if planted by a master gardener. The setting sun blazed a trail through the leaves, spotting the ground, rays dancing into the shadows, pinpointing a family group of impala beneath the trees. Slender, elegant creatures, the impala cavorted, leaping and running as they browsed. Perhaps sensing danger, they moved frequently, like a well-orchestrated ballet making room for the principal dancers. Kudu, wildebeest, waterbuck, and elephant moved through the shifting scene, often together, trusting one another but wary, watching for predators. The pachyderms and antelopes were part of a diorama so perfect that Sela found herself whispering, leaning over Jonathan to see, touching his arm, pointing, smiling.

"I have seen paradise," she recorded that day, the tape sent by plane daily to Harare and relayed by satellite to the U.S. So what if the big shots in the studio smirked when they heard her words, Jonathan's smile told her he was pleased.

Another day, watching the park setting, she saw baboons come down from the trees, troops of them adding to the herds of elephant and gazelle-like impala.

"I can hardly believe what I'm seeing. It's all so peaceful. No sirens. No screeching traffic. No shouting."

Tears of emotion dampened her eyes, and she ducked

her head to brush at them. When she looked up, Jonathan was watching her, all traces of arrogance gone, only a deep understanding showing in his eyes. A surge of tenderness tightened her throat.

His voice was soft. "It affects some people."

Sela glanced quickly at Jennifer, perched in back on the top seat, to see if she was listening. Confident she couldn't hear—the others were riding with Matui—she confided to Jonathan, "I guess it got to me."

"I'm glad you like my Africa."

"I do." But it sounded as if he meant, I'm glad you like me. She raised her eyes to his face, drank it in quickly: the sculptured lines, the wide mouth, the dark holes of his eyes in the black of his face. A vertical dimple cleft his chin. She hadn't noticed it before and almost reached out to trace it with her fingertips. At home there was a pecking order of color that had no bearing on the safari. She felt the competitive striving to succeed leave her, soften like Grandma Minnie's home cranked ice cream on the 4th of July.

Eyes narrowed against the sun, Jonathan leaned closer to her. She could smell the faint aroma of him, a fragrance not comprised of aftershave or cologne, but pure male, strong, inviting. Yet something more than animal magnetism attracted her to him, a tenderness she surprised at odd moments when she realized he was looking at her, not at the jungle.

Later she remembered those feelings when she saw Sheba and her family again. From the first, the elephants in camp were her favorites and brought feelings of tenderness exploding within her. Going to early-morning breakfast, she often passed Sheba and her siblings and children nibbling the foliage along the trail. The matriarch was dignified and noble, guiding the others, leading them with nudges and gentle touches, looking always for stragglers, helping those youngsters who had difficulty, waiting for those who strayed.

At night Bump often nibbled at the tree in front of Sela's chalet. Sometimes she left her bed to watch. Twice he stopped to look at her, and now she fancied he recognized her. When she watched the family during the day, she looked first for Sheba, then for him. The two were at the extremes of the group, the baby and the old lady. At times Sheba moved slowly, ponderously, but never floundered, but Bump wobbled at times, his legs going one way, his head another, so that he seemed awkward, unbalanced. Sheba, or one of the other adults, often rescued him from danger, brought him closer to the herd. Even Madonna, who seemed to flirt with danger, was protective of Bump.

Sela poured her feelings about the animals into a tape recorder, but to no one, not even her journal, did she mention her growing feelings for Jonathan.

When they were out with the Landrovers as the sun flared toward earth, Jonathan parked facing the west, choosing, usually, a promontory or bluff where they could watch the setting sun leave the earth. Matui pulled his vehicle alongside, and from the ice chest passed out drinks and snacks, long stemmed glasses for wine, cut-glass tumblers for highballs, smoked salmon, English biscuits, scones. The English tradition of "sundowners" became a favorite time of day.

On the last night, Jonathan didn't get out when the others stretched their legs, walking cautiously in the vicinity of the Landrovers, and Sela kept her seat beside him, feeling comfortable and a little sad. Only a night and three fourths of a day left before she and the crew would start back to the States.

As the sun flared to a show-stopping blaze before it dipped below the horizon, she felt Jonathan's hand upon hers. After a while he lifted hers, examining it.

The poinsettia-red polish showed even in the darkening light.

"You have the nails of a woman who doesn't work," he said, his voice not quite trailing off.

"Meaning?" she asked, hearing the but.

"It's a contradiction. You work hard."

Her brows raised. "You didn't think I would?"

"I wasn't sure." He grinned. "Remember, I saw you in Washington. Boss lady. Calling the shots."

"So?"

"I've watched you here. Nobody works harder or is more enthusiastic about the camp."

She felt the warmth of his words. "I'll take that as a compliment."

He chuckled, dropping her hand. "It is. Or maybe it's a way of extending the conversation. I don't always know what to say to Americans. The English I know better."

"Because they used to be here?"

"Some of them still are. It's the rulers we ran out."

Of course. The revolution. "You don't seem to have trouble talking to me."

"Sometimes I'd rather just watch and listen."

"My Grandma Minnie says I was born talking." Was this the way it was to end? He talking almost formally, she answering in kind? She wanted to throw herself into his arms, make something happen, but stiff pride made her go along with his lead.

"You be sure and give your grandmother my regards when you get back home. Your parents, too."

"Of course." Tomorrow, the flight back to Kariba. Then to Harare, London, and home. Her heart did a flip and, without thinking, she allowed herself to look Jonathan in the eyes. Lately, when her eyes met his, she had trouble letting go. "I'm going to miss all this," she said, determined not to do anything foolish. For some reason, she was feeling weepy, and that seemed ridiculous, not anything like the weather woman who had become a television interviewer because she could keep her cool.

But then he said, "I'm going to miss you," and the soft, mushy feelings seemed all right. He'd merely said the words, but they sounded like a record repeating in her head, echoing back and forth rhythmically. She sneaked a look at him, but he was sweeping the meadow in front of them with his gaze.

"Look," he said, putting one hand on her knee and pointing with the other. His touch caused a wave of heat to pass through her thigh and up her body, drenching her with excitement. She trained her binoculars in the direction he pointed. The increasing night breeze made patterns in the grass, and she didn't see anything else immediately. Then a full-maned lion sauntering through the elephant grass took up the space in her glasses. Padding slowly, its head up, alert, it moved silently.

"He's been alternately sleeping and dozing all day. Now, he's getting ready to see what's happening," Jonathan whispered.

Outside the vehicle, Matui brought the others to a watchful silence, even though the lion was too far off to be a threat.

Sela swept the field ahead to where a herd of impala gamboled, gentle-seeming as sheep. "He's after them," she said. "I thought only the lionesses hunted."

"Lionesses hunt more often, but the males hunt, too. Right now, no use crossing him either," Jonathan said, his hand on her leg tightening. She shifted slightly, and his hand dropped away.

Sela leaned against Jonathan as she followed the lion's progress through the meadow.

"I don't think he's hungry enough yet to be a threat,"

he said, and it was almost as if he spoke of himself, his words a soft whisper in her ear. Her own lips felt dry, and she licked them as she watched the lion pad silently along.

Jonathan moved and, for a second or two, her head was almost cradled on his shoulder. An accident or impulse? She stiffened inside, even as her body went soft, speaking a language of its own, knowing what it would be like to have the touch linger, become a caress.

"See, he's going on, and the impala are poised for flight." Jonathan's dark gaze flicked over her face. "Like you."

She moved back into her seat, breaking the contact. "It's late. Hadn't we better get back to camp?" The sun was setting precipitously, and Jennifer and the others were vague shapes in the afterglow.

He shrugged. "You're the boss." He put his hand briefly over hers and winked.

"So are you," she said, the wink allowing her to relax, become her most professional self. She felt a kiss building up between them, soon, but now it would be lighthearted as the wink, nothing to worry about, a safari remembrance only. She had no need for a long-distance romance, or men who knew revolution firsthand.

She rode back to camp in easy silence.

That night after dinner Jonathan invited everyone to his stilt house. Camera and taping equipment with them, Sela, Art, Jim, Ezra, and Jennifer piled in the Landrovers with Jonathan and Matui and rode the mile and a half through the wakening nighttime jungle. Above, the sky flashed stars, and Sela thought it a fitting last-night tribute.

Jonathan parked beneath the tree house, and Matui flashed a light on the stairs leading up.

"Just to make sure we don't have any visitors," Jonathan explained. "There's a family of baboons in that tree next to us. They sometimes climb my stairs or swing over from their tree to my deck."

The surrounding trees creaked and groaned, and the deep velvet night at ground level hid whatever animals were present.

Jennifer stuck a foot out in front of her. "I shouldn't have worn these shoes," she said, surveying a sandal. "It's vaguely spooky tonight so maybe the sight of my bare toes will send the beasties running."

Everyone laughed, and Sela was glad she had stuck to wearing traditional safari garb, her boots firm on the tread going up to Jonathan's living quarters. She wasted no time climbing, wanting the comparative safety of well-lit surroundings. A generator supplied Jonathan with electric light.

After the lamps were glowing, she passed through his bed-sitting room to the deck, the others in her crew following. Shortly, everyone was ensconced in canvas chairs, watching while a full moon bathed the meadow with silvery light, and the eerie feeling of darkness fled before an overwhelming sense of peace.

"This is what I call living," Art said, shooting film of hippopotami coming from the river, and a herd of cape buffalo drifting like black ghosts across the lighter-colored ground of the dry riverbed. The trees near the banks converged, became one.

"It's gorgeous," Jennifer said.

"The buffalo almost look beautiful," Sela said.

"*Nyati*, not buffalo," Matui explained, hunkering down on a three-legged stool near the cooler where he dispensed bottles of beer and soda.

"That the way you say it in Shona?" Sela was aware of Jonathan talking to Art, chatting with Jennifer, moving from one person to the next in the best tradition of a host with guests.

Matui said, "That is their real name."

"Meaning you were here before the British came in and renamed everything," Jennifer said. "Like we planned, be sure and weave some of this into our show," she muttered in an aside to Sela.

Sela nodded, realizing that history depended upon whose version was being related. When Jennifer went inside to browse through Jonathan's bookshelves, she moved closer to Matui. Maybe now was the time to tell him about Grandma Minnie's stories. At the far end of the deck Jim and Ezra, sounding as if they were still in D.C., were drinking beer and razzing one another, Air Jordans clad feet resting on the railing, Redskins caps back to front. Jonathan was helping Art set up a time exposure, their concentration on the camera and the game. No one was paying attention to her and Matui. "From the time I was little, my grandmother told me the story of the big water and the rainbow," she began, a good feeling working its way through her as Grandma Minnie's kitchen floated up in her memory, good smells and bright colors melding, becoming part of her story, part of this night that would always stay with her.

Matui became instantly alert, intent, no doubt, on enjoying the story.

As she told him the story, leaving out nothing, she felt the link between her and Africa tighten, pride in her family and her heritage connect, especially when he nodded his head and said, "My people have many such tales, different but similar in some ways."

"My grandmother thinks her people originally came from somewhere near a big water."

He nodded again, his grizzled head closer to her this time, his face in the dim light having the look of crushed leather.

"It was all so long ago," she said. "I kept thinking she should have been here, not me. I don't have any memories of my ancestors, not even of *her* mother or her mother's mother, the people who passed on the stories from Africa."

"Long ago, they say my people came from elsewhere. I have no memory of this either," he said. "But your grandmother's story sounds like stories I have heard of the falls, the rushing water our people saw long before the English came."

"You think my ancestors came from here?"

"It is possible, many, many generations ago."

"You pass the stories on to your children and grandchildren?"

"Yes, it is the only way."

"You're saying I should, too."

He smiled, opened two beers and handed her one. "But first you must have children."

She laughed. "I'm not married."

"So you need a man." Laughter lurked in his eyes.

She hoisted her beer bottle, anxious to change the subject. "Tell me, what do I call this in Shona?"

"Doro." His face took on a mischievous look as Jonathan approached. "And you call him *baba*."

"Baba?"

"It means mister," Jonathan said, balancing one leg on the bottom rail, his stance shutting off the rest of the deck, making a threesome of him, Sela, and Matui. "What's this old warrior been up to?"

"Actually, we've talked of many things, and he's been very helpful." Sela smiled at the grizzled old man before she turned back to Jonathan. "If I call you *baba*, will you call me late for breakfast? For once I'd like to sleep in." She knew her voice had the deliciously teasing tone Grandma Minnie said would make anyone do anything.

Jonathan's laughter harmonized with the deep rich sounds of the jungle. "The last day you're here we let you sleep as long as you like. That suit you?"

"Sounds wonderful," Sela murmured, smiling at Jonathan and wiggling her toes when he caught the smile and returned it with an added measure.

Coming from the house, Jennifer announced her presence with a clearing of the throat. A line of freckles were almost lost beneath the red of a recent sunburn, and her pale hair had preternaturally white highlights. "I hate to break up this party, but I'm for getting my beauty rest tonight."

Matui offered to drive her back to camp, and Art, his eyes beginning to droop, said he was more than ready for a little shut-eye.

"Hey, man, I'm taking a ten-hour *siesta*," Ezra announced, pushing to his feet, and Jim said that suited him fine.

Not wanting her last night in camp to end, Sela looked studiously out over the railing to the meadow below, but nothing she saw registered.

Without taking his gaze from her face, Jonathan spoke in a slow, easy manner, saying, "I'll drive Sela back later."

A fine tingling shot through her as she heard him see them off, a proper host, murmuring niceties, his voice coming back to her like bubbles in champagne. As the Landrover purred into the jungle, he came to where she stood at the railing. "You sad about leaving?"

"Yes, is it that apparent?"

"I told you Africa gets to the good people."

She lifted the weight of her hair from her neck, a warm suffocating feeling striking her. The musk of his presence filled her nose, and she was overwhelmingly aware of his arm grazing hers. Like a prelude to a symphony, she told herself. Get a grip. But the night was magic, a moment to treasure in old age.

"I really meant it when I said I'd miss you," he said softly, his voice in harmony with the night noises, the hippos roaring, the lions snuffing, the sigh of the wind in the trees.

"And I'll miss you."

His tone changed. "No, I'm serious. I'm not making polite chatter. After the war I had trouble trusting people, especially strangers. But these last two weeks, with you here every day, I felt different. I thought you felt it too." He shrugged and looked away. "Well, never mind. Sometimes I talk too much."

"No, tell me."

He made a clicking sound with his tongue and then spoke while facing the meadow, not once looking at her, as if confronting whatever demons scourged his mind. "In the beginning I was positive you were a spoiled American. I wanted nothing to do with you. You represented all the things I fought against. The British one step removed. But now I think about not seeing you again, and I don't like it." With a quick violent motion, he turned back toward her. "So, now you know, I like you. A lot."

"I know," she said, all the things she wanted to say and do crowding her mind. But was it fair to speak them? She hesitated, opened her mouth, swallowed and shook her head.

"So that's how it is. Shall I take you back to camp so you can record it for posterity? How the African humbled himself before the American, made a damn fool of himself, and she said nothing?" He moved slightly away from her. "After all, you're a celebrity, probably used to men falling all over you, stumbling like wounded animals when they're around you."

She heard the hurt and the ambivalence, heard things that corresponded with what she was feeling. "Hush," she whispered, leaning toward him, putting the fingers of her right hand over his lips. "Don't say that. You didn't. It's not true. You couldn't make a fool of yourself for if you have, I have, too."

He frowned. "What are you trying to say?"

"I'm trying to say I like you, too."

For a long moment, while the breeze fingering the trees set a branch rubbing against the house and, from far off, an elephant trumpeted, Jonathan stood poised above Sela. "Oh, hell," he said finally and leaning toward her suddenly like a giant tree falling, he put his arms around her.

For a time they stood, awkwardly, and then she gave in to the warmth and comfort of his embrace, closing her mind to the words whispering in the back of her mind. His kiss had lingered on the periphery of her thoughts too long to deny, and it was good, his mouth making a tender assault on hers, not frightening but joyous, a celebration of friendship, a beginning, nothing more. It would be folly to let it go further.

His body pressed against hers, taut and muscular, bending her so that she was tight against him, chest to chest, thigh to thigh. His torso was as lean and hard as an athlete's, and the core of her being quivered and ignited to his touch.

He drew her to a large chair, held her across his lap, ran his hands over her breasts, and explored her mouth with his until she thought she would break into a million tiny pieces of longing. It had been a long time, and she needed reassurance, needed to know that what she was doing was right.

Gently, she pushed his hands away, her breath hot in her chest, her voice weak. "I think we're racing before we've even strolled the neighborhood together." Moving languorously, stuporously, she went to the rail. The moon was gilding the bush with magic, making the meadow seem benign, inviting. She stiffened her spine.

"Will you write?" he asked, coming to stand beside her. "I'm pretty good with postcards."

"I'm not much of a correspondent. Can I telephone? Grandma Minnie swears I was born attached to a phone."

"I suppose they could relay it by radio. Anyway, you'll be back."

"Sure," she said, knowing no such thing, but knowing that this was the way to handle it. Be light, be sophisticated, and remember with an ache in the gut. "You predicted my return." With his arms around her shoulders it seemed simpler than she knew it was. "I'll make them send me to do all my shows here," she teased. "Seriously, you'll be in America again soon for your book tour. I'll see you then."

"Seeing you would be my prime reason for going to America."

She felt his lips on her neck. They traveled down to the hollow in her shoulder blade, tasted, tongued. Quickly, she turned into his arms, let her lips cherish his with passion as well as assurance. "That's a promise," she said, breaking away. "I'm going to miss you, too. But now I think you better get me back to camp." Before she collapsed into a mass of jelly.

He chuckled. "Or you won't have the will power to go?"

"Stop reading my mind," she said, going back through his living quarters, the thought stabbing her: How could he laugh, as if what had happened was inconsequential, unless safari romances were routine? Well, she would keep it light, keep it manageable, too. He'd not be able to look back later and say she'd cried, clutched at him and acted juvenile. Tightening her jaw, she raised her head and surveyed his room. She'd not inspected his shelves of books or the maps on his walls, neither had she studied the pictures of animals mounted in frames. The loss struck her like a fist in the belly, and the thought followed, *I don't know him, but, oh, how I want to.* Yet pride kept her from letting him know the depth of her feeling.

At camp, the hippos were already grazing along the riverbank, so Jonathan drove as close to her chalet as possible. She sat for a while, looking at the surreal landscape, all grays and silver, the animals seeming like shapes from an ancient past, the whole trip a dream best forgotten—no matter that she wanted it to be real.

She kissed his cheek and reached for the door, needing to escape.

Grabbing her by the wrist, he pulled her back. With a sigh, she settled in, took his kiss and gave one in return, while her mind pondered her actions. Was it the glamour of the bush pushing her into action? How could she know? She reached for the door.

"The planes don't come until afternoon. We have almost a whole day." He put one hand on her neck, the other on her face. "In America I thought you wanted to fight me. Now, I don't think so."

She didn't think so, either, knew only that she wanted him to kiss her once more.

He did, and it was better than before, tasting of cinnamon and cloves. She closed her mind to the wonder and slipped through the door before he could kiss her again.

The next day she slept until sun made the chalet warm and sent the row of frogs perching on the shower's rim toward the shadows.

When she appeared in the dining area, Jonathan was there already, pouring coffee and consulting with his guides. Light filtering through the trees dappled his arms, and for a moment she fantasized that he'd smile in a special way, but the image faded as morning hellos reverberated, shutting out for a time the sounds of the daily bird songs. It was just as good that Jennifer and the others were converging on the tables, she mused, greeting everyone with a professional smile, leading the conversation into safe areas. Jonathan had made it clear enough that he wanted nothing more than a romantic interlude.

She relaxed over breakfast, a long and lazy feast, and welcomed the languor that settled over everyone. Talk was desultory and unimportant and, while everyone lingered over their coffee, Sela knew a moment of supreme contentment when Sheba, leading her family to the river, moved majestically down the dry river bed.

"It's pure magic," Jennifer said.

Sela nodded, too much in awe to speak, and concentrated on the elephants until they were lost to sight below the bluff.

"Man, they are *big* animals," Jim said, shaking his head.

"I ain't arguing with you about that," Ezra muttered.

"I ain't arguing with them, and that's a fact." Jim laughed and they both went off to visit with the kitchen help. Soon, Sela and Jonathan were left by themselves as Jennifer and Art went off to check photographic lists and make sure they hadn't missed any shots.

"Want to go watch Sheba and her family?" Jonathan asked, his voice, his stance casual.

"Sounds good," Sela said smoothly, not meeting his oblique glance.

He drove her in a Landrover to a promontory near the Zambesi, turned off the key and gestured below. Sheba and her family cavorted in the shallows, showering one another with water, splashing, drinking, and rolling in the sand.

"Bath powder," Jonathan said as the elephants dusted one another with sand.

Sela nodded. A lethargic peace was settling over her,

and she didn't want to remember that, in hours, she'd begin the trip home. Occasional lazy conversation drifted from camp, while the cape turtle doves called and, high in a tree, a weaver bird wove a gossamer nest.

"It's so peaceful," Sela said watching Bump blow sand and dirt over himself, learning by example what to do. She held her breath, but thoughts of the days ahead began to intrude. The television ratings had been spectacular, and now the pressure would mount. The powers that be would want bigger and better shows. How could she stay on top? Improved formats took more than planning. She'd have to get Jennifer an assistant, some clever, creative person, someone who wouldn't be swayed by the excitement of television. She shook her head ruefully and for the first time that day, she looked straight at Jonathan. His eyes had a guarded look she wanted to penetrate. "I love it here. Really love it." Pleasure gleamed from her eyes.

Jonathan's smile slid slowly over his face, and his eyes probed hers. "You truly mean it."

She nodded. "I do. After this," she gestured toward the trees, the water, the elephants, "I can't imagine battling the traffic in D.C." Or not seeing Jonathan again for months.

He looked thoughtful, his mouth softening a second after his eyes. "We have a good life here. Sharing it with the animals just adds another dimension. I like to think the camp is in harmony with nature, not fighting it."

"Oh, you're so right." She dug through the pockets of her safari jacket, found a notebook and pen. "If you don't mind my borrowing it, I want to make a note of what you said and use it in the opening segment essay when I get back."

"Essay?" He stretched his arm along the back of her seat, and she was reminded once again of his guest appearance on her show. She had been enormously aware of him, and now she was again. The men in Washington faded, became invisible in her mind, none worthy of her attention. "I do a monologue at the beginning of my first show on return." She leaned confidentially toward him, wanting his praise as well as his attention. "I usually write my own material. Not many hosts do the same."

He snapped his fingers. "I keep forgetting you're a celebrity back there in America."

She almost flinched, but then she saw that his black eyes had teasing lights that matched the sudden upturn of his mouth. She found herself leaning closer. "So are you. In two places."

"I doubt it. I got the feeling all life in America was on a fast track. People will have forgotten about me already. I think it's a lot simpler here." He grinned at her.

For a while she got caught up in his look. It was as if he were giving her the opportunity to take the moment beyond easy camaraderie if she wanted. She hesitated, trembling on the brink, seeing the pulse in his neck, remembering how it had felt beneath her fingers last night. Then from the corner of her eye she caught movement.

She straightened, trained her binoculars up the dry river bed. A big bull elephant, its tusks gleaming, came rushing toward the river, sending everything in its path running.

"A rogue?" she breathed, leaning forward.

"No. A bull in musth."

"I thought it was 'in heat.' "

"That's for a female."

"He seems angry."

"Frustrated. He wants the females and they're not sure they want him."

"Sounds familiar." Her words sounded silly even to

her ears. But if Jonathan noted the innuendo, he didn't let on, keeping his attention with the elephants.

The bull pushed into the herd, but Sheba nudged him away, moved her group downstream a little.

Sulking, he moved off to a place where he could watch.

After a while he was joined by the juvenile male in Sheba's family.

"Sometimes two or three males travel together. It's about time for Sting to leave the family group. He may not go now, but sometime soon."

Sela sighed again. "Speaking of leaving, seriously, these two weeks have gone too fast. Tomorrow we fly from Harare to London, and then home."

"I should go to Harare next week. A cousin's getting married." He indicated the elephants. "They reminded me."

"A wedding's usually fun," Sela said, wondering about his family. "Are you and your cousin close?"

"I never knew him well, but he and my mother are all that's left in the family. She says he's still getting the bride price together."

"Bride price?"

"The woman he's marrying is educated, so she comes high."

Sela frowned at his words. Jonathan looked modern, his speech with its British accent was clear, but he sounded like he was speaking in an earlier time and in another place. "You're serious."

He blinked. "What do you mean?"

"Bride price?" She waved her hands. "You're saying that in Zimbabwe you pay money for a bride. You buy your wife?"

He shook his head. "Nobody buys anyone."

She felt as if she were drowning in sand and dirt and shallow water. "You just said . . ."

"It's a mark of respect to the family. If the woman is famous, like you, her family, of course, would expect more money." He straightened. "My father spent fifteen years paying the bride price for my mother."

Shock waves raced through Sela like an earthquake. Jonathan looked proud, pleased that his mother had been so expensive. She shook her head. "I thought that sort of thing went out long ago."

He looked puzzled. "We aren't buying women, if that's what you think."

"I don't know what else you'd call it." She pressed her back against the door.

He stretched his long legs. "Hey, the woman doesn't have to marry the bloke just 'cause he asked. They choose, just like Americans."

"But in America there's no money involved," she said, annoyed that his gaze went over her, swept up her bare legs, to her calves, and over her thighs. "Not for over a hundred years." She folded her arms over her chest and was pleased to see a frown cut his forehead and, after a while, he, too, folded his arms over his chest.

For a time neither one said anything. Staring out at the horizon, the distant mountains blurring in her gaze, Sela thought, *I was right not to get in too deep.* This is just a sexual attraction, a summer fling, and in weeks I'll have forgotten him. How can two such culturally different people get along? Dipping into her professional persona, she smiled, made a comment about the elephants, and brought the conversation back to an easy place again. But, underneath the casual chatter she sensed the difference, while her mind repeated: no matter what they call it, people don't buy people.

Later, as she waited her turn to enter the airplane for the flight to Kariba, a group of tourists who had come in from Britain blended their voices with Jonathan's in a way hers never had. Still, standing at the edge of the airstrip while Matui loaded the newcomers' baggage in the Landrovers, the tranquillity of the previous two weeks prodding her sensibilities, Sela's gaze drifted to Jonathan and clung there. The tourists were asking in a totally refined way if they were going to ride in "that open vehicle." Matui was reassuring them that animals never attacked the Landrovers. Jonathan was a lone figure etched against the jungle, an overwhelmingly handsome man, a charismatic figure she had kissed, wanted to kiss many times more, and she realized with a start that she might never see him again. What difference did things like bride price mean in the long run? She walked over to him, knowing he watched her move, his gaze raking her, not with insolence, but interest she didn't want to deny. She touched his hand and said, "I wanted to say farewell, and thank you for all your assistance."

For a moment his expression didn't change, a man remote but approachable, friendly as he'd be with anyone he'd guided. Then he nodded, as if affirming something to himself, and the light she'd grown to look for in his eyes touched the brown with liquid gold as he said, "Until we meet again." She, too, nodded, but she knew that no matter how poised she appeared—her tan twill pants suit and boots so proper—that a sneaky, pleased smile was crossing her face. She turned away swiftly but, later, as the small plane landed in Kariba, she recalled Jonathan's kisses. Cool as a summer shower, they held fire at their depths, like a volcano ready to explode.

Seven

On the flight to London, the thought of Jonathan stayed strong and clear in Sela's mind, never losing its potency until the final leg of the flight across the ocean to home. The in-flight movie showed Kevin Costner romancing Whitney Houston. Western music played as the flight attendants joked and laughed with Sela about American happenings, and Africa, with its tribal customs seemed another world. What did she think about Tupac Shakur? The latest conspiracy theories about government? And did she want a Diet Coke or care to try this new mineral water? The jungle, the quiet life and customs like bride price were a dream, not real; her world and Jonathan's differed as much as vanilla and chocolate, Sela told herself. She had to forget him.

With the plane humming along, the ocean invisible below, she consulted with Jennifer and watched and listened while Jim and Ezra joked with one another. Their legs stretched out, too long for the space allotted, they were like Jonathan, but not like him at all. Talking with them might help. A wide-awake spell gripped her, made up of jet-lag and the rapidly approaching land of her birth. "Before we wrap this up, how about giving me your impressions of the trip?" she suggested, knowing they had little choice. In camp she'd had little time to get to know them, and their wisecracking ways would help rid her mind of Jonathan. Soon the familiarity of home would block her perceptions of the man. Even if her feelings about Jonathan were only infatuation, her feelings about the country and especially the animals, wound deep and true within her.

As she stopped by Ezra's seat, his butter-colored face broke into a smile. "Hey, this flying around is all right. I could get used to being waited on." He grinned and pushed cellophane honey-roasted peanut wrappers to the side of his tray table.

His smile faded when Sela asked him his impressions of Africa, and especially the camp. His lower lip extended in exaggerated fashion and he cocked his head in an attitude of consideration. "Let's see now, that was more than a day ago."

"Come on," Sela said, putting on a stern, older woman's look, "what did you think?" If she'd been younger, less important, he would have called her 'baby,' joked with her. As it was, he regarded her in a semi-teasing way, his eyes saying she was being far too serious for his liking.

She turned toward Ezra.

He rolled his eyes. "After a while, you see one elephant, you see them all."

He grinned, and Sela knew she'd never get his or Jim's true feelings. Two weeks did not a friendship make. Anyway, he'd grown up where crime had run rampant and help was not always available. Trust came hard.

"You feel the same way?" Sela asked Jim, not letting her irritation show. She had not kept silent about her affection for the family group of pachyderms. At least Ezra could have named some other animal, not picked on the elephants. But damned if she'd let him get to her, not when she had bigger problems to contend with.

Besides, both of the men reminded her of her brothers when they were young, and she even younger.

Jim straightened. "It's the kinda work I could get used to. You know?" His smile was not as challenging as Ezra's.

She smiled back. It was primarily through her family's instigation that the Neighborhood Center where they belonged had begun. Her father had lobbied the mayor, and her mother had offered to volunteer time staffing a medical clinic in connection with the Center. After a few influential citizens made donations, a fund was started, and the Center got off the ground, with recreation and training programs. "How about Africa?" she asked, feeling like Grandma Minnie, especially when Jim began to look uncomfortable. "You know some people call it our spiritual home."

"Hey, I was never into worrying about the past," Ezra said with a slouching shrug, and Jim's eyes shifted toward the window and the drifting cloud bank below.

"But you were both talking up a storm with the people working in camp."

"Passing time," Jim said, his brows knitting. "Those dudes know from nothing. You know what I'm saying?"

Ezra nodded and fixed his gaze on Sela as if to say, you asked, we're telling. "Fr'instance. I say movies, and they say, 'how about that double o seven?' I mention hip hop and they talk about some dude from Jamaica. It's like they're brothers from another planet." He laughed.

"You got it," Jim said. "We don't, as you say, commun-i-cate."

Their words underscored Sela's own feelings. No matter how much she and Jonathan seemed to be on the same wavelength, it was evident that they weren't. The contradictions were vast. Tribal drums and CNN. Wild animals and sleek airlines. Skyscrapers and bride prices.

No, Jonathan had to be a pleasant episode in a working vacation. Nothing more. A one-time friend who had kissed her.

She returned to her seat, shaken but determined.

At last Dulles was rushing at her, and the beltway traffic, the colonial residential areas, the numbered and lettered streets, and the feeling of being in her home city again encompassed her.

At KDCA she strung out the "living in harmony with nature" theme throughout her first week back from location. Following the segments she'd filmed in Africa, the shows were a big hit, viewers calling, faxing, sending E-mail messages. Her first guest was a woman who raised wolves, followed by a man who never killed insects, and then came a man who had transformed his ranch into a refuge for buffalo. Sela thought, "I'm over the hump about Jonathan," and then giggled at the unintended pun. Her guest had raised over a hundred buffalo and said he had room for a thousand. The woman brought one of the wolves on camera with her, a big, gray, shaggy animal Sela petted. Thoughts of the hyenas pranced around the perimeters of her conscious being. She shoved them into the unconscious.

She worked with no time off for jet lag, she still felt hardly fatigued. "I guess I've got the magic touch," she said.

The owner of the wolf agreed.

Other guests said Africa had rubbed off on her.

As the wolf put its head in her lap and growled at the male assistant producer when he got too close, Sela chortled, "I've got Africa in the soul."

She hadn't meant to say that, but the ratings shot sky high, and Bowles, evidently pleased, came into the studio often, wearing his smiling face and most effusive manner. She'd come back with broken nails and hair that needed a beautician's touch, but a visit to her favorite beauty shop had fixed that. Nothing had fixed her ambiguous feelings about her boss. At one time she'd have been overjoyed to have Andrew Carrington Bowles, CEO, on set. Now, she felt ambivalent about his appearance after the buffalo show when he personally congratulated her. "Great stuff from Africa. I also like the follow-up you did this week. Fantastic." He wanted her to do more of the positive "save the whales" stuff. Maybe go on location more. "The public is eating it up."

It seemed she could do no wrong. So why was she feeling as if she had blown it? Environmental groups were vying for spots on her show. Those opposed to spending more money on the environment picketed the studios, carrying signs that said, "People first, animals second."

"If they weren't there, I'd pay the pickets to appear," Bowles chortled, inviting Sela, Jennifer, and Art to his suite for drinks. A panorama of Washington people were there, among them Carol Moseley Braun, the first black woman elected to the U.S. Senate.

Sela gravitated in her direction.

"You're doing a great job," she said.

"Keep it up she'll knock Oprah from her perch," Bowles said, speaking about, not to, Sela, even though she stood in the group.

It wasn't the first time such things had happened. She'd learned to ignore them. Now, especially it didn't matter. That afternoon a call had come from the Oprah show. Oprah wanted to interview her. Sela was telling the woman she'd have to check her schedule when Oprah came on the line. In five minutes it was final; Sela would appear on Oprah's show.

She flew to Chicago.

Wind sweeping through the city was counteracted by Oprah's warmth.

"Girl, you have done it," Oprah said on the show. "I mean Africa and those guides in those itty bitty shorts." She smiled into the camera.

You don't know anything about it, Sela thought.

"Miss Sela, you know you got us all envious."

Sela merely smiled, although for the first time since her teenage years she felt the hot blood move up her chest and into her face.

"How did it feel, really being there?"

"It felt wonderful. A little like home, a little like a strange land."

"Would you clarify that?"

"The big cities are much like big cities anywhere. Unfortunately, I didn't get to any of the outlying villages, but I was much taken with the safari camp where we shot most of our footage."

"Why was that?"

"It was so peaceful, the animals respecting one another, so like a paradise."

"That was Jonathan Mokane's camp, wasn't it?" Oprah lifted a copy of Mokane's book.

"Yes." Sela nodded.

"It must have been wonderful. Your shows from there were splendid." Oprah looked out at the audience. "I'd recommend you all read his book, and if you missed Sela's fine shows from Africa, this will fill you in."

And then before she welcomed her next guest, slides of Sela's show were being shown in a montage as Sela left. It was a kind thing to do, and Sela sent a note of appreciation when she got back to D.C.

Bowles, who was not adverse to publicity, said a raise was warranted for the team: Sela, Jennifer and Art.

"I'm making more money than I ever thought I would," Sela confided to Jennifer. She'd bought gifts for all of her family—extravagant and expensive—such as mink stoles for her mother and Grandma Minnie and two sets of encyclopedias for her nephews.

Jennifer admitted that she, too, was making more money than she'd dreamed about as a kid. "Not quite as much as you, but almost."

"But you the star," Grandma Minnie said, her eyes shadowed, rhythm and blues music keeping time with her lament, blackberry dumplings simmering on the stove. "Don't seem right somehow. I bet Oprah makes *a lot more'n* her producer."

Sela made herself move around the kitchen, making busy work, avoiding her grandmother's eyes. Some things she didn't like to talk about. "She's been around longer. Paid her dues, so to speak."

"That African man, he paid his dues, I bet." Grandma Minnie didn't let her avoid *that* subject. "That man is *surely* special," she said. "You see much of him in that camp?"

"Every day. You saw the shows. But speaking of special . . ." Sela said, and used the words as a segue to Matui. Maybe by the time she finished her grandmother would have forgotten Jonathan. "Remember the old man who was at the camp? I told him your story." By the time she finished repeating Matui's remembrances, Grandma Minnie's eyes brimmed with unshed tears, and talk of Jonathan was put off again.

Grandma Minnie looked off, beyond Sela. "Sounds like what I heard. I surely would like to see some of them places," she said.

Sela finished setting the table, while her mind whirled. Next year she'd take her grandmother to Africa. With the raise there'd be more than enough money, no matter that it should have been more.

* * *

Sela had just finished a television hook-up with Michael Jackson—he in Southern California, she in Washington, D.C. Not everyone remembered his animal loving side and, although she had not been able to get him to tell her anything new, still she felt the interview had been successful. Jennifer did a thumb and forefinger circle, Art gave a thumbs up approval, and Bowles called to say, "Good girl. I think you've got Oprah on the run."

Sela wanted to say she didn't want Oprah running anywhere, but the words wouldn't form. "Thank you," she muttered before hanging up and moving slowly through the back offices. She wanted to drop off some souvenirs and make some personal thank-you's to the people who had kept the home fires burning while she was gone. It was Friday, and she planned to catch up on her sleep, do family things. It was the first opportunity she'd had.

In the back office where desks and people were jammed in tight, a teletype story caught her eye, brought her to a stop.

"Zimbabwe's government claims elephants a menace. They trample gardens, eat produce and trees and are a threat to the local population. Culling—killing chosen herds—will begin soon."

The areas targeted were listed, and Jonathan's camp was among them.

A knife blade, sharp and pointed, pressed relentlessly into her heart. The room spun momentarily, and she reached out, caught her balance against a filing cabinet. It felt cool to the touch, and she leaned her forehead there while she tried to regain her bearings. Kill Sheba, eliminate Bump? Rain was turning to sleet outside, and the weather man was predicting snow. A great time to go home, hole up. But she couldn't. Snatching the printout, she rushed to Bowles's executive offices, praying he'd still be in.

She caught him at the door to his suite, pink and

white jaws showing a faint five o'clock stubble, his eyes hooded but alert. She held out the paper. "Would you read this, please?" The look in her eyes turned the question into a statement.

He cleared his throat. "Ms. Clay, I'm due in Leesburg for dinner in less than two hours. It will be snowing soon, and the Dranesville Road is narrow and winding. I don't have time for any discussions."

Ms. Clay, not Sela. At one time she would have applauded his use of the title, now she heard it as it was probably meant, a way to distance her. "I only need a few minutes." She moved closer, forced him back inside the office.

"Very well." He glanced at his watch. "Begin."

"They're killing elephants in Zimbabwe. Probably the very ones I featured from camp. I want to go back. Do a follow-up story. Stop them if I can."

He frowned, but she could see she had captured his interest.

He held out his hand. "Let me see that damn paper."

She gave it to him, watched him scan the article.

He shook his head. "I can't authorize a trip without a board meeting. How do you propose I justify the expense?"

"The elephants are the subject that boosted our ratings. We're a show about animals, and this is an animal-rights issue. I think it will help us, not hinder us. And," she nodded her head, as if reaffirming her position to herself, "I want to do it."

He considered her without speaking. She knew he was seeing her plum-colored suit, the pearls circling her neck, the seed-pearl-and-diamond earrings, her false nails covering up her own that had all broken in camp.

For a time, he drummed his fingers and looked past her, before saying, "Okay, I'll back you."

She grinned, relieved.

"In a limited fashion, that is." Standing next to his desk, he reached for his phone, and then pulled his hand back. "I was going to place a quick call to the members of the executive committee, but I don't think so. Instead I'll unilaterally authorize a week."

"A week! It takes a couple days just to get there."

"Combined with your vacation, it would be more than enough time. How much vacation time do you get? Three weeks a year?"

She nodded.

"Take one or two of them and you'll have time left."

"Yes," she said, knowing she was being shafted in a civilized way, but also knowing that this was the best she could do. She'd not come this far to back out now.

"Take Art and Jennifer with you, and this time take some technicians, too, people who can glue things together if you run into problems."

"Thanks." The shows from Africa had been less than perfect technically, but no one had objected because the drama had been so high. But, now, a fuzzy picture might not be accepted.

"We'll rerun the original footage of the camp until you arrive in Zimbabwe. Then we'll resume regular broadcasting."

"You won't regret this," she said, her mind whirling with all the things she had to do to prepare, an image of Jonathan growing in her mind. Together they would work to save Sheba and her family. Bump would grow up, go on to father his own family. Misfortune would bring them all together again, and this time she was ready for it, ready for Jonathan. She sent a telegram saying she and a crew were returning.

Jonathan was waiting when she arrived in Kariba for the second time. He saw her as she got off the plane and walked across the tarmac. Her hair was smooth and wavy again, her lips a carmine red, her eyes mascaraed and shadowed, but her smile was broad, and he knew a moment of real hope.

This was more than an assignment, he thought, she wants to be here, and a spurt of energy rushed through him. But she looked different, more like she had in Washington, D.C. In camp, without access to beauty shops and makeup people, she had almost looked like she belonged, a Shona. But now, except for her smile, she looked like someone else. Her white pants suit had the expensive look of show business, white satin stripes trimming the outer leg seams, pads making her shoulders broad as a stevedore's, and her initials twining from the décolletage that showed the fullness of her breasts.

"I bet you didn't expect to see us so soon," she called, avoiding his handshake, kissing him on the cheek, and holding firmly to his arm.

He wasn't sure he liked this forward-appearing action, so assured, as if she were taking charge, not only of her show, but of him. "No, I didn't, but we have a saying; an elephant returns to the best water holes. How was the trip?" he asked politely, smiling at her as she squeezed his arm. Like ripe cherries, her lips begged to be kissed, and a jolt of longing ripped through him. Later, he thought, when Art, Jennifer, and the others weren't crowding around, he'd put his lips to her, taste the honey within. He hugged Sela's hand to his side. "I see you're getting into the mood." He indicated the leopard-print scarf blowing like a flag from her throat, the matching leopard print shoes and bag decidedly Fifth Avenue.

"They're fake—favored by the station's big-wigs." She rolled her eyes, and then giggled, obviously pleased to be back. "They have this thing about image. But they don't know it, before we leave for camp, I'm changing my clothes."

"Good." Jonathan nodded, not sure what else to say for Art was shooting, and Sela was recording, explaining for those who hadn't seen the first shows. "We'll be on our way soon." He turned to the others, welcomed them back to Zimbabwe. "I'm glad you were able to return so soon."

Jennifer said, "Like you told us, it gets in the blood." Her blond hair seemed even blonder, her skin whiter.

"Amen," Art added. "Wish we could make it without that long trip in between."

Jonathan agreed that it was difficult to escape jet lag, but he was only partially aware of anyone but Sela. Breathing in her fragrance, aware of her soft curves, like a touch to his groin, he wanted to bury his nose in her hair, gather her supple body against his, and take in her scent. He waited while she disappeared into the W.C. When she came out wearing a khaki shirt and pants, he led the group toward the place where Matui was gathering together their luggage. "You realize I'm closing camp now, packing and boarding things up. Any day now, the rains will set in, and I'll have to head back to Harare."

"We won't stay long," Sela said. "Just long enough to see and photograph Sheba and her family. They're okay, aren't they?"

"Last time I saw them, they were ruling the camp, as always." He made a face. "Here I thought it was me she missed, and now I learn it's a herd of elephants." He grinned at the others, pleased he was able to maintain the light tone Sela had affected, that they both had opted for earlier.

Art introduced the rest of the crew who were ready to go to work.

Jonathan glanced at Sela. It was clear, no matter that

it was her job, that she really had empathy for the animals. The trip wasn't just a television gimmick . . . or was it? He was unable to speak for a moment as that thought struck him. Every night since she'd left, he'd dreamed of her, and in the morning, as the harsh call of the francolin bird announced the dawn, he'd tried to forget her. But Sela was there every time Sheba and her elephant family came through camp, every time he glimpsed a leopard, every time he saw a lion. He'd saved her life, and she was grateful. But was that all she felt about him? Before she left he'd find out once and for all if she returned his affection, not superficially, but in the same deep Shona way that was all he knew.

"How long will you be in Africa?"

"Two weeks tops, counting travel time."

Not long enough, Jonathan thought, as Matui appeared with their luggage and Sela turned to greet him. Soon the two were engrossed in talk about the city.

"Tell me again about Kariba," Sela directed Matui, signaling to Art to record the moment.

Matui's face got the serious look it did when outsiders mentioned the sacred city, but he spoke softly, explaining that to the old ones Kariba was the navel of the world, the center of the land of the Shona.

Jonathan felt a tightening in his chest as Sela said, "I see, it's a myth." How long would it take Westerners to see the dignity of their beliefs? Quickly, Jonathan led them all to the waiting planes. The overflow crew would come out later, as the airstrip at camp was too small to accommodate large airships.

This time, as they flew over the bush, Jonathan watched Sela's enjoyment of the changing scene below. Her gentle touches of his hand drew his attention every time she spotted something exciting, they emphasized her smiles, and made her fragrance even more heady.

He breathed in her aroma in long draughts, liking

the blend of spicy and clean. A floral perfume overlay the sweet scent of her skin, and he wanted to press his nose into her shoulder and inhale every nuance of richness, suck it in through his mouth as well.

Damn, she was getting to him. "I'm glad you're back so soon." He tried to keep his voice neutral, but he had to speak above the growl of the engine, and he felt as if he were shouting.

"I had to see if Sheba and her family were all right," Sela shouted back.

Was it her way of saying she wanted to see him, or of denying his importance? He pointed out the Zambesi River, the dividing line between Zimbabwe and Zambia. "For a while we had trouble with people crossing the border. Poachers practically wiped out the rhino."

"What?"

He put his mouth to her ear. "They wanted them for the horns," he repeated three times.

They both laughed, and he didn't try to make conversation the rest of the way in. Neither did she. But he touched her as often as possible, drawing her gaze to a group of giraffe, their heads in line with the treetops, to a bank where alligators lazed in the sun, to a vast dust cloud rising from the plains where zebra, wildebeest, kudu, and waterbuck ran, their hooves scarring the land, pulverizing the dry earth. Sela's skin felt moist and warm and smooth as satin, and he leaned close, his eyes drinking in her sultry gaze.

When they landed at the airstrip, Sela was the first one out, and while Art filmed, she made a preliminary statement. "Publicity junk," she said, shrugging, as Jonathan's gaze crossed hers.

"I think you better film quickly as possible." The dust was thick now, rolling through camp with each puff of wind.

She nodded but said nothing, and was silent all the way in.

Dinner was being set up under the trees when they arrived. Jonathan watched with amusement as the Americans gathered for drinks and toasted each other's luck in being back. He had the cook bring out all the delicacies left in winter storage, and felt a small thrill as Sela commented favorably on everything. They feasted on caviar, Yorkshire pudding, lamb chops, and hearts of palm salad, and Jennifer said it was better than the Four Seasons.

"Oh, it's good to be back!" Sela cried as Sheba and her family began their trek down the trail and through camp, walking almost silently on their big feet. Sela jumped up, hand to her mouth, watching, calling out the names of the elephants she recognized, her eyes misting when Bump came into view.

Jonathan wanted to hug her, kiss her, convince her to never leave again.

"Wow!" she cried. "My kids came to see me." Her gaze was frankly flirtatious.

Jonathan took her glances and returned them with alacrity, playing host and erstwhile boyfriend, too. They could always sort out differences later, couldn't they?

As the elephants progressed through camp, he held her hand, sat on the same bench with her.

Sheba had her sights set on a tree past the chalets. Everyone watched until the elephants had passed. Then, quietly, they sat down, their voices hushed.

Art photographed the evening, concentrating on Sela as she explained safari terms. "A diurnal animal is one that comes out at night, although I don't see many at this time." Everyone laughed, as Jonathan said the obvious, "We're surrounded by wildlife even though they aren't always visible."

"Where?" Jennifer always played the straight man.

Jonathan pointed. "You just have to look in the right places to see them. On the perimeter there's a pair of cape buffalo roaming around, and if the cameras will swing out toward the dry creek bed, that's a troop of baboons returning to their homes in the trees."

A pale pinkish-beige dust cloud rose.

"Oh," Sela said, her hand gripping Jonathan's as the baboon's loud vocalizing carried. Art photographed for ten minutes, and all the while Sela's look of enchantment increased. Jonathan watched her, intrigued. She had on tan shorts and a safari shirt over a sleeveless T-shirt. Her smooth creamy-colored legs curved toward the swell of her hips. She walked in the loose-jointed way of athletes, and stood beneath the trees at the bluff while looking out over the dry river. For a time she was in silhouette, the trees framing her, her curves defined, her chin up, her mouth slightly open.

Jonathan's body tightened with renewed desire.

Art got up. "What a picture. If I were a photographer, I'd take it," he joked, clicking off frame after frame of still shots.

Laughter dwindled, and quiet descended. The kitchen help cleared away the dishes and disappeared. Jonathan built a fire and asked if anyone wanted an after dinner drink. He had dry sherry and some port. Art and Jennifer said it was bedtime. Matui escorted them to their chalets, and then went off to his hut. At last Jonathan was alone with Sela.

"I keep trying to figure out exactly why you're back," he said as bird song and the rustling forest were all that disturbed the night.

She settled into one of the chairs that faced the fire and the fringe of trees that separated the camp from the dry riverbed. "I thought I made that clear. I want to make sure the elephants are all right."

"As you saw, they're fine."

That wasn't what she had read in the States, but now was not the time to discuss it. If she could stop their slaughter she'd need Jonathan's help, not that she was thinking of anything but him now.

He moved his chair close to hers, sat quietly while the fire popped and crackled and then settled down to a steady glow. Gradually, he moved closer to her, so close his legs and hers became tangled when he turned to her. In the firelight's gleam her mouth was wet as if she had just licked it, and he wanted to do the same: test the sweet curve of her lips, explore the soft inner side. Her skin had the rich lushness of a peach, driving him without thought to press his lips to hers, to taste and probe, a being only of emotions, mind whirling with passionate images, unplanned.

"Oh," she breathed, his image uppermost in her mind.

He put the heel of his hand against the tautness of her breast. All during dinner he had been aware of her nipples pressing against the thin stuff of her T-shirt, like the appetizer at a feast to follow. Leaning quickly, he opened his lips over one jutting tip and breathed deeply, feeling the warmth and smoothness of her skin through the cotton of her shirt, feeling the nipple rise and grow hard. He kissed and tasted his way to her mouth, with an agonizingly slow movement that filled him with cravings not easily assuaged.

"My, oh, my," she said, her lips going slack as his hovered over hers.

No matter why she had returned to Africa so soon, she was here, and the kiss sending a jolt through him greater than an electrical storm. He gathered her in, held her as close as the two chairs would permit. She was warm and soft and wholly wonderful, and he wanted to kiss and fondle her all night. He knew he wouldn't. Not yet. Too many things remained unresolved, unanswered.

"Wow," she finally said, coming up for air, looking up at him with those big eyes wide, the lashes fluttering like butterflies over her cheeks.

"Agreed," he whispered.

Her fingers hovered like weaver birds on his face, his shoulders, and his chest.

Her touch and her body felt so good; his thoughts kept pace with an image of taking her there, in the dust at the edge of the elephant trail. He would kiss her bare breasts in the silver moonlight, touch her secret places, know them, make her quiver and shout with longing.

Groaning, he pushed back the image and restrained himself.

She pulled away, her voice like a crescendo of musical notes, muted but rich. "I think it's the moon. My grandmother says it influences our actions."

"I think your grandmother is a wise woman." His own voice harmonized with hers.

"Yes."

"But not entirely right. I'd feel the same, sun or moon."

"Me, too," Sela confessed.

Her whisper sounded like music, a whistle of willow reeds, a cry of ecstasy in the night.

He let his husky laugh out. "You make me feel bloody good."

She chuckled. It sounded like pure melody, rhythmic and on key. "I think I better call it a night. It seems like a long time since I had a real night's sleep."

"Since Washington, D.C.?"

"At least."

"I'm an ogre, keeping you up." He was sure she was smiling. "You want to sleep in tomorrow morning?" He spoke softly, wanting to be gentle with her, and yet wanting to make her go wild along with him.

"No, I want to get up at the usual time. I don't want to miss one minute here."

"Good."

She rose, slipping from his grasp sensuously. The feel of her breasts, her hips, her lips stayed with him.

"I was thinking, we could go see the authorities together—you and I. Talk to them about this culling thing. We could go to Harare—anywhere it's necessary."

He frowned, brought his mind back from its erotic trip. "What are you talking about? I don't follow you."

Her voice light, confident sounding, she continued, "My television show's been well received everywhere. I understand it's been seen in reruns in Harare. I think the authorities might listen."

"To what?" He was really puzzled.

"To my feeling about this killing of the elephants."

"What killing?" She was adjusting her clothes, moving slightly away from the chairs.

She turned back, her face lost in shadows, her voice reaching him sweetly, but the words confusing. "Maybe I said it wrong. Culling. Whatever your government calls it. It's all over the papers at home, and your embassy assured me it was being done."

He stood. Her figure was barely visible in the dim light, her face unseen, but the feel of her still in the tips of his fingers, sent spasms of memory shooting through his arms. "So that's it." She simply had misplaced concern for the animals. "Culling is not new."

Her voice lost its musical sound, grew drum-like, repetitive. "You don't sound very excited. I mean, killing off a whole herd at a time is genocide. Animal genocide." She picked up her jacket and turned in the direction of her chalet. "I don't understand you at all. I feel deeply connected to those animals, and I thought you felt the same way I do about Sheba and the rest. For God's sake, you're the one who named them. They're family."

"You don't understand. Culling's necessary. The elephant herds have become unmanageable."

"Unmanageable!" she cried as he stirred the dying coals and covered them with sand.

He turned from the dead fire. "Yes, unmanageable."

She shook her head vehemently. "Now, you're into *managing* elephants. What happened to the live-and-let-live philosophy you quoted, not too long ago?"

"For Heaven's sake, Sela, they're a nuisance and a threat, overrunning towns, eating trees bare."

"So you just pull out a gun and start shooting, is that it?" She stood, legs apart, head up, hands on hips.

Hurt slammed into him like a fist in the gut. She had become a different person, someone he didn't know at all. Obviously, she had returned because of the elephants, and not because of him. Sighing, he clicked on his flashlight and started down the path. "I'll see you to your hut."

She hurried after him. "I don't believe I heard you right. Did you say you approve of the government maybe shooting Sheba and the whole herd?"

"I do."

"I can't believe what I'm hearing."

"It's the humane way to do it. And if Sheba and her family's been selected, there's not a damn thing either of us can do about it." How could he have been so stupid as to fall for this American, her with her white suits and raft of flunkies following her, doing her bidding? She had fooled him, made him think she liked him, and all she wanted was to launch some crazy crusade.

"Sheba? You want them taking out Sheba?" she cried, pausing in front of her chalet, her voice full of burrs.

"Don't be ridiculous, of course I don't."

"I don't understand then. Why not do something about it. Perhaps if we went to Prime Minister Mugabe . . ."

"You don't know what you're talking about. We would get as close to Mugabe as we can get to a herd of impala."

"How can you say that? You haven't even tried, have you?"

"No, because I know better."

"Maybe I don't, but that won't stop me. Now, I'll say goodnight, and if you don't mind, use that radio you have and get planes in here to get us out just as soon as possible. The sooner I get to Harare the better."

She faced him head up, glaring, and he felt the starch enter his backbone so fast she didn't have a chance to hurt him any more. "Good, the sooner you leave the better I'll like it. I don't need greenhorns in camp while I'm trying to close it down for the season."

"Great. We don't want to be here."

"You shouldn't. Anyone dumb enough to go running on a game trail shouldn't be anywhere near a safari camp."

"You bastard," she cried, and glared again before disappearing inside the chalet.

He wanted to run after her, force her to listen to all the things he had to say and then force her to accept his embrace. For—god help him—he still wanted her.

Eight

At the University in Harare, Sela looked out over the audience and the anger she'd been feeling since she left Jonathan's camp dissipated slightly. Many people had come to hear her. But he was right; she hadn't been able to get anywhere near Prime Minister Mugabe, and his assistants had said they wanted to help her, but did nothing except ask for her autograph, sniffing around her worse than American groupies. She was glad she had scheduled the lecture before she'd left home. Maybe here she'd have a chance to say something about the elephants. *An Evening With Sela Clay* had sold out immediately. After her first trip to Zimbabwe, she had become an instant celebrity, known throughout the country. Concentrating on what she had to say helped alleviate the pain and bewilderment she had felt at Jonathan's camp. How could she have been so wrong about him? He had seemed to be so in sync with her, so sympathetic to the plight of the animals—when he probably was no different from the Great White Hunters who had gone out for trophy game, nailing horns to walls. It made her sick to think of it. She, apparently, had been one of the trophies.

The lecture was going well. Twice, the audience had stopped her with prolonged applause, and they had laughed at the right places. She had only had to explain Americanisms a few times.

"You all don't understand what grits and black-eyed peas are?" she asked when a thousand persons stared at her without comprehension.

They shook their heads in concert.

"How about sadza?" she asked, referring to Zimbabwe's staple food.

"Yes," they thundered, and they laughed along with her when she said, "Grits are an American's sadza."

Again laughter.

She waited until it became a trickle, and then she moved across the platform, trailing the cord from a hand mike. Her tangerine silk dress turned iridescent in the light. She'd bought the gown in Harare. Worn with matching shoes and big, chunky jewelry she'd purchased at a kiosk in the city, she had said from the stage that she was a walking advertisement for Zimbabwe's designers. The audience had responded with enthusiasm. Now they were leaning forward respectfully and with anticipation. "Okay. So, let's see: so far I told you about my growing up years and my family. About sweet potato pie and barbecue. About my mother pinching my arm when I was a kid and didn't behave in public. No one knew anything had happened, but let me tell you, I did. Oh, yes, I guess you know: despite those pinches, Grandma Minnie ruled the roost. She's the one told me I should get that job as a weather 'girl,' and how it finally led to my present position. So now it's your turn. You can ask me anything you want. I might not answer it, but you are free to ask." She chuckled, and a few people laughed along with her, and she relaxed more, knowing they were with her even though they might not agree with what she had said about the animals. She looked toward the far reaches of the hall. "Can we have the lights up, please?"

MIDNIGHT SKIES

As the lights illuminated the audience, Sela shook her head and looked out over the room. "Good to see you." She leaned down and shook hands with several students in the front row. "Glad you came. How are you? I'm just fine," she said, straightening, facing out, smiling broadly, enjoying herself. From the first time she had stood in front of the class in first grade and told a story, she had known that the stage was where she belonged. With faces turned toward her, applause sounding in her ears, she felt almost as treasured as when she leaned against Grandma Minnie's knees and listened to the old stories. During her scripted talk, standing mostly at the podium, with the house lights off, she had only seen the audience dimly. Now individuals stood out, women in brightly patterned dresses, men in tropical suits, younger people in jeans and T-shirts. Two standing mikes had been set up in the right and left aisles, and people were lining up for the question and answer session. "Let's start on this side," she said, motioning. "Your question first, please."

The bare-legged woman, her young face serious but friendly, leaned toward the mike. "I wonder how you manage to affirm yourself daily. I know you're successful, but it seems there are other forces at work. I mean in Zimbabwe I just look around and I get affirmation for being a black African from almost everyone. But you come from America where you are the minority. Maybe you can explain how you keep a sense of self-importance."

Sela nodded and walked to the edge of the platform. "From my family and friends, of course, but I also remember Rita Dove, my African-American sister who's a poet laureate of our country, Carole Mosley Braun who's in the U.S. Senate, Lena Horne who helped blaze the way for all of us. I think of Maya Angelou whose wisdom and creativity gives an example for all of us to follow. I'd like to quote from a poem she wrote called, 'Our Grandmothers.' "

Bowing her head, she took the applause that followed, for she had recited the words well, the passion and richness of the words ringing from her subdued but strong voice.

"I also think that African-Americans have to have self-love first, and then the rest comes. When I find the going tough, I just let Maya's poem ring in my ears." She glanced toward the other mike and nodded at the first person in line.

The young man said, "But aren't people whose families originally came from Africa doing anything to make things better for themselves in America?"

"Of course. One of the organizations I know, Urban X, is a group whose members are young and ethnically diverse. They work for racial and sexual equality. And of course the Urban League and the NAACP and many others have been active for years. Also, we can't discount individuals who don't receive national glory, but whose work is just as meaningful."

The next questions were easier and less political, and Sela took them in sequence, going back and forth from side to side. She'd just fielded a fashion statement—how best to support African designs in the West—when Jonathan Mokane fell in at the end of the line on the right. Seeing him, she tried to still the sudden hot blood racing through her veins, the rapid beating of her heart, the wish to pull back the angry words she'd said in camp. She tried not to grin like a silly schoolgirl or frown like an angry woman. He must have taken a flight from Kariba to the capital shortly after she left. He wore a straw-colored linen suit, with shirt to match, beige shoes, a Panama hat, and looked city-wise and elegant, and it bothered her that her heart leaped with joy at his appearance. His handsome head was higher than most of the others, and his gaze drilled into hers with the might of a power tool.

Panic hit her. His mouth made a firm, long line, the lips compressed as if anger had driven him, his eyes narrowed, his nostrils flared. Trying to forget he was there, she answered the other questioners automatically, thankful she could do it with half a mind. Yes, the United States and Zimbabwe had many similarities, she said while Jonathan shifted his balance, a hand going to his hip, his eyebrows lifting as if he were amused by her answers. The state of California resembled Zimbabwe in weather and topography, Sela said, her breath coming faster. Damn him for showing up. "Except our seasons are turned around. We have winter when you have summer, for example." She didn't bother to say California was just as big and twice as rich, and carefully she avoided meeting Jonathan's gaze again.

"You've really made our elephants famous," a tall, slender man said, moving closer to the mike. "And we owe you a debt of gratitude for that. Tourism is one of our biggest industries and, in that regard, you've certainly helped us. But I wonder if you realize how big a nuisance the elephants really are. My brother saved for years to buy a house in Kariba. A nice place, three bedrooms, room for the kids to play, for his wife to grow vegetables and flowers. So he erected a fence to keep out animals. The elephants knocked it down, trampled his garden, ate all the leaves from his trees, and ruined his yard. It's not so simple as you Americans seem to think. Would you comment on that?"

"I sympathize, of course, with your brother, and all who have had similar experiences. But I tend to think there has to be a way to accommodate both the people and the animals without harm to either side."

The man frowned and from behind him, Jonathan glared. With gratitude, Sela saw the timer signal that time was up. She moved back toward the podium and put on an automatic smile. "I seem to have used up all my time, but I want to take these last few moments to thank you for being such a great audience, and for sharing your time with me. Believe me—I love your country and you. I will be back."

She took the applause with bowed head, and when she looked up, Jonathan was moving to the side of the room. Relieved that she had avoided an open confrontation with him, she gathered her notes together, shook hands with the university personnel who had gathered, answered still more questions from the students, and prepared to leave. Like a swimmer coming up for air, she moved quickly through the last die-hard questioners, tossing off one-liners, shrugging, smiling, but always moving.

A woman asked her to autograph her program. Others thrust theirs at her. Automatically, she signed, Good luck, Best wishes.

And then she was free, no one in front of her. She started out, moving rapidly.

The hall was three-fourths empty now, the lights dimmed. She didn't see Jonathan until she was almost on top of him.

He blocked her way.

"Excuse me," she said moving to the side,

He moved, too.

She moved back.

So did he.

"Do we really have to play this game?" she asked, annoyed at the maneuvering and also because his aroma was filling her nose, and she wanted to bottle it, take it home with her, wallow in it to her heart's delight. But that was stupid thinking. He angered her, and she was silly to think of anything else. "Let me by."

"Not until I've had my say. You effectively shut me up. Didn't even let me speak. It's my turn."

"So speak." She glanced at her watch. "But I don't have much time. We have an early flight."

"You had time to listen to others."

She smiled. "Do I detect a note of self-pity? My, oh, my."

"Your sarcasm doesn't become you. Neither does your stance on the elephants. I look at you and I see a rich American who knows little about privation. As for the elephants, I was going to say essentially the same as the other man did, but now I don't think I'll add a damn thing. I'll just let you find out by yourself how stupidly you're acting."

"That's enough," she spit out. "You're impossible. Insufferable. Let me by or I'll. . . ."

"Scream? That's classic. Protest to someone? Most people believe as I do that Americans, no matter the color of their skin, are impossibly arrogant."

"Step aside, or do you want me crawling over the seats?" She took a half step, began to move faster.

"I hate anyone making a fool of themselves." He moved to the right.

Her shift to the left was already in progress.

She collided with him before she could compensate.

She dropped her briefcase. Lost the grip on her purse. Knew nothing but the hard muscled feel of him, the lips so close, the eyes with their puzzling look of concern, the arms that held her for a moment. His hands were firm and his chest was solid, and she wanted more. The kisses and touches in camp flooded her mind, made heat rise like a fire flaming up from coals she'd convinced herself were dead.

"I really have to get going," she whispered.

"I'll see you to your hotel," he murmured.

"I can manage by myself."

"A woman shouldn't go around by herself after dark."

"I do it all the time at home."

"But you're not at home."

"I am constantly reminded of that."

She let him take her arm, and usher her to the door, where he hailed a taxi. "Is that what the bride price is all about? Making sure the woman doesn't go around unescorted?"

Not answering, he handed her into the cab and then got in beside her.

She was enormously aware of his pants legs brushing against her nylons, his linen hip pressing against her silk-clad one.

"The driver can take you directly to your hotel, or we can go to my apartment."

Jonathan's gaze startled her, it was so hard. Too proud to move to the side of the seat, she let herself get locked up in his look, even as she felt anger at his arrogance. Dreamlike scenes played in her mind. Naked together, they flowed down a stream, she floating on her back, the current rippling over her like satin touching her skin, he beside her, his arm going around her, his fingers touching her, teasing her.

Absorbed by the dreamlike quality of her emotions, she drifted toward him, let the movement of the cab throw her against him. "I'm not spoiled," she said through clenched teeth.

"No?" With a laugh, he put his arms around her and pressed against her. His torso was as lean and hard as an athlete's; her breasts flattened against his chest, and her legs quivered. Pushing aside warning notes, she burrowed closer, obeying some elemental longing deep inside her that wanted him. The core of her being had been ignited by his touch, and was becoming a burning conflagration she didn't care to put out. Not yet.

He'd unbuttoned his jacket and, like a woman possessed, she ran her hands up under the lining, wanting the feel of him without layers of material. His shirt was soft and welcoming to her touch, his body firm beneath. She imagined him unclothed, the image wanton, majestic.

His lips were nibbling at hers, his hands doing things she didn't ever want to end. She groaned as the irresistible urge came to trap his hand between her legs, capture his lips with hers, open her mouth and plumb the depths of his.

"My apartment?" he asked.

She hesitated, caught by her desire. To continue this way was delicious, but folly, nevertheless. He was too different. *They* were too different. If she told him about eating beans and sharing a room with Grandma Minnie when she'd been growing up, she was sure he would recount war stories that would make her hair curl. Since she'd met him she'd read books about Zimbabwe, knew the bloody history. What could she say that could compare?

The driver called, "You want me to just drive around?"

"Yes," Jonathan growled, passing a wad of paper money forward.

The cab wound in and out, past the National Art Gallery, the Botanical Garden, the Houses of Parliament, through neighborhoods, and back to where they'd started. A sprinkling of students were still crossing the campus. Embarrassed, Sela pushed away from Jonathan. "Meikles Hotel, please."

"So that's how it is." His words rumbled with disappointment.

"Yes, that's how it is." The gulf between their two worlds was so large that the actual physical geography separating the two countries seemed small.

Jonathan moved to his side of the seat. "Sounds as if you're moving up in the world. Meikles Hotel." His words taunted her, the sound challenging as a lion's roar.

She could never resist a challenge. "I thought we deserved old world charm and deluxe accommodations," she said, quoting the ads, using her most high-toned voice.

"Of course. You wouldn't want to go slumming. Isn't that what you Americans call it?" He buttoned his jacket. "When do you leave?"

"In the morning." It was as if they had never touched, never kissed. She wanted to cry, but that wouldn't do. She straightened her clothes, and applied fresh lipstick.

At the hotel, she jumped out before the doorman reached the car, and then, steeling herself, she managed not to look back as she raced into the lobby.

She'd never know if Jonathan watched her, but with a perverseness she recognized and didn't admire, she liked to think he did.

Nine

The last thing Sela did before she left Harare was to tape an essay relating the plight of the elephants. KDCA aired the segment while she was winging back over the ocean.

On arrival at JFK in New York, she was mobbed by animal rights enthusiasts who claimed her as their champion. They loved her. "Hey, Sela," they called. They shook her hand, pressed against her and declared, "You're the greatest." Although their words rang sweetly in her ears, she wished they would admire from a distance. She was tired; the grit of sleeplessness still plagued her. She wanted just to change planes and head for Washington, D.C. But a representative of the THIS IS YOUR DAY Show cut her out of the crowd, and gave a spiel she couldn't ignore. The next day at pre-dawn she was to be interviewed by Katie Couric.

Walking through the canyons of New York City, she told herself that a man thousands of miles away didn't matter. The gray light where sun never filtered down, the cement and concrete buildings and walls of glass were the sentinels of another world. She would have her say and cleanse herself of Jonathan Mokane.

That next morning a bevy of New Yorkers and tourists looked in through the broadcasting studio's huge windows. Bundled against New York's cold, the fans held signs saying, "You tell 'em, Sela," and others that read "Sela, we love you."

"Did you ever see yourself as leading a cause before?" Couric asked in her traditional hard-hitting but friendly way, a gamin-faced woman on the top of the heap of television morning shows. At one time, Sela had dreamed of this moment, but no sense of triumph perched upon her shoulder or filled her mouth with longing.

She barely remembered to smile. "Never. I'm not the type. I look on from afar. I report about a cause, give facts, do interviews, maybe stir up people's emotions."

"You have certainly done that now." She sifted through and held up papers that had printed articles about the elephant culling.

"Once one becomes personally involved, it puts a different perspective on the whole matter of advocacy," Sela said. The problem of the elephants seemed solvable with the jungle at a distance, so why wasn't she feeling elated? She talked easily, convincingly, and concluded her remarks by saying she wasn't starting an organization, merely hoping people would plug into the organizations already in existence. "I'm not a leader."

Couric raised his eyebrows. "Merely someone pointing the way?"

"Yes."

Couric said Sela might not consider herself an activist, but anyone who had such powers of persuasion *was* one, nevertheless.

She shrugged prettily.

The NBC host smiled at her and, then looking straight into the cameras said that tomorrow they'd address the elephant problem from the opposite perspective, that there was definitely another way to look at culling.

The interview was over. She'd been on camera three minutes in all. She caught the commuter plane to D.C.

The city had never looked better, the capitol dome gleaming in an unseasonable warm spell. Tourists strolled the mall, the buildings of the Smithsonian looked regal and majestic, and the houses of Anacostia sparkled after a recent rain.

When she got home, Grandma Minnie said it was too bad Couric hadn't given her more time.

Sela shrugged and said, "I don't mind. It's just good to be home." She was determined to forget all about a man from a different continent, a different culture. Mokane was not for her.

"You see the falls this time?" Grandma Minnie asked, taking a package of pork chops from the freezer. The kitchen was an oasis, the spider plant and ivy green in the window, steam from the water boiling on the stove steaming the glass.

"No," Sela said.

"You feel better 'bout the whole thing once you see them."

"Grandma, you got falls on the brain."

"That ain't what you got on yours, that's for sure,"

Sela shook her head. "Grandma maybe the falls in Zimbabwe and your falls are two different places."

"Makes no difference, I still got the words passed down to me, and they're your falls well as mine."

Sela had a feeling her grandmother wanted to make an issue of it. If not that, she'd pick at her about Jonathan Mokane. To avoid either, she went to the studio as soon as possible, convinced it had to be the first day of her new life. No more thinking about a man whose actions belied his words.

Driving familiar streets helped. But when she opened her office door, she found the room filled with flowers. Her hand shook as she reached for the card nestled among the baskets and vases of tropical blooms: birds of paradise, orchids, anthuriums, and myriad sprays of flowers she couldn't identify created a heavenly fragrance while Jonathan's name repeated in her mind like a musical refrain. Jon-a-than, Mo-ka-ne, Mo-ka-ne. Jonathan Mokane.

The flowers were from Bowles. "For the good job," was written on the card.

It was ridiculous to feel disappointed.

Moving like an automaton, she pushed her way through the blooms, calling to her secretary to arrange to have them sent to the nearest hospital immediately. She had a show to get ready for.

When she entered the studio, it was filled with animal rights activists, animal rights lovers, animal-rights protesters, animal haters, anarchists, nuts, and the press— all speaking, waving signs, and shouting protests.

"We've had to organize overflow seating," Jennifer said, rushing to adjust Sela's mike. "Smile. Everyone expects you to sparkle."

"I am smiling."

"Not so you'd know it."

"Sparkling wasn't on my job description." Her smile dazzled. Never in her weakest moments would she let Jennifer know what she was really thinking.

"God, you are a bear." But Jennifer's voice was light.

"I'm thinking to early days. Did I ever tell you about Josh who took me to my high school prom? Gave me my first corsage. A far cry from what I found in my office. Did you see it? It looks like an undertaker's parlor."

"Bowles was trying to be nice."

"I'm not forgetting he made me use my vacation time

MIDNIGHT SKIES

to go to Africa. Anyway, I'd rather have a raise than flowers."

"I'm working on it. For all of us on the Africa Team."

"It seems like years ago." Sela took her place, checked the TelePrompTer, looked over her personal notes. The noise level was high; everyone in the audience trying to get her attention and the attention of the cameramen who were moving into place. A slight pounding was beginning behind her eyes, and Sela found it hard to concentrate.

A middle-aged woman with a hawk's nose broke past the demarcation line between audience and staff. "I'd dearly love to have your autograph, Ms. Clay." She held out a piece of paper backed by a copy of Jonathan's book.

Sela felt her face go numb, and the pounding behind her eyes increased.

The woman grinned. "Just sign it to Alice. That's me. Sorry I don't have a pen."

Jennifer handed her one.

Sela signed, "To Alice, from Sela Clay."

"No love?" Jennifer asked as the woman returned to her seat.

Sela grinned.

"Well, that's close to a smile." Jennifer said. "You going to be okay? Or do you want me to stick pins in a doll and call it Mokane?"

"Yes and no to both questions."

"I think you love him," Jennifer said as the countdown to show time started. An assistant was warming up the audience, giving them instructions, and Jennifer was looking straight at Sela, missing nothing.

"I hate him," she said in her lightest, most breezy voice.

"No, you don't."

"Okay, I don't," Sela echoed, not knowing what she

really thought, only that a relationship with Jonathan was impossible.

Jennifer squeezed her hand and Sela squeezed hers back. In America friends could come in many colors. Was that possible in Zimbabwe? She took her seat.

The guests for the show came in; the first two she had met in other places, allowing her to wing it while her mind played a song of its own—Harare, Kariba, Lobengula.

The show proceeded nicely, no matter that Sela felt removed, far away. Jennifer cued her when she faltered. Art cut away when she forgot to smile enough.

With a Herculean effort, Sela got hold of herself, and lost her detachment. She would give Art something for his new apartment, have a chatty lunch with Jennifer, call old friends and in that way get back into her own world. Africa was her grandmother's dream, a rainbow Sela wouldn't chase anymore.

The next-to-the-last guest, a woman, had red hair, freckles, and a smile that added to her friendly appearance.

Sela smiled into the camera. "Darcy Wentz writes a book column for the Washington Post. Now, you might be wondering what a book reviewer is doing on our show. It's because Darcy is also an animal-rights supporter, and she's going to update us on wildlife reading we may have missed. Welcome, Ms. Wentz. It's a pleasure to meet you. Can you tell us, in a nutshell, what books our shelves should contain?"

The woman shed her smile on Sela and the audience before turning to the camera. "I can give a few guidelines. I'd start with the basics. Then . . ."

Her voice went on—listing, defining, taking questions from the audience with Sela's guidance. *She's a pro*, Sela thought, not having to dig, as was necessary with many interviewees. As Wentz held up book jackets and told

MIDNIGHT SKIES

anecdotes, Sela thought ahead. If the weather held, she'd take Grandma Minnie to Roosevelt Island on the weekend. Her grandmother loved the nature trails and the monuments to Teddy Roosevelt. They could take a picnic lunch. But if it turned cold again, they'd go to Frederick Douglas's house, to which they made a pilgrimage once a year. Sela turned to Wentz, not having missed a bit of the woman's monologue, but shocked by her next words.

"This new book by Jonathan Mokane contends that government-sponsored culling, killing a whole herd at once, is necessary," Wentz said.

Sela jumped to her feet and shook her head in disagreement. "As you know, I'm opposed to that stand. I understand that sometimes there's a need to do away with the old and infirm, the matriarchs, perhaps. And of course, if it's done humanely, with sympathy and kindness. But wiping out a whole herd is reprehensible and cruel. Animal genocide." She shook her head, and with hands out, palms up, appealed to the audience. They burst into applause and, smiling with satisfaction, Sela took her seat.

Wentz's smile became even broader. "Those are strong words, but I thought exactly the same way until I read the first chapter of Mokane's new book. The publisher sent me a pre-publication copy. Mokane reasons that if one kills the matriarch, the whole herd perishes, for she directs and leads the herd's actions. Without her, they flounder, suffer, and eventually die, sometimes a lingering death. It's not a pretty sight to watch. Culling is essentially the humane way to go."

Sela felt as if a balloon had burst in her head, ideas moving so fast she couldn't process them all. As smoothly as possible, she ended the segment, cued her last interview, and rushed out as soon as the show ended. If only Jonathan had explained it to her. Or had he thought she'd known? Or had she given him a chance to say much of anything? Maybe she should call him, apologize.

She hurried beyond the set, but Bowles's assistant stopped her before she left the studio. "Mr. Bowles says you made us look idiotic, not knowing the full story about the elephants. He wants you to bring it out on the next show, talk about it fully, explain how you were so mistaken. And then eat crow if you have to."

She twined a red and white scarf around her neck, buttoned her coat. "I feel idiotic enough and you're saying he wants me to do a *mea culpa*?"

The assistant lowered his voice. "If I knew exactly what he wanted, I wouldn't be doing his dirty work for him. I'd have his job."

"Thanks loads," she said, hurrying out. As always, traffic was awful. Cars entering and leaving the beltway were backed up a quarter mile. She jockeyed into place and, before she could lose her nerve, she dialed Bowles's home phone on her cellular. She'd never called the unlisted number before.

"Who in the hell has the audacity to call during dinner hour?" he growled.

"It's Sela Clay, and I'm wondering what you want me to do."

"Ms. Clay, I personally don't care what you do. For the show I want you to be contrite and then get out of the damn pachyderm business. Cozy up to wolves, coots, coyotes. Even llamas. Whatever will keep the ratings up. Understand?"

She shifted gears. "You're coming in loud and clear."

"Nothing personal, Ms. Clay, but if the ratings fall you'll be interviewing aardvarks in Timbuktu."

"Aardvarks were never my thing," she said, zooming into the line of traffic, her red car drawing glances from people who recognized her. She waved back, smiled automatically. She'd contact her agent tomorrow and begin looking for another position.

"Good girl," Bowles continued, "you've got spunk."

"In the world I come from, spunk is necessary." As she changed lanes, it occurred to her for the first time that maybe she should make a career change, too, and leave television. But for what?

Jonathan might help. She would write to him and explain. What? That she was looking for another job? That she had been wrong about the elephants? That she had been wrong about him from the first? What if he read her letter and discarded it, or only read a sentence or two and tore it up? Or, worse yet, read it when he was with another woman?

For hours that night, she tossed and turned, words and phrases, sometimes sentences forming, but the final form of the letter never seemed right. She kept putting it off until even the thought of picking up a pen and writing to him terrified her.

One day, a month later, she sent him a card showing the Washington, D.C. monuments at night. "Thanks again for your hospitality while we were in Africa," she wrote impersonally. And then, incongruously, she added, "My family sends their regards."

Three months later, she strolled along the grand corridor at the Kennedy Center, cocktail glass in hand, at a benefit for the Dance Theater of Harlem and wished fervently that she wasn't with KDCA. Her show had taken a dive after those wonderful weeks during and after Africa. Now she was barely holding her own in the ratings game. Bowles barely nodded when he passed her in the studio, and she felt stressed from the constant need to stay ahead of the pack. She was keeping her ears open for other possibilities, but tonight she didn't want thoughts of the studio plaguing her. She was here with her family and she would enjoy it.

Meandering along with her sister Nefari at her side, she smiled at acquaintances, called to friends, and felt the distinct possibility of good things happening. Her tangerine-colored dress sparkled with sequins, and she felt decidedly glamorous—if a little lonely. The long scarlet carpet and the vast amount of glass at the Kennedy Center seemed a fitting background for the hundreds of women and men in stylish evening attire. The concourse was filled with important and famous people who had received the ballet company's gala performance of *Dougla* with wild enthusiasm, thunderous applause leading to a standing ovation. Performers and audience were the cream of African-American society. Arthur Mitchell, the elegant force behind the Dance Theater and a former dancer himself, moved with the courtly refinement of his station and soon became the center of a group who watched him with looks of adoration on their faces.

Nefari whispered, "I bet he was something when he was the only black man in ballet."

Sela said, "Girl, he still is something."

Jesse Jackson was smiling at her; Quincy Jones called, "Talk to you later," and the extreme feelings of loneliness she had felt since last she'd seen Jonathan lifted somewhat. She nodded to Quincy, even as she listened to Nefari, a slight smile on her face.

Her sister squealed and suddenly gripped Sela's arm. "My gosh, Mitchell's speaking to Cicely Tyson. You know they used to be an item."

Sela spoke carefully, glad that the hollow aloneness was fading, before someone suspected the depth of her unhappiness. She forced an even tone to her speech, one that canceled all inner anxiety. "I know they used to date. Come on, I'll introduce you."

"No, I'd rather just watch. Isn't Cicely's hair great? Still, I'm glad I wear braids. Suits me, don't you think?" Nefari's self doubt was not always so evident.

"You look fantastic."

"You think so? I'm jealous of Cicely Tyson's clothes. In case you're not aware, she's wearing a Tracy Reese original. Think I'll ever design anything as great?"

Sela said, "One day you'll make your own mark on the fashion world."

"I'd do it differently, though," Nefari announced with the arrogance of youth. "Less jacket, more skirt."

Smiling, Sela led her toward Mitchell, but supermodel Naomi Campbell got there first, her head a riot of curls, her mouth a pout of red, her bare arms clanking with bracelets, her curves in abundant display.

"Oh, wow!" Nefari said, looking down at the outfit she had created for herself. "Makes me feel dowdy."

Before Nefari could become too crestfallen, Sela hugged her. Only the warmth of her family had sustained her since she'd returned from Africa. "Truthfully. Your satin shirt dress with that gray silk blazer is really striking."

"I think you sound like a fashion-show host," their mother, Miriam, said, joining them, her ample curves covered in flowing material that glittered almost as much as the sheen of excitement in her eyes.

" 'Cept Nefari don't know who she is," Grandma Minnie said giving a twitch to her own quilted jacket. "Few months ago it was an Egyptian princess."

"I'm just glad she isn't bleaching her hair," Samuel Clay said, fingering his tie. "I think this thing is going to choke me before the night is over."

"You look good in a tie, Dad. As for light hair; some women can carry it off, some can't," Sela said.

Grana Minnie bobbed her head emphatically. "Ain't that the truth."

"The truth will set you free," Louis said, a paper plate full of hors d'oeuvres in his hand. Pulling paper napkins from his pocket, he passed them around.

"You savin' my life," Grandma Minnie said, helping herself to a goody.

Everyone laughed. As Lawrence and the younger members of the family congregated, Sela let her gaze sweep the room. With a coterie of admirers swarming around her Nikki Giovanni stood not far away. She pointed her out discreetly to the family while a few gutsy people collected autographs. Most just watched the celebrities from a distance and Sela realized—not without a smidgen of pride and gratitude—she, too, was drawing attention. While Grandma Minnie pursed her lips in an attitude of ownership, Sela signed a program for an admirer, looked up, and spotted Jonathan Mokane standing near the sculpted bust of John F. Kennedy.

For a moment her heart did a familiar rat-a-tat-tat, while an infusion of hot blood spread up her neck and through her face. She'd never seen him in evening attire before, and he stood with a group of people she didn't recognize, his white shirt making his mahogany skin that much richer, that much darker. Perhaps his companions—people she didn't recognize—were from the Zimbabwe embassy. Or the publishing world. Tall people, ebony and chocolate, a sprinkling of Caucasians, they spoke with animation that seemed natural, not forced: people who moved with authority. Jonathan's dark face, his form, his bearing—so utterly confident, so indisputably sure of himself and his actions—made the others seem lesser than he, shadow people in his play. As he talked, his hand gestures adding to the story, she wondered what he was saying. A riptide of emotions, from A to Z, washed over Sela while Jonathan's laugh carried, moving through her mind with familiarity, awakening the feelings she had deliberately hidden.

Grandma Minnie gave her jacket a twitch and put a hand to her hair before saying, "Why, there's that African man." Her voice hummed and echoed with pleasure.

"Well, so it is," Louis said, squaring his shoulders. "I haven't seen him since he came to the reunion. Sorry, Sis, but I missed your shows from Africa."

"I forgot to pay you to watch," Sela managed, her laugh coming out forced.

"We should see about getting together with him," Louis said, his gaze going to Brenda Mae.

"Great idea," she said, sliding her social calendar from her purse and consulting it. "I promised him some homecooking next time he was in town. Remember?"

"Sure do," Grandma Minnie said quickly.

"You think Friday, Louis? If he's still here. Or we could shuffle things around and be free Thursday."

The family crowded in, everyone offering suggestions.

"Excuse me," Sela said, the need to be alone expanding like a balloon within her. It was clear that Jonathan didn't want to see her, or he'd have written, gotten in touch with her before now. The card she'd sent had been far from subtle. Mentioning her family, using them in that way still made her flush. "Be right back." No doubt Brenda Mae was already planning a menu and the guest list.

Sela veered down a connecting corridor—narrowly avoiding a collision with General Colin Powell, who was saying he had no interest in a political position—dashed into the women's room, bypassed the women who crowded the makeup mirror, and locked herself into a cubicle. If Louis and Brenda Mae wanted to entertain Jonathan, Sela could plead another engagement. No one would know she was avoiding him, and there'd be none of that push and prod language, albeit well-meant, that came from family who would like nothing better than to see all single members married.

When she heard the other women leave the powder room, she eased out and took her time refurbishing her makeup. Guerlain of Paris was brushed on her cheeks, she ran a comb through her hair, dabbed perfume in the crook of her elbows, and took her time applying lipstick. Emerging into the hall again, she had her feelings in check and she allowed her luminous eyes, freshly made up, to sweep the hall as if she owned it.

"Sela Clay!" a baritone voice cried and, for a moment she thought: Jonathan. Relief spread through her. Yes, she wanted to see him. Then a hand on her arm spun her around, and she saw the thin, wiry man who had taken her to her high school prom. He'd been studying for his Ph.D. when she'd started college and had always, in some not quite clear way, wanted more than a platonic relationship with her, but she'd had eyes only for Frankie. "Why, Josh Hughes, I haven't seen you for ages!" His caramel-colored face with its broad mouth seemed little changed, his smile as infectious. Disappointed, but her fears about a face to face meeting with Jonathan somewhat allayed, she felt the constriction in her heart ease.

"That long? In some ways it seems like yesterday." He steered her over to the side, next to the wall, away from the stream of ballet dancers who were now circulating among the paying guests, the ballerinas and principal dancers seeming very young away from the glare of the stage lights where their artistry had rendered them ageless. "I see you on the tube now and then and tell everyone I knew her when," Josh said, his smile broad. "Gosh, you look good, you little animal lover, you."

Sela pressed her lips into a reasonable facsimile of a

MIDNIGHT SKIES

smile. "I do my bit for nature. And you! You made a movie, didn't you?"

"Several, to be exact. One that caught on, and a couple that scored big in Cannes." He grinned. "Damn—it's good to see you. I'm doing a new picture. Me and a dozen investors. Spectacular, if I must use the word." He waved his hand, and the rings on his fingers glittered.

"Doesn't sound like you've been letting anything get in the way of success."

He looked thoughtful and, for a moment, she supposed he was remembering her as she had been the days they'd both scrimped through college.

"I'm going to make it big with this African picture. Drama, history—all that. But heck, you been over there, you know." He fixed her with a penetrating gaze. "You gonna be in my picture, Sela?"

She shook her head. "I'm no actor."

"Too bad. You got the looks for it."

And then, before she realized what was happening, they talked about other positions behind the camera. As technical assistant she would be up to her eyebrows in new territory, borrowing their expertise from others. But she could do it, she knew. A new job would be demanding, giving her no time to think, and working with Josh would be a way out of KDCA, a way of forgetting Jonathan.

"I congratulate myself for thinking of it," Josh said. "The minute I saw you, I said to myself, she could be a great help on my new show."

"Josh!"

"Okay, okay, I apologize. I didn't think about it until you opened your mouth. Let's talk seriously tomorrow about getting you a job in Jo-Dusk Productions, my company," Josh said, giving her his card. "Call me. We'll do lunch or happy hour or something." His gaze swept the hall. "Right now, I've got this investor . . ." He looked back at her, smiled, winked.

The same old Josh, she thought as he strolled off with his signature bounce still in his walk.

Returning to her family circle, Sela's step was light. If things worked right, she would never go to Bowles's office again. If anything, Josh was loyal, and the thought of working with him was a good one. All she'd have to do would be to say no and he'd stop any unwanted advances.

As she hurried down the hall, conscious of admiring glances, she was again relieved and disappointed when she didn't see Jonathan. Now, she would feel encumbered, the duties of a new job serving as a wedge between them. With gratitude, she rejoined her family.

Five minutes later, trailing a group of young hangers-on, Josh came rushing up announcing that there was a party in Gaithersberg, Maryland, and Sela had to attend with them. Everyone would be there, including the ballet dancers. He wouldn't take no for an answer.

Forty-five minutes later as Josh's chauffeured limousine swept into the circular drive in front of the white-pillared mansion, Sela glimpsed a familiar-appearing man going into the house. He was surrounded by a group of people, but there was no mistaking that head, that stance, that walk. It was Jonathan Mokane, and there was no way she could avoid him, and she knew that in truth she didn't want to. In the big entrance hall, he turned just as she entered the door. As her eyes grew big, his narrowed, and then softened, and he said, "Here she is now."

As if he'd been expecting her.

Ten

During the next few minutes Sela felt as if she were on auto-pilot, having no control. Jonathan took her by the arm and never let go. She found herself guided, through rooms of gleaming parquet floors, white molding, delicate flowered wallpaper, silver sconces, candelabra. Along with many of the celebrities she had seen at the Kennedy Center, the East Coast African-American social set were here in full force. People who had led the summer exodus to Martha's Vineyard as early as the 1920's rubbed shoulders with New Yorkers and those prominent in Washington, D.C. circles. All recognized her and most had heard of Jonathan Mokane.

"How nice to see you together. You must have much in common."

Sela found herself smiling and saying yes. What else could she do? It was impossible to speak to Jonathan without an audience listening. Reluctantly she allowed him to lead her through the glittering assembly to the vast dining room. Through grammar school and high school, she had been a leader, not a follower, and the trait the family said was inherited from her grandmother had increased. She didn't like what was happening, and that she was also getting a peculiar pleasure out of his touch angered her.

Playing it as cool as possible, she circled a table laden

with good things to eat, all tastefully displayed on crystal and china, Jonathan at her elbow, his eyes drinking her in, his words addressing others, but the sound belonging to her. Background music bubbled along with the champagne. Carnations in vases sweetened the air, and everyone was smiling at everyone, talking about the benefit, of the grace and ability of the Dance Theater. Mitchell had made it a success, against overwhelming odds.

Sela kept her voice low but urgent, her face noncommunicative as the people nearest her moved on. "Let go of my arm, please."

Jonathan popped an olive into his mouth. "Why? So you can run away again?" His voice, too, was soft, but he smiled, his gaze going over the people assembled as if nothing was happening between him and Sela.

"Why should I stay? Things haven't changed between us. You set me up to be humiliated about the elephants, and now you lead me around like I have a ring in my nose." She managed a smile, as if she were conducting witty repartée.

Before he could reply, a woman cried, "Jonathan Mokane!" Small, white-haired, and expensively dressed, she clutched a book in her hands. "My students read your books, and so few catch their attention these days." She held out a copy for him to autograph. "Your latest straightened me out about the elephants." Her smile went from him to Sela.

Sela smiled, too.

Jonathan scrawled his signature while holding Sela next to him, and joked and laughed with the woman.

Sela thought she would suffocate, his aroma like an aphrodisiac tickled her nose, his strength made her want to melt. But that would be giving in, and she'd never capitulate without a struggle.

After the woman left, Sela muttered, "I'm glad you

straightened her out. Now, how about me? I came off like an idiot on television, not once but twice." Smiling, she tapped his arm. She imagined the muscles beneath his coat bulging, but he didn't budge an inch.

He cocked his eyebrows, and a look of quiet amusement hovered around his mouth. She almost expected him to laugh. Instead, he took another olive, offered her one, holding it delicately between the tips of two fingers.

She shook her head. "You're impossible." Would she have to make a scene to make him let go? She knew she looked well, the mirror in the powder room at the Kennedy Center had told her so. Now the look in his eyes showed his appreciation. She frowned more confused than ever.

He shrugged, popped an olive into his own mouth. "The way I heard it, not knowing everything about Zimbabwe's elephant policy didn't appreciably hurt your ratings. Isn't that what television's all about? Ratings?"

She kept her voice low, her mouth tucked in a smile. "It's also about being efficient, competent, and knowledgeable. I came off looking like an ill-prepared, know-nothing jerk." She hissed the words.

"Sorry. I assumed you knew what culling meant." He reached into a bed of ice, speared a shrimp. "You arrived in camp acting as if you didn't need explanations about anything." Swallowing the shrimp, he moved down the table, sampling mushrooms, pickles, quiche, pulling her along with him.

Taking a quick glance around, she saw that, except for a couple at the far end of the table, they were alone. "I came into camp being myself, as prepared as I could be." Her staff had fed her all the latest information available. It had left her with understandable gaps in her knowledge.

He grinned at her, released her so suddenly she stumbled after him, catching her balance like a high-wire walker.

"Being yourself is pretty good," he said with that brown-sugar voice making candy of the words.

She was startled into staring up at him, a question in her eyes. Was he switching gears, changing his strategy? His expression was bland, mild even. Again, she felt intrigued.

"There was something about you I liked." His voice had a husky quality, like fur brushing against bare skin, warming it. Or a pot simmering, ready to boil.

Startled, she muttered, "Liked. Past tense."

"You haven't been exactly ingratiating lately." His voice suddenly assumed a bored sound, but his eyes gleamed in a taunting fashion.

She felt renewed righteous anger. He was playing with her, and she felt let down, put upon. "Neither have you."

The smile left his eyes. "No."

"You admit it." She was genuinely surprised.

"No. I admit other things. Such as I like my arm around you. You feel good." He leaned down and whispered, "Admit it, Ms. Clay, you like it, too."

She felt her cheeks sizzle, her head spin and none of the arguments that gave her an excuse to be angry with him had legitimacy anymore. "You're impossible." She grabbed a cream puff, bit off a large hunk to keep from laughing, letting him know she was enjoying the moment.

The cream oozed from the crust, some settling on the edge of her mouth. Before she could lick it away, he said, "Here, let me."

She looked like a fool again. She could stomp on his foot, so elegantly clad in shining patent leather, but she liked being held in the circle of his arm, although she wouldn't admit it.

Sensually, he wiped the cream from her lips. "There."

She caught the gleam of laughter in the back of his eyes, the smile breaking like sunshine across his mouth. Her own eyes responded, and a chuckle came unplanned from her lips. Beneath his elegant and urbane exterior, his sometimes rough unknown African ways, she glimpsed a relaxed and kind man.

He hugged her. "How about we find a place where we can sit, drink champagne, and I can apologize?"

Her heart did a tripping action. "Did I hear you right? You said the A word?"

He nodded, loosening his hold on her. She could walk out of the room, cut him out of her life forever, but she lingered, standing tall, her gaze meeting his full on.

His face serious again, his eyes shadowed, he said, "I really thought you understood about the elephants. And when I realized you didn't, it was too late to explain." He moved away a few steps, and toyed with the edge of a napkin, folding and unfolding it.

He seemed as nervous as she felt, rocking back and forth on his heels, a smile skittering around his mouth and then disappearing.

For a few moments they were the only ones in the large dining room. Through the open double doors she could see other guests swirling in party configurations in the two front parlors, surrounding the piano in the music room, crowding together in the den. Other people, voices ringing, were taking the stairs to the downstairs recreation room. "I suppose I was as much to blame for the silence as you. I never asked for details," she admitted, discarding the witty quips that came to mind.

Jonathan nodded.

Their host, a man who was somebody with Josh's film

company, stuck his head in the door. "Everything all right in there? Need more food, champagne?"

"Everything's fine," Sela said.

"You mean that?" Jonathan asked as, with a wave of the hand, the man disappeared. "Everything's fine?"

"I was talking generally."

"Me, too. Generally, I like you. A lot."

A waiter came through with glasses of champagne on a tray. Jonathan captured two, handed one to Sela. His fingers were square-tipped, strong. She imagined them on her neck, touching her as he had in Zimbabwe. His last words repeating in her mind, she sipped from the fluted glass, let the bubbles go up her nose. People were congregating around the table again, two couples, followed by a gaggle of lone men all talking film-making.

"I glimpsed a small room down the hall," Jonathan said. "I guess you could call it the library."

"It is. I doubt my ancestors got anywhere near a library in the early days. We weren't even allowed to learn to read then."

He took her arm. "When Zimbabwe was still Rhodesia, the British brought their schooling to us, segregated, of course." He led her down the richly carpeted corridor, pictures of nineteenth century people on the wall.

"Grandma Minnie only went to third grade, but she's one of the wisest women I know."

"I'm sure she is."

The room was tucked beneath the curving stairs. Books, two overstuffed chairs, a desk. Small, cozy. She liked it.

Smelling like the outdoors and reminding her of big open vistas, Jonathan seemed to fill the space. She was conscious of him with all her senses, hearing the rustle of his pants legs, seeing the glint in his eyes, and feeling the texture of his skin in her hands. Tough, weathered.

He kissed her as soon as they crossed the threshold, and she knew it was what she'd been waiting for, longing for. She wanted to melt into him, never let go . . . and so she held back slightly.

He wooed her with lips and hands, his body becoming slowly insistent, his hands moving down her arms, over her shoulders, caressing her face: her neck like a summer breeze touching a chiffon dress, lifting a skirt, tossing a ruffle, his hands both cool and warm upon her.

She felt his heat, his masculine firmness, his hard muscles and then his tongue.

It met hers, wooed and won, drove away all thought. A tender touch to her lips, licking them, cherishing them, sucking them, until they looked like crushed roses when she glimpsed them in the mirror, the beveled edges catching the light like jewels and sending it through the room in a shower of refracted glory. Her surrender seemed precious, totally right. "I never was a 'swooning' type, but you're making me feel almost woozy," she whispered, clutching him, a white hot heat swelling her breasts, driving her nerve ends wild.

His hands traced her sides, touching briefly, passing on to her waist, her hips, drawing her close against him. Reaching behind him, he slammed the door shut, turned the lock.

She melted.

Her breasts pushed against the thin stuff of her dress. He put a finger beneath the plunging neckline, and her nipples became hard. "My mother warned me of moments like this," she murmured, sagging against him.

"I came on this book tour because of you," Jonathan whispered, his breath sweet in her ear, against her cheek, her neck. His British accent, melodious and exotic, excited her. His body and lips thrilled her.

Footsteps approached; she heard the door rattle. "I think we'd better join the party," she said, finding the pulse in his throat with her lips.

"I don't want to let you go."

"I don't want to go."

"I want to find the fastenings of your dress and undo it. Let it slip to the floor."

"You're wicked."

"But you like it."

"Yes, and I don't want you to answer the door."

"Then we won't."

"We should."

Sighing, he released her, backed from her, waited until she straightened her dress, fluffed at her hair. Then he unlocked the door. "It must have been stuck," he said, with an innocent expression, as their host and General Powell entered, nodding at them, the host taking a book from a shelf and handing it to Powell.

Sela, hand-in-hand with Jonathan walked to where the main body of guests filled the double parlors, people perched on chairs, standing in clusters, jammed together on sofas.

A fire burned in the fireplace, yellow and red and green flames.

"Fake," he said. "Like the American animal parks."

She nodded. What had once seemed attractive seemed full of pretense. "We could leave," she said, taking hold of the evening, moving it in ways she knew he hadn't expected.

"What do you have in mind?" he asked, his eyes saying he was pleased, but surprised.

"We could get a cab, ride through the District. Everyone needs to see the national monuments at night. Of course, the taxi will cost a fortune."

"It will be worth it if you show me your capital at

night." His emphasis on capital made the whole thing sound clandestine but enticing.

The butler, a cinnamon-colored man who spoke British English as well, called the cab company for them. He was from Jamaica and traded stories with Jonathan while they waited for the taxi.

Outside, snow was feathering down, large flakes that were beginning to accumulate.

"It seems like magic," Jonathan said as the car made tracks over the newly blanketed driveway.

Sela turned her face up, let the flakes touch her cheek.

"They thaw so fast," Jonathan said, his voice thick as he handed her into the automobile.

On the trip back to the city, Sela was hardly conscious of the passing suburbs. Brick row houses, neighborhoods with pop and mom stores whizzed by. Christmas lights trimmed the windows of a liquor store, and showed inside a dry cleaners. Jonathan's arms were warm, encompassing, his lips demanding, his hands gentle but insistent.

"After you left Zimbabwe, I could think of nothing but you. I came here thinking, perhaps I could scoop you up, take you back with me."

Sela leaned away from Jonathan, needing the space, and yet wanting to capitulate fully, say, yes, I will go anywhere with you. "What exactly did you mean?"

His gaze stayed on her and he spoke softly, barely moving his lips. "I could see us together in the camp."

"And?"

He looked away, his profile firm yet gentled by the warmth of the moment. "Together always."

Arranging her coat around her, she managed to put distance between them. Was he talking marriage?

In the District, the Lincoln Memorial appeared blue white in its bath of lights. Majestic, a shrine.

She turned toward him and found his arms waiting to receive her.

Jonathan's lips teased hers again, his hands under her wrap, molding her waist, rubbing her back. The slow, steady beating of his heart increased and thumped with anticipation as his hands played up and down, over her hips, defining her like a sculptor molding clay. She heard the sliding sound as he pulled her dress's zipper slowly down her back, and she felt the two sides separate as his mouth pressed against hers, firm and insistent. Only the pressure of his chest against hers held her gown in place. She imagined them both nude, on the banks of the Zambesi River. She thought she would burst from longing.

"We're right together," he murmured.

The taxi was circling the Washington Monument, when he finally murmured as he traced the line of her shoulder with his lips, touched his tongue to her breast. "Come back to my hotel with me."

"Yes, oh, yes," she murmured. As he leaned forward to direct the driver, she agreed, "We are right together."

Jonathan hadn't thought anything would be this good again—this feeling of newness and discovery riding his emotions, making him tremble with the sheer wonder of it, After the loss of his first love, he'd been sure that nothing could equal it, ever. She'd been as young as he, untutored, unaware of the feelings that would eventually rip through them and bring them together—awkwardly, but so sweetly loving that he'd carried the memory for years. They'd come together during a time of crisis, a time when terror and death had become a way of life, and they had comforted one another. Night after night, crawling into one another's arms, sometimes making love, more often just whispering their fears and their hopes and their love. Later, he'd found her dead body, mutilated, used and tossed aside. He'd gone on a rampage of killing the enemy and eventually anger had made him whole again. But he'd been wary. Women had drawn his attention but never had he let his emotions follow. Until Sela.

Now he stood in the doorway of his small hotel room and held her tight in his arms, kissing her. A soft light from the bedside light cast shadows across the bed, over the carpet. His fantasy had been to undress her slowly, see her soft milk-chocolate body in all its glory a bit at a time. But something in him spurred him on. Whatever it was moved through her with just as rapid a pace, wild and wonderful in its insistence. They were not two young people barely out of childhood but adults, with a man's and a woman's needs.

He felt her hands on his shirt buttons as he found her zipper again, worked it down, released her upper body.

The dress must have cost a fortune, but as it fell in folds around her waist, she pushed it down, stepped out of it, and kicked it aside. Hurriedly, he undid his belt, loosened his trousers.

At last nothing came between them but flesh, flesh so hot he felt as if his fingers would ignite when he touched her, send sparks shafting through the night. Half walking, half carrying her to the bed, he fell with her onto the quilted comforter and kicked the covers away, for the satin was not half as smooth as the silk of her body.

Her lips were open and giving, and he dived in, the kiss taking him to a place where his hands had a life of their own, moving over her body, her breasts, her abdomen, the silky place between her legs, feeling, enjoying, feasting, and his mind told him it was but a prelude.

She moaned, and his mind drifted on a cloud of feelings so good he wanted them never to end. Her hands were on his body, too, touching like gossamer, and he felt as if she were blind and reading his body with her hands lightly, then insistently, over his chest and buttocks, exploring until she finally, eventually, ultimately found the center of his passion. He floated in a world of sensation as she caressed and fondled him, even as he pleasured her. She. He. Their arms, bodies, lips and beings were all of life. Were life.

When he entered her, she was ready, meeting him with whispery kisses, feathery touches, an open sweet body that felt soft and supple and strong.

She was so right. So positive. So wonderful. So uninhibited. And probably unobtainable. A celebrity. An American.

Afterward, he lay quietly, looking at her, admiring her and wondering. The sweet, full breasts, the tiny waist, the wonderful swell of her hips. Would he ever know them again? Her legs wrapped about his had been a poem; now he saw each stanza complete within itself. With an ending.

"I don't ever want you to leave," he said, the words both false and true.

She snuggled into him, traced a line dawn his jaw. "I don't ever want to leave."

He heard the small core of doubt in her words. Alarmed, panicky, he began to make love to her again. How could he live without her?

This time they slept as soon as it was over, pressed tightly together. Facing one another.

He could hardly believe it when he woke, her naked body in his grasp, her lips a millimeter from his. Night was fading, day pressing hard, light leaking in the window where the draperies remained open.

Her breath was sweet, like flowers in spring, a breeze coming from a cool lake. Dark lashes fluttered against her cheeks. When she opened her eyes, her smile lit her face.

"Well," she said, getting up, a thoughtful expression on her face.

He watched her walk around picking up her clothes, arranging his, depositing her purse on the bureau, her shoes close by. He wanted to run to her, pull her into his arms and again make love to her. With a playful smile, she disappeared into the shower. He wanted to join her, to cry out his pleasure, tell her he loved her, but the words were slow in coming. He'd always expected to marry a woman who understood African customs, spoke Shona, understood what it was like to live in his world. But this was the woman he wanted, the woman he was going all out to obtain. When she came out of the bathroom, his voice loud in the lingering hush of love, he said, "Earlier, when I said I wanted to take you home with me, have you be with me always. . . ."

"Yes?"

He could hold the words back no longer. "I was talking marriage."

"That's pretty big talk," she said.

"I know."

"Serious talk."

"I'm quite serious."

She looked both pleased and mildly upset. He wondered whether it was this women's rights thing he had heard was so big in America. "I have an idea," he said, feeling nervous now. "In Zimbabwe we'd go see your parents." It was how things were done.

"But I've never said yes or no."

"Isn't that irrelevant? You care for me, I know you do."

She shrugged and shook her head.

A frown moved across his face, settled in.

Sela shook her head again. "Sorry, if I appeared to take your proposal lightly. It is a proposal of marriage?"

He nodded, lips tight together.

"Really?" She met his gaze and looked away quickly. As if amused? Embarrassed? He couldn't read her. Neither was he sure how things were done, miles away from home. So far he'd not had to think much, just follow the schedule the publisher had lined out for him. It said nothing about personal relationships. At home he would have drunk beer with her brothers, talked politics with her father, hunted and fished with him. He would have spent less time with the woman, more with her family.

Sela seemed to have recovered her surprise, if that's what it was. "It's almost dawn," she said, smiling in a self-assured way. "If I don't get home soon, my family will be worried. They keep forgetting my age." She picked up her purse. "Don't get up; I'll grab a cab." She paused near the door. "We'll talk about this later. Okay?"

Pleased that her family would have missed her and that she cared, he watched her from the bed, the air charged between them. "No, we have to talk about this now." He got up, pulled on shorts and pants. "I love you, and you love me. You know it." In two steps, he stood by her.

"You shouldn't have done that," she said, as he put his arms around her. "You make me forget all the sensible arguments, the reasons why we couldn't make a go of marriage."

He stopped her words with a kiss. "Go on home, I'll follow you later," he said, his eyes telling her that now she was his. He must tell her about his mother, relate stories about his father, who had died in the war. Zimbabwe seemed far away, not as important in this fast-

MIDNIGHT SKIES   163

moving, different society, and so he would hold tight to it to keep from feeling unsure.

When he arrived at the Clay house, Sela met him at the door. For a time, he just looked at her and she at him.

"Two hours since I saw you," he said.

"Seems like a damned lifetime," she said, breaking the look, her breasts rising and falling in time with her rapid breathing.

He drank in her movement, all grace as she whirled, grabbed a coat from the hall rack, and slipped it on before he could help her. "Grandma Minnie wants us to take her to church," she explained, adjusting a strap on her shoe. Her skirt hiked up slightly, allowing him a brief glimpse of black lace, a shapely thigh. His mind spun backward, remembering. She had met him touch for touch, kiss for kiss, like a woman committed. Her vitality added to the soft look of sensuality in her eyes. He said, "It would be an honor to accompany your grandmother."

"My parents attend a different church, but occasionally we all go with Grandma." She took a long scarlet scarf from a peg.

He took it from her and draped it around her neck, holding firmly to the ends to pull her close. As he kissed her, cherishing her lips, he heard footsteps approach from the dining room. Sela's mouth had the swollen, crushed look of a kiss. Wild thoughts of her escalated in his mind before she pulled away.

Grandma Minnie came in. "Well, if it ain't that African man," she said, her hand going to her gray hair. A small hat with a veil rode the top of her head. "How you doin' this fine morning, Mister Mokane?"

"Very well, Mrs. Clay," he said greeting her with the respect he'd accord his own mother.

She shook her head in admiration. "How was that party you and our Sela went to last night?" she said, grabbing her cane and pointing with it toward the door.

Jonathan opened it for Grandma Minnie and waited for Sela to precede. "It was a party in Maryland," he said to Grandma Minnie, who hesitated on the stoop.

Sela said, "Go ahead. I have to get all the locks."

"We lock things tighter than a tick on a hound dog," Grandma Minnie said, taking his arm. "Some a them no accounts around here'd steal you blind iffen you let 'em."

In a moment Sela joined them and led the way to her car parked at the curb. Once again, she wove in and out of the traffic.

Grandma Minnie shook her head and glanced back at Jonathan, in the back seat. "We're heading to the Church of True Believers. Sela's mama and daddy think they's outgrown it, and Sela, she don't hardly go nowhere. But Mister Mokane, iffen I was a bettin' woman, I'd bet you might like it fine."

He smiled diplomatically.

Inside the white frame building, it was close and warm, and they were late. An overflow congregation packed the room. Women in purple choir robes beat their tambourines, the organ thundered, and the people clapped in rhythm.

"Y'all ready to show your 'preciation of this service?" shouted the Deacon.

"Yes," roared the congregation in unison.

"Pastor, we're ready," Grandma Minnie cried, moving down the aisle, holding on to Sela's hand and dragging her and Jonathan along with her.

"Sister, shove on over and let Miss Minnie and her

MIDNIGHT SKIES

family sit down," the Pastor cried, "while I talk to you about Judgment Day."

People in a pew halfway down the aisle moved over and Grandma Minnie sat down, Sela next to her, Jonathan on the aisle. He was conscious of Sela's hip pressing against his, her legs encased in nylon stockings so sheer her legs looked bare. A gold chain circled her left ankle, and her delicately arched feet were shod in high heeled shoes. Aware of her deep in his gut, he barely heard the sermon.

"My parents say the pastor has verbal diarrhea," Sela whispered. "He goes on forever." She grinned.

Jonathan smiled. "Once I heard Mugabe speak for three hours. We're used to long speeches in Zimbabwe."

"Knew he would know what's proper," Grandma Minnie said, nodding her head righteously.

A delicate frown etched Sela's forehead.

All through the service, Sela was conscious of her body as she had never been before. Her skin, even the bones underneath, felt special—alive in ways they never had before. Her muscles were tired, but elastic, ready to expand and contract, make love. She could think of little else but Jonathan, his body, hands, arms, lips. He was appropriately clad in a gray pinstripe suit, a white shirt, and gray-and-red striped tie that shrieked West. But he smelled of a spicy aftershave and cologne that reminded her of the jungle, of foreign and exotic places. Last night had happened too fast. One moment she was firm in her mind, the African episode was merely that. Now . . . Her mind drifted, spun away to last night.

The congregation jumping to their feet jolted her back to the moment.

"Stand on your feet and put your hands together," the Deacon shouted.

The choir began, "Where you gonna run to on Judgment day?"

The people joined in, and when the song ended, Grandma Minnie cried, "Hallelujah."

"Sister, praise be," someone shouted.

"Amen, amen, yes sir." someone else said.

"We are working here this morning," the preacher cried. "Getting out the sin. Casting out the devils."

A woman two rows ahead began to jerk. She fell. A man toppled over. Others followed him, sliding to the floor. The ushers ran around to care for the parishioners.

"I should have warned you," Sela whispered to Jonathan.

"It's a little like a spirit ceremony at home," Jonathan said. He seemed not at all put out.

"Praise be," Grandma Minnie said, clapping vigorously and finally sitting down. "I'm too old to be slidin' to the floor," she explained, "but I used to shake it up good when I was young."

"And you?" Jonathan asked looking at Sela.

"She never take no active part," Grandma Minnie said.

Sela pretended not to hear. Grandma Minnie's church was a sore point. Her brothers were embarrassed by it, but the rocking, loud ceremony apparently didn't offend Jonathan at all. Indeed, he seemed to like it.

Later that morning, Sela and Jonathan sat with her parents in the living room, cups and saucers in hand, a coffee urn on the table. Outside, the sun was shining a winter bright, all traces of snow gone, but she felt chilled and tired. The glow of the past night began to dim. Jonathan, in a low-voiced exchange with her, had insisted he had to speak to her parents. "For your hand."

"You don't have to do that here," she'd whispered back. She admired—no loved—Jonathan Mokane, and a life with him sat like honey on the tongue. So sweet. But could they surmount the vast distances between their countries, the differences in their cultures? She needed time to think about that, but if she said nothing, let him speak out, she'd be forced to face what she probably would have demanded he examine minutely. He seemed determined, and in an inexplicable way, she liked his stubbornness.

She looked around the room. Her parents had a calm, scrubbed look from a benign sermon, a social lesson, not a fire and brimstone affair.

Now, Jonathan leaned forward, the cup and saucer in his hand seeming small and fragile. "I want to speak for your daughter." He addressed Sela's father.

"Speak for?" Sela's mother Miriam said, an edge to her voice. "What are you talking about?"

"I want to marry her." Again, Jonathan looked at Mr. Clay.

"I told him asking your permission wasn't necessary," Sela said. "Anyway, I haven't said yes yet."

Jonathan's mouth formed a grim line. "But talking to your parents, telling them is necessary."

Miriam shook her head and leaned back in an evident attempt to remain calm. "Well, now, I can't say I'm exactly surprised, but marriage is a big order." Her cup jiggled on the saucer. She set it down on the table and said to Sela, "It must have been very sudden."

"It was, sort of." Sela glanced at Jonathan, who sat rigidly upright as if needing to impress everyone with his posture. She felt like poking him, telling him to relax, but the whole sequence seemed like a dream. Of course, she wanted, to be with Jonathan always. Yet, details that had popped into her mind during the night began to insinuate their presence into her mind again. Had he considered where they'd live? What did he think about his wife working? She certainly wasn't a stay-at-home woman. And as much as she loved being at the camp, and as much as she liked Zimbabwe, it wasn't America. But she was not about to say anything now with everyone looking on like it was the first act in a play they hadn't planned on attending.

"Last night," Jonathan said, "we spoke of our futures but, of course, we didn't make any plans until I could speak to you." Again his gaze went to Sela's father.

So that's what it was all about, Sela thought watching her mother take a deep breath, her more than adequate bosom rising.

"Last night. You just realized your attraction last night?" Miriam said, her eyes widening.

Jonathan shook his head, his easy smile lighting his face. "No, no. I always noticed Sela. I just didn't say anything." He glanced at her, a proprietary look on his face.

Even though she exchanged a smile with him, Sela felt a trickle of exasperation pass down her spine. He was not acting like anyone she or her parents knew.

"I always noticed the woman next door," Sela's father interrupted. "Didn't mean I wanted to marry her." He shook his head.

For several moments no one said anything. Sela stared at the pictures on the wall—Louis when a baby, his children, a painting of Jesus. Jonathan sat as if struck dumb, and Sela heard her parents go into a long discussion about the merits of long engagements. They used Louis and Brenda Lee as a case in point. Hadn't they waited years? Jonathan's posture grew even more rigid, his face noncommittal. Sela stared at him, willed him to look her way. He didn't.

Grandma Minnie came in from the kitchen, a plate with a crumb cake in her hands. She set it down on the coffee table and folded her hands in her apron. "I think they tryin' to say you two hardly knows one another."

"Your daddy's family and mine knew one another for years," Miriam said. She brushed invisible lint from her flowered crepe dress, eased her feet from her high-heeled shoes, an action she never did in front of visitors. Sela watched amazed.

Miriam continued. "He knew I like to take off my shoes soon as I come from church." She forced a laugh, and then, as her husband turned to smile at her, it became a genuine warm laugh filled with the memories of years. He chuckled.

"I think your mother means you should get better acquainted," Sela's father said.

Sela shook her head. "Wait a minute. Jonathan was only trying to do things as they're done in Zimbabwe. Plus, we're hardly underage kids. We'll discuss these things between us. And as for knowing one another, we do know one another." Last night had been laced with the leavenings of heaven. In between coming together, they had whispered words of love and of sharing. It was then that an awareness of self had begun to move through her like water finding its level, and now the dreamlike state only enhanced her appreciation of what they had shared. She smiled across the room at Jonathan, confident he'd smile back, a powerful look of love radiating from his face—but, no, there was a slight frown on his face, his gaze stayed on her father, and she felt again strange pricklings of apprehension. "Isn't that right, Jonathan?"

"Yes." The word came with a bluntness she hadn't

expected. He leaned toward Mr. Clay. "I'm ready to do whatever is customary."

Miriam slipped her shoes back on, smiled at Jonathan as she got up and moved around the room, adjusting the mini-blinds and doing chores that didn't need doing. How many times can you re-stack the Sunday paper? "That's certainly good to hear, Mr. Mokane. Heaven knows I have nothing against you; you're a good man, I'm sure. But you must admit you and Sela haven't had much time to get acquainted."

"I thought they was acquainted," Grandma Minnie said, cutting the cake with exacting efficiency.

Miriam's voice grew brisk. "Sela and Jonathan are talking marriage."

Grandma Minnie paused, knife in hand. "So they's ready to jump the broom."

Jonathan looked puzzled.

"An American slave term," Sela muttered, impatience battering at her equanimity. She avoided looking at Jonathan.

Miriam raised her eyebrows. "You can never know one another well enough," she said, "After all these years, I'm still learning things about your daddy."

"He favors *his* daddy," Grandma Minnie said. "Nothing much to figger out. Nothing much to figger out 'bout Sela and Mister Mokane, either. They in love."

"Love is one thing. Long distance romance another. Sela's got a career. She's worked hard for it."

Mr. Clay held up his hand. "Miriam, if you don't mind, we are all proud of Sela. But if she wants to get married, that's her business. And, of course, we should hear her and her young man out." He looked directly at Jonathan. "Perhaps things are handled differently in Zimbabwe."

"Slightly," Jonathan said, looking a bit embarrassed.

"I really don't know why we're having this discussion

at all," Sela said. It was premature; she should have insisted that Jonathan keep his mouth shut.

"I believe it's a matter of respect," her father said. "Jonathan seems to realize that."

"And what about me?" Sela said, getting up, wanting the whole conversation to cease. "No one has asked me what I think?"

"You hush while I get this all straight," Grandma Minnie muttered. "If I 'member the stories rightly, in Mister Mokane's country they done pay a bride price."

"Bride price?" both Sela's parents cried in unison.

Jonathan smiled and shook his head. "A custom in Zimbabwe. Not to offer a bride price would be an insult." He leaned toward Mr. Clay. "I just wanted to assure you that I am solvent and of good character. I own the safari camp free and clear, and the books are paying nice royalties, and I'm prepared to pay whatever figure you name."

"You've certainly been successful." Mr. Clay's gaze climbed the wall. "I don't have any doubts on that score. And I'm sure you'd be very generous."

"Yes, of course," Miriam said.

They both looked past him, half-smiling, an uncomplicated, spontaneous coordination of lips and eyes that was almost genuine. It didn't confuse Sela. If this was the way they handled things in Zimbabwe, it was antediluvian and had nothing to do with modern America. And her parents were right to begin to shut him out. No matter how much his touch made her tingle, his voice enthralled her, his kindness and genuineness thrilled her, she would not take part in this bride price charade.

Jonathan continued, his voice rumbling pleasantly. "I have this book tour to make and then I can come back, seal the agreement with an engagement ring. If it would make everyone happier, we can talk about the bride price later." His smile took in Sela.

"Bride price!" she cried. "Don't be ridiculous." She clenched her hands. He was acting as if she had no say in the whole affair, and her parents, by sitting there and not complaining, were suddenly falling in line like elephants walking through camp, elephants Jonathan had given up without a fight. He hadn't cared enough about her to treat her as if she had a word to say in making her own decisions and plans for the future.

"We can talk about this later if it bothers you that much," he said. "Or dispense with this part."

"How nice," she cried, her voice tinged with sarcasm. "Marrying me will save you a bunch of money. I'm sure you'll be the envy of all your friends at home. No bride price. Of course, they will also think I'm not worth much, isn't that the way it goes?"

Her parents frowned, and Sela saw the hurt in Jonathan's eyes and the bewilderment, and she felt like crying for both of them. She had wanted a Romeo, and he had disappointed her miserably.

Jonathan's eyes grew opaque as stone. "The bride price is an honorable institution in my country." His glance slid off Sela's. "If your parents wish, we will follow the custom, no matter how high a price they put on you." A look of glacial tolerance slipped over his face like rain sliding down the side of a canvas tent.

A sudden, brutal silence followed. Only the soft thud of someone coming down the stairs was heard. Nefari—leotard, tights, and leg warmers proclaiming her new-found admiration for the ballet—glided into the living room. "Did I hear someone say bride price? It sounds deliciously wicked." She strolled in with the turned out walk of the ballerina, and with a wave of the hand, grinned and sat down on the floor next to the coffee table. "Who's paying whom?"

"No one," her father snapped. "I think Mr. Mokane needs to explain this bride price thing."

Miriam dabbed at her face with a napkin. "Don't know why I feel so hot all of a sudden."

Jonathan rose, "I didn't mean any disrespect."

"Wait a minute," Sela said getting up. "I prefer all of you to stay out of this."

Jonathan frowned and turned away to speak to her parents. "I'm sorry if I brought up unpleasant memories, but I only meant to honor the customs of my country and yours, not provoke an argument."

"I think, Mr. Mokane, you understand very little about America."

"Or about American women. Do you think my input in this conversation, dialogue, whatever you want to call it, is unnecessary?" Sela asked, her head high, her eyes sparking dramatically. "For the past thirty minutes or hour or whatever, you conveniently left me out. All of you."

Jonathan frowned. "I don't understand. Of course your input is necessary."

She waited, only just managing not to tap her foot in frustration, as she gave him time to explain, amplify, mollify her parents, spread soothing syrup over her jangled nerves.

The clock ticked.

Her mother shifted and sighed.

Nefari said, "If this is about marriage, I never thought Sela was the marrying kind anyway."

Sela said, "When and if I marry it will be my decision."

In one fluid movement, Jonathan got up. "I think I should leave,"

So this was how it would all end? He was being obtuse, and she was tired of the whole preposterous scene. "Unfortunately, I have an engagement this afternoon." She glanced at her mother, at the others, willing them to say something that would make sense out of everything. But no one met her gaze and no words came from their mouths. Anger at them rose in suffocating waves, and she wanted to shout and stamp her feet as she had as a child. "It seems the studio gets more and more demanding." She turned to Jonathan. "I could drop you off at your hotel on my way." There, that was the way to do it, businesslike, impersonal. No one could say later that she had caused a scene, screamed at him, thrown accusations at her parents, cried, beat her fists against Jonathan's chest.

His frown grew deeper, making his face grim and even more unreadable, a stranger's visage. "That would be considerate," he said, his tone as conversational as hers even though his face had the look of a man who'd been blindsided. "I thank you for your hospitality, Mr. and Mrs. Clay. Grandma Minnie, it's been a pleasure. Nefari, I wish you well with your studies."

Sela's parents nodded at him, Miriam's hands fluttering as if they wanted to do something, but she didn't know what was proper. Mr. Clay's face grew solemn, his eyes guarded.

Nefari did a *plié*, her technique crude, but graceful nevertheless, her eyes bright. "Good-bye, African. You sure got the pot to bubbling."

Sela grabbed her coat and purse and went to the door, a river of emotion seething within her.

Grandma Minnie followed Jonathan to the door. Sela heard her say something about the rainbow, saw him nod and then kiss her on the top of her gray head.

In the car, Sela had trouble finding words to express the frustration that kept pace with her mounting irritation. She wanted to kick and scream. But at whom? Jonathan? Her parents? The differences in their two cultures? "I'm sorry things got so hairy."

"What?" He looked even more puzzled.

"It's a way of saying . . . Oh, never mind. It all adds up to one thing. A person's experiences mean one hell of a lot, and ours certainly couldn't have been more different. We don't even speak the same language."

He nodded. "If you expected all beads on a string to be alike, you're probably right"

Damn it, he didn't have to agree so rapidly. Didn't he know she was just talking, saying words to fill the silence? When he said nothing more, she turned on the tape deck, let the sounds of an old Stevie Wonder album take over.

Near his hotel, Jonathan said, "I'm off tomorrow. Philadelphia, New York, Boston. Then stops in Atlanta and Dallas before I head for home."

She almost said: what a nice long speech—you can talk, can't you? But his gaze was on her, and she felt it like a white hot heat. She nodded, and then before she could stop herself, the night and all its glory filled her mind, and she asked, "Are you coming back to Washington?"

He said nothing for the space of thirty long, miserable seconds before adding, "My plane leaves from Dallas."

She felt tears dampen her eyes, and willed them not to drop. The hotel was looming up in her vision, blurry. She blinked and pulled up to the entrance and braked to a stop. "Well, this is it," she said, forcing a hearty sound to her voice. He could have come back from Dallas, given them time to talk this out.

"Yes," he answered.

For a second, she felt his gaze on her again.

She turned to look, ready to tell him they could work through all their problems if they wanted to badly enough. They could leap across the chasm so recently cut, build bridges with their love.

But he was looking toward the hotel and, as a car pulled in behind her, he said, "Thanks for the ride," as if she hadn't slept in his arms last night, drank deeply of the love he'd offered, given as fully of herself.

"Don't mention it," she muttered as he swung the door open and got out.

As he nodded toward her, she tromped on the gas and zoomed off. Watching him in the rearview mirror, she saw him enter the hotel without looking back. A sense of déjà vu and then grief, and finally anger overcame her. Together they had made a mess of their future, let stupid, silly obstacles come between them. No matter how much she wanted to believe it, she knew she'd not be better off without him. She'd miss him always, but at this moment, in some way, she'd have to learn to live without him. Tomorrow, or the next day, when she had thought it through she'd find a way to make it all right again. She had to.

Eleven

Sela refused to discuss Jonathan with her family, and for the most part—except for Nefari, who said Sela was acting stupidly and Grandma Minnie who walked around with a contemplative look bordering on sadness—they respected her wishes, making Sela feel a little bit guilty. So, she threw herself into her job, but even though exhausted at the end of the day, she still dreamed of Jonathan. Once again he smiled at her, kissed her, saved her from lions. But always afterward, he turned his back on her, left her. She would wake drenched in sweat.

Then one day, twenty minutes before the end of her broadcast, a half-dozen vocally abusive people put her on the defensive. Speaking up from the audience, they argued against the Endangered Species Act. First a woman declared Sela was protecting animals at the detriment of people. "Honey, we got hungry people walking the streets." Then a man took up the cause, and soon they were swaying the audience. Sela listened respectfully before giving the show's official policy. Still, she felt as if they had gotten the best of her.

Afterward, Bowles said she'd handled it poorly. She should have known when to soft-pedal her own extremism. Play it more diplomatically. Ratings were falling. People were watching sex-and-tell-all shows. From behind the broad expanse of his desk, he said, "I'm beginning to think animal shows are passé." His perfectly manicured and polished fingernails caught the light as he toyed with a pen, pushed papers around his desk.

With a sudden, gut-wrenching sureness, Sela was positive he was planning to scuttle both her and the show. "Get me something, anything," she said to her agent. But nothing surfaced, not even a gig reporting the weather.

Then the day Jonathan left Dallas for Zimbabwe, a review about his book appeared in *Essence*. The accompanying photograph showed him in safari wear, standing next to a Landrover. Sela studied the photo. He looked relaxed, at ease, and he was smiling, leaving her with a great, mind-tingling loneliness.

She was avoiding Bowles as much as possible, and trying to avoid the unemployment line, when Josh called.

"Excuse me." She went to the other side of the office, a few paces away from where Jennifer, Art and the crew were trying to come up with a format for the show that Bowles might like. They had brought in ever more exotic animals, creatures that looked as if they belonged in Jurassic Park, had guests who were controversial. Nothing worked. "Hello, Josh," Sela said, forcing lightness into her voice. She listened while he explained that he was calling from "the friendly skies" on the way to Hollywood.

She pictured him wearing torn jeans and a French sailor shirt, sitting in first class, a pile of manuscripts and papers overflowing his briefcase.

He said the backing for the African film he'd talked about had come through. Was she ready to go to Hollywood and talk turkey, tell him how a movie about Africa should be filmed?

Her heart did a quick tap-dance. "I can certainly try."

"A round-trip ticket is waiting for you at National Airport, and I'll send the script for you to look over on the plane. It's just a working script at this point. I've got this idea about animals and people, symbolic images making historical statements. You still with me?"

"You bet I am," she said. Ten minutes later she was giving Bowles notice. She knew it was more than he would have done for her. "Two weeks, three, whatever you need," she said, looking him directly in the eye. No more gazing past his shoulder.

He came out from behind his desk and contemplated her as he moved toward the door. "I gave you a break and now you leave me high and dry."

"I didn't think I was leaving you high and dry. I merely turned in my resignation."

He shrugged. "Whatever. It's leaving a bad taste in my mouth. Monday Jennifer can handle the whole thing. Far as I'm concerned, you're through now." He went back to his desk, picked up a paper and began reading it.

Words rose in her mind like magna in a volcano, sputtering, heat-tinged words, and she let them out in a self-contained way that brought surprise and then a grudging respect to Bowles' face. All the pent-up irritants of the past years, the times she had bit back a reply came out in a flow of words so appropriate they amazed her. Finishing, she shrugged, raised her head high and stepped with dignity to the door. Pausing there, she said, "You won't ever have to patronize me again, and you know something, *dear, dear* Mr. Bowles, it feels wonderful." Chuckling, knowing her laughter hurt him more than any words she could shout, she left.

At home she told the whole story to her parents. They said she should have been more careful, not closed all those doors behind her. Of course they were pleased that she would be connected with the movies, but someday she might need a recommendation from the station. "You young people are too impetuous, too ready to spout off." They looked troubled. Grandma Minnie said a movie job sounded fine to her, but only Nefari was completely supportive, wondering in her youthful way if Sela could get her on as an extra. "Not a speaking part right away, of course . . ."

It was the one thing that brought Sela a real chuckle.

Two days later she sat in Josh's office listening as he took phone calls, put people on hold, called them "darling" and "honey" while commenting to her in between calls. He wore Dockers and sandals and a T-shirt printed with the title of his first film: *Sister.* His office was a Hollywood extravaganza of glass and wrought iron, of gray leather sofas on pale green carpet, of meat-eating plants in Grecian urns and a floor-to-ceiling cartoon framed in mirrored glass. The line drawing depicted stars of another era.

"Know who that is?" Josh asked, pointing to a slash of red above two épaulets.

Sela shook her head. "Who?"

"Joan Crawford."

"Oh, sure."

"And this is Mary Pickford," he said, indicating a pair of soulful eyes above a daisy. He cradled a telephone to his ear and crooned into it, continuing a conversation he'd momentarily interrupted to speak to Sela, "But, sweetheart, you'd be so right for the part." Catching Sela's gaze, he pointed to a sword and a mustache below the Crawford shoulders, "Douglas Fairbanks. The father, not the son." He rolled his eyes and spoke into the phone, "Yes, darling; your loss, but not our gain." He hung up, and his eyes blazed from his thin face. "Bet you don't know who this is." He pointed again.

"Josephine Baker."

"Yep. She's probably better recognized now in America, than when she was alive." For a few seconds the lines in his face went down. "Says something, doesn't it?"

She nodded. This was the side of Josh she had known.

The full-watt smile came back to his face. "So tell me what you know about wild animals."

This was the Josh she hadn't known, the man who had climbed to the top of the Hollywood heap. "You suddenly have doubts about my abilities?"

He grinned. "I have to know you won't be more flash than substance. Give me an example." He waggled his fingers.

"Okay, everyone says male lions don't hunt. Right?"

"Sela, that's what they all tell me."

She shook her head. "They're all wrong. Most people assume male lions only trot out for a meal after the lioness makes the kill. Not true. They all hunt. Females hunt more often, because they have to provide for their cubs."

Josh shook his head in admiration and looked across the room, where two of his cronies lounged. "Can I pick 'em, or can I pick 'em?" As they nodded emphatically, he turned back to her. "I stand corrected." He picked up a file with her name on it. "Knowledge keeps me from looking like a horse's ass on film. That's what we'd be paying you for." He named an amount three times higher than her current salary. "You think that will do you?" A shadow of a smile played across his mouth, and she was reminded again of their school years and his sometimes brilliant ideas proposed with just such diffidence.

"It's a good start," she said, smiling just enough to show that she was flexible, but not enough to let him see that she was ecstatic. "But my agent handles all that. I'll sign a contract after she's looked it over."

"Baby, I wouldn't have it any other way." His smile was full now, his eyes gleaming.

She smiled back.

"Good." He held out a sheaf of papers. "Contract. My attorney's idea, not mine. He says I'd be cut to ribbons if I didn't insist on John Hancocks. I'll send copies to your agent."

"Great."

He got up, shook hands with her, then grinned and gave her a hug. "Welcome aboard," he said as he pressed an intercom button. When a secretary answered, he said, "Ms. Clay will be needing a hotel. Give her the red carpet treatment." He winked at Sela. "You like Mexican with American flavor? They serve terrific *fajitas* at Casa Pepita's. I'll pick you up sevenish tonight." He walked slowly to the door, opened it for her, waited for her to go through. "I'm really happy to have you with us. A week soon enough to get your ducks in order and fly out to the dark continent?"

"A month would be better."

He walked out into the hall, pressed the elevator button, smiled at her. "Only if you had to make all the decisions on your own. I forgot to tell you. You'll be working for Jonathan Mokane. Terrific guy. Just what this studio needs." He hugged her again. "He'll be expecting you a week from today." He snapped his fingers. "In that city whatever it is, the capital of Zimbabwe."

"Harare," she muttered determined not to let him see he'd just kicked her in the gut like a mule.

"Yeah, sure, Harare."

The elevator door opened, he reached around and pushed the lobby button, waved her in, and said goodbye. She realized he had no intention of going to the ground floor with her, just as she had no intention of working for Jonathan Mokane. But did she have a choice?

* * *

Trying to play it cool, Sela left the plane in Harare head high, a half smile on her face. But rain was pelting the tarmac, and Jonathan Mokane wasn't among the people waiting to greet her. Josh, wearing striped shorts, a flowered Hawaiian shirt, an Eddie Bauer jacket and baseball shoes with the tongues hanging out, spurted out from the waiting room. He held an umbrella that half shielded her as he talked excitedly about his movie, telling her it had to be a winner.

"Of course it will, but who will believe you? You look like you should be back on the sandlots," she said, hugging his arm.

"I don't want to give these dudes an idea I'm made of money," he said, waving toward the hangers-on waiting inside. "Anyway, these duds are pure *style*."

"Josh-style," she said handing him her carry-on case.

"God, a pushy broad." He grinned and steered her through the waiting room, out the opposite door toward a car and driver idling at the curb. "I'm devastated," he said when they were both seated. "No welcoming kiss when I spent the past ten years pining for you."

She kissed him on the cheek. "There."

"I guess I have to settle." He shrugged his shoulders. "Seriously, Sela, if you ever feel romantic . . ."

"Please, Josh," Sela sighed.

"Okay, just wanted to remind you . . . I still feel the same." He leaned forward, told the driver, "Don't spare the horses."

"What?"

"I'm in a hurry." He turned to Sela. "I see a black face and think 'brother' and then come up against a brick wall."

She wanted to say she knew first-hand, but sometimes

it was better to keep quiet. Once again she was whisked the ten miles from the airport to the hotel, this time Josh talking a kilometer a second about his ideas for the film.

She felt both relieved and anxious that Jonathan Mokane hadn't been at the airport. Out the window she saw the city through a blur of rain, palm trees and jacaranda trees blending, street-corner vendors running for shelter.

The driver stopped at the Monomatapa Hotel, a modern high-rise with lots of glass.

"Old home week," Sela said. "I stayed here before."

Josh grinned, his thin face going round. "My staff took over the whole thing. Made me feel like some kind of big shot. You know they remade *King Solomon's Mines* in Zimbabwe?"

She had just read that in her research. "And put 4000 extras to work."

"You got it, baby. Since then the government rolls out the red carpet for filmmakers. I got permits and licenses like this." He snapped his fingers. "Try the same thing any place else and they tie you up for months." He handed her luggage and room key to a bellhop. "If you feel up to a meeting tonight, Mokane's here and is anxious to get going."

She shook her head. "I'll meet you in the coffee shop in the morning." Rested, she might know what to say to Jonathan.

Not for the first time in Africa, she went to sleep watching CNN. In the morning, the screech of the telephone woke her.

"Time moves on big cat feet," Josh said.

All she wanted was to curl up and go back to sleep. "I'll be right down."

A weak light seeped in from outside. She showered, dressed in bright yellow, and went to the coffee shop.

Josh waved from a table behind a potted palm next to a lattice-work divider. Jonathan Mokane sat opposite him. She hesitated, the past staying her steps, making an awkwardness she hadn't entirely anticipated. In the world of television, social façades made daily life possible.

"Good morning, sunshine," Josh shouted. "You make us pale to nothing, you all decked out in yellow."

There was nothing to do but walk quickly, quietly, and with composure across the large room that spilled out to the patio. All the way, she was conscious of Jonathan watching her and, no matter how hard she tried, she could not pry her own gaze away.

He wore boots, safari shirt, and pants that defined his torso in a way she hadn't noticed before. She remembered the last time they'd kissed, he had cupped her chin before touching his lips to hers. His had been surprisingly soft, but with an underpinning of granite.

She dragged her gaze away. "Morning, Josh. How are you, Jonathan?"

"Fine, thank you," he said, his smile pleasant but detached.

Two acquaintances greeting one another, she thought as he rose, held her chair for her. All so circumspect, so civilized.

Josh waggled his fingers. This morning he wore pink and violet sweats and a scarlet head band. All had Jo-Dusk Productions printed on them. "Now that that's over, let's get to my movie." He wiped his brow with his handkerchief and grinned at her. "I was the only one jogging this morning, seeing as how you declined my invitations to join me." He grinned at Sela. "Everybody stared like I was some kinda freak." He stuck his handkerchief in his pocket.

Sela kept her face bland. Jogging was not a subject she cared to pursue with Jonathan sitting next to her.

Josh said, "Back to the movie. I see a modern fable." His hands made pictures in the air. "A blending of old and new." His voice went on, describing, embroidering, conjecturing, painting images of America and Africa together.

Sela nodded at appropriate times, scanned the menu, ordered, all with the devastating knowledge that Jonathan Mokane sat next to her, his knee an inch from hers. It was difficult keeping her mind on Josh's rambling monologue. She wanted to be angry at Jonathan, wanted to bring up that last scene in her parents' house, but she knew she had to be professional, get through the job as if she worked with ex-lovers every day.

Reaching for the salt, Jonathan's arm grazed hers.

She jumped as if shot, but he did, too, both of them fumbling for the shaker like awkward children.

"Sorry," he said.

"My fault," she mumbled.

Josh looked from one to the other, as if just realizing there might be something going on between the two. He took papers from a briefcase on the chair next to him. "Let's continue," he said. "I'll want your ideas and feedback on a couple things. As you probably know, Sir Richard Attenborough directed one of the first films made in Zimbabwe. I mean—that's a class act to follow." He nodded at the waiter, who set a plate of bacon and eggs in front of him. "But he's not a brother."

Sela spooned into her fruit cup. "How can we help?"

Jonathan's head swiveled swiftly toward her as she said, "we." Why had she used the plural?

Josh swallowed and looked thoughtful before saying, "Listen to the name Attenborough gave his movie. *Cry Freedom.*" He looked from her to Jonathan, as if gauging the impact of the words on them. "What a name. To say so much in two words. If I can just come up with something as great."

Jonathan said, "Zimbabwe means stone house in Shona. Maybe you can do something with that."

His eyes were dark as a sable antelope's as he glanced toward Sela, his look unreadable, distant. She determined to keep her gaze on Josh, her pronouns singular. "Maybe we can use *stone house* as a springboard to something else."

He looked thoughtful. "Perhaps. Jonathan wants you to go out to Masvingo, scout out locations for photographing the ruins at Great Zimbabwe. I have this idea for the beginning of the movie. The stone houses of—what was it, the 12th century?—as a backdrop when the movie starts. Then show Livingston plodding through the bush. Finally dissolve to Vic Falls. All while the credits are flashing."

Jonathan said, "I thought you were going to have Livingston meet Stanley at Victoria Falls."

"I was going to. Show two white sahibs and one saying the famous 'Dr. Livingston, I presume,' line. Big whoop-de-do scene of white men discovering one another and the widest damn waterfall in the world. Then show, by God, *show* the real people of Zimbabwe who were always here." He grinned. "What do you think?"

"Sounds great," Sela said. "I assume you're referring to the ancient ruins called Great Zimbabwe."

"Right."

"Everything I know about Great Zimbabwe I read in books. I do need to go out there."

"Jonathan can fill you in on current information, provide government pamphlets and maps, stuff you can look over on the plane."

Jonathan looked straight at her for the first time and nodded.

"What about staff?" Sela asked.

"Some of our people are already there," Josh said. "And Jonathan has local people lined up who can help smooth the way. Our camera people will go with you and shoot some preliminary shots. As you can see, I'm doing this by the seat of my pants. I want you to get the feel of the past even if I start the film with shots of the falls. Maybe I'll show the spray shooting up, that sort of thing. You know, ephemeral Africa." He leaned across the table. "Let me tell you about the latest refinements in the working script."

As Josh lowered his voice, glancing at manuscript pages as necessary, Sela leaned closer in order to hear. Slowly, she relaxed, caught up in Josh's tale of people and animals, and when her knee accidentally touched Jonathan's leg, she let it stay there, warm and companionable for the space of a long moment. Then, aware with her mind as well as her body, she withdrew it. Like a mahogany statue, he sat quietly, except that she could see his chest rising and falling, and she wanted to put her hand inside his shirt and feel the beat of his heart, as she had done that one glorious night.

"Epic progression, Africa to the Indies to America. Reggae music fading into America the Beautiful. *Finis.* The End." Josh finished his story, rocked back in his chair.

"I love it," Sela said, the images moving through her mind, unclear but powerful.

Jonathan's nod came a few seconds later.

Josh shrugged. "Like I said, it's seat-of-the-pants stuff."

Sela shrugged, in imitation of him.

Josh grinned. "You know you're my toughest critic, Sela." His gaze was warm. He looked at Jonathan. "She knows my warts. Once, in college, I copied her paper. Got an A, but she's never let me live it down."

Both men turned to look at her, and Sela felt her cheeks grow warm as Jonathan drank in her face as if memorizing it, while Josh's held the same flickering of hope it always had when he spoke to her.

Josh said, "So what about that night scene in the bush? The one where two main characters get left alone out there, with lions making a kill nearby, predators all around them." He looked from one to the other. "Can it be done on a low budget? Everyone here tells me it would be tricky."

Jonathan said. "And perhaps dangerous."

"Why, particularly?"

"No time to really acclimate the animals to the lights and equipment necessary." Jonathan leaned his forearms on the table. "I'd have to scout the best location. Somewhere as close to my camp as possible. Use it as headquarters, go out from there."

"I didn't think that location was known for a large concentration of predators," Sela said. "In order to get good pictures, wouldn't you need a lot of animals? I doubt that they act on cue, no matter how used to you they are."

Jonathan frowned and pushed back slightly from the table. "Predators never get 'used' to people. They acclimate to vehicles, equipment, things that offer no challenge or that aren't seen as a source of food." He spoke to Josh, not to her.

Sela felt constrained to add, "I'm sure there are better locations than your camp for such scenes. What did we see, two leopards, three lions, when I was there?"

"Two lions stalked her," Jonathan said, once again addressing Josh. "She was jogging." He threw her a challenging look. "Can't get more exciting than that."

Feeling justifiably angered, Sela, too, addressed Josh. "I'd think that for your purposes a large pride would be necessary."

"You make a point, not necessarily the best. Film-wise either way can be made impressive."

For a time, all three sat quietly. The hum of voices and the click of utensils on pottery sounded around the room.

Sela leaned forward slightly. "Why not film in Botswana? According to an article I saw in the *Geographic*, the lions there are ferocious. They don't bother with people, but bring down elephants, buffalo, hippo."

"Baby elephants," Jonathan amended, turning to look at her, his eyes wary.

Josh glanced at Jonathan. "Is that true?"

He shrugged. "You go out every night for ten years or so here, as they did in Botswana, you'd find the same things. Animals are animals." His gaze went back to Sela.

Sela glanced quickly at him. "Animals are animals? I can't believe I'm hearing right."

Josh held up his hands. "Let's not you two quibble." He shook his head. "Anyway, it would take too long to get permission to go to Botswana. What I want is for you to duplicate the same excitement here. Can you do that?"

"Guaranteed," Jonathan said.

"Good."

"How long do we have before you bring out the stars?" Sela asked.

Josh got up. "Three months, tops."

"It's not enough time," Jonathan said. "You want elephants, you want lions, you want storks and hornbills and baboons, and none of them act on cue."

"Sorry, that's all the time we have," Josh said, getting up.

"No problem," Sela said, determined to make things work if it killed her.

Josh grinned, stuck out his hand. "I got faith in you, sweetheart."

Jonathan's frown looked as if it would cut his face in two.

Josh winked at Sela, shook hands with Jonathan, and was talking his way across the room by the time Jonathan turned toward Sela.

"Can we do everything he wants in such a short time?" she asked, rising.

"If we start before the rainy season ends."

"But won't that be dangerous?"

"Anything in the bush can be dangerous."

"You're not answering me."

"Going into the bush when the grass is high. Filming at night when animals are hunting. Hell, yes, it's dangerous. The worst kind of danger." But then he turned to her, looked at her as he hadn't really done all morning, and all the prickliness, the underlying anger she'd felt, dissolved like sugar in water. She felt a jolt of recognition slash through her. His eyes were filled with worry, but underneath the concern she read awareness of and for her. "But . . ." she said, feeling as if she were teetering on top of a precipice and could go either way.

"We'll talk about it when you get back." His words were soft, and he sounded as if he were talking about a lot more than background shots for Josh's movie. He reached out a hand as if to touch her, but it fell halfway to her face. For a moment more, he stood staring at her and then turned on his heel and left.

Two hours later, Sela was leaving for the airport and a small commuter plane bound for Masvingo, with a tangle of mixed emotions like a knot in her chest. In her own mind, she'd never thought of Josh as anything but a friend, yet it was clear he wanted more, while Jonathan . . . She wasn't sure what Jonathan wanted.

Twelve

Afraid it would take off without her, Sela ran toward the twenty-passenger plane sitting on the runway. The copilot, who doubled as major domo, boosted her aboard, and directed her to one of the tail seats, the only ones not occupied. Eighteen passengers looked over their shoulders at her, as if needing to identify the woman who had held up the flight. Within seconds, the copilot was back in his seat, but still the plane didn't move. Then a long leg thrust itself into the plane, and Jonathan was climbing into the seat next to her. As he buckled in, the plane taxied down the strip, narrowly avoiding a jet that was landing. A roar of the engine, and they were in the air.

Sela shouted to Jonathan above the continuing noise, "I thought you weren't coming."

"Changed my mind."

"Obviously."

He shrugged, and pointed to the earplugs in the pocket back of her seat.

She put in the plugs and took out the materials about Great Zimbabwe. But it was difficult to concentrate with Jonathan so close. His heat was hers, his right arm, leg, and hip tight against her left. As the plane skimmed low over the city and then the countryside, she tried to avoid looking at him, her gaze on the scenery below. A few traditional houses built of mud, cow dung, straw, and reeds stood in isolated fields, but most village houses were of modern construction, with pickup trucks parked nearby. The *highveld,* or high plateau, stretched beneath her, green from summer rains that were slowing down, signaling the dry season—winter— to come. It couldn't come soon enough, she thought, her mind going to the movie scenes they would have to set up before it was completely safe to do.

She had barely started reading the material Jonathan gave her when the plane landed. The other passengers deplaned first, leaving Jonathan and her to try gamely to avoid one another's eyes. "I saw a review by a Dallas reporter. Sounds like your book tour went well," she commented as the wait in the sudden quiet grew increasingly awkward.

"I suppose it was successful. The tour went quickly. In that regard it was good," he said, getting out and then reaching up to help her alight. His hands on her waist were firm, but his cool gaze did not linger.

"Thanks," she said, turning aside swiftly, resolved to be as impersonal as he. Papers whirled in a sudden breeze, and the taste of rain was in the hot, humid air.

"You're welcome," he said, but he looked away.

Of course, helping her down was the polite thing to do. No need to read more into it. She smoothed back her hair and followed the crowd.

Along with a dozen Germans, two women from Ireland, and a small group from Harare, she and Jonathan were loaded on a bus that bumped along a two-lane road.

"Look, I won't bother you out here," he said, as the bus sped forward. He kept his gaze to the front, glancing at her only when absolutely necessary. "I have some things I have to do. Matter of fact, someone's here in Masvingo that I have to see."

She nodded.

"I just wanted to make it clear I wasn't following you."

"I didn't think you were." She didn't know what to think, a tingling was working its way through her, irrespective of the logical reasoning her mind was following. He was tall and warm and handsome, and it would be pure pleasure to give in to lust. Kiss, make love. Another episode in a summer romance? Was she that modern? Her parents would disapprove but say nothing, Nefari would act sophisticated and then giggle, and Grandma Minnie would shake her head.

Eleven miles from Masvingo and the airport, the bus stopped on the circular drive facing a complex of buildings—the Great Zimbabwe Hotel. Sela dragged her mind from its dangerous meanderings as vervet monkeys swung down from the trees that bordered the manicured grounds, a peacock wandered into the lobby and was shooed out, and weaver birds looked from nests hung like baby cradles from the trees. She didn't need to remind herself that she was in the tropics.

A ball of excitement growing within her, she checked in, made contact with Josh's staff, and, with relief, realized that Jonathan was not in sight. She put on stout hiking boots and rushed to the ruins a quarter of a mile away, walking between trees peopled with monkeys, past fields thick with grass to the foot of the mountain where tourists gathered. She was back in Africa and reveling in it. She felt almost as if she were home.

Off and on since she'd arrived, rain had streaked windows and had run like streams down gutters. Now the rain had stopped, and the sun was trying to break through a cloudy sky. She paused and looked around her—up to where the ancient stone village meandered to the top of the hill, around to where tables sporting thatched umbrellas sat beneath sheltering trees. A refreshment stand offered drinks and snacks, and an information center furnished guidebooks and guides. She decided to explore on her own, forming impressions free of outside influence.

Two hours later, she finished crawling up, over, and through the stone rooms and passages. Standing on top, she looked down at the ancient corrals and the great stone tower. The sun had come from behind fluffy, voluminous clouds, and a breeze sent the clouds drifting as lazily as lions resting after a kill. The sense of peace was staggering. Somehow, some way, she had to bring her family to Africa, let them see and experience the feelings Grandma Minnie had tried to articulate without ever having been there.

Back on the valley floor, happy now that she was back in Africa, Sela hiked to the reconstructed Shona Village set in the meadow a short walk from the base of the cliff.

"This is how we lived a hundred years ago," a sculptor explained, as he worked on a soapstone carving of a bird. "Many carvings of birds were found in Great Zimbabwe, and they give us an important link with the ancient ones. In fact, we have a bird on our national flag."

She bought a souvenir before going on, passing communal buildings and a vast array of smaller huts. In one, she found a fortune-teller.

"Come in, come in," he said, as she bent down to peer through the door.

She crossed the threshold into the dim interior. The corners were lost in shadows. The crouching man wearing a leopard skin and woven and fringed grass arm and leg bands smiled at her reassuringly. With a long finger, he pointed to a straw mat. "Be comfortable, lady."

She sank to the mat.

"I tell your fortune?"

Why not? She nodded, handed him five Zimbabwean dollars.

He took bones from a pouch and shook them in his hands. The multi-layer bone and shell necklaces around his neck hung away from his chest as he swayed hypnotically, his eyes closed, the bones and shells clicking together.

He threw, watched the bones land, pointed to their positions, clicked his tongue against his teeth before taking stones from a pottery container. He passed the stones from hand to hand before tossing them out, too.

An image suddenly flashed before her eyes, her and Jonathan together.

"Ah," said the fortune-teller, observing where the stones fell. "You will have a very good life." He pointed toward the stones. "You came a long way, to find good things. From America?"

She nodded. Easy enough to figure out. She smiled. "What else?"

He reached above him, pulled a rope connected to a balance. He put a stone on one side of the balance, a bone on the other, jiggled the rope and raised them both. The rope went almost to the top before it spilled the stone off.

"A long life," he said.

She smiled. "No misfortune? All good things?"

He frowned, studied the configuration in front of him.

She leaned forward.

He shrugged. "A little problem with your back."

"That's all?"

"If you do not heed your heart who knows?" He picked up two of the stones. Pointed to the pattern remaining.

They roughly formed the shape of a heart, but removing one of the bones threw the whole illusion off.

"What does it mean?"

"I cannot tell you more," he said looking away.

Then she noticed that another woman sat in the shadows. Had she been there the whole time? As Sela left she saw the woman get up, move into place in front of the witch doctor. Evidently the native woman had given way for the American.

"Thank you," Sela said leaving. "I certainly didn't mean to take your place."

The woman gave no sign of hearing.

Sela wandered through the village, watching the crafts people again before taking the path that led back to the eating area. A slight breeze nipped at the signs advertising soft drinks, pressing against the trees and rustling the leaves. In the dappled sunlight falling on the outdoor tables, she didn't see Jonathan until she was almost on top of him. He rose, his voice husky with feeling. "Sela, my mother's here. Come meet her."

The woman who had been in the fortune-telling hut nodded slightly. "So this is the lady from America," she said. "Pleased to meet you. Won't you join us?"

"I'm honored to meet you," Sela said. "Didn't I see you in the reconstructed village?" Mrs. Mokane's dark face was lost in the shadows, but when Sela sat down next to her, she could see that she was old enough to be comfortable in her maturity, a flowered dress stretching over her copious bosom, her hands folded quietly in her lap.

Jonathan's mother smiled. "I heard you get your fortune. You must like our country, to keep coming back."

"I do."

She smiled. "I do not think that is all. My son has feelings for you. A mother knows these things." She looked from Sela to Jonathan, who was still standing.

He shrugged as if to say, what can I do?

Mrs. Mokane said to him, "I know I speak out when you'd rather I didn't, but I speak only the truth."

"Mother, sometimes your honesty can be overwhelming," he said, smiling, conveying his obvious affection for her.

She confided to Sela. "He thinks I don't know how to talk to foreigners. Believe me, if I can talk to the people in the villages, I can talk to anyone."

"Mother lectures to women in outlying places. Convinces them to get educated, go to school."

"I don't lecture, I talk," Mrs. Mokane said, looking from Jonathan to Sela.

Sela smiled. "That's wonderful. My grandmother insisted on schooling for her children, and my parents made sure my brothers, sister and I got an education." Sela rested her arms on the round table. "So your schedule takes you all over the country, Mrs. Mokane?"

"As you know, I was in Chiredzi," she said to Jonathan. "It's southwest of here," she explained to Sela. "I am traveling now, making initial contacts. But last week the group that sponsors me sent a girl to school in California. I had first talked to her and her mother two years ago. So we make progress. Before that we sent a woman to Washington."

"Washington's where I live," Sela said. "The U.S. capital, not the state." She opened her fanny pack, took out a mini photo album showing pictures of the capital, and handed it to Mrs. Mokane while her mind mulled over the woman's words. His mother had made it clear that Jonathan knew her schedule, knew she'd be in Masvingo when he was here. Was that why he wanted Sela to make the trip, in order to meet his mother? His mother talked as if his feelings hadn't changed, no matter what had happened in America.

Mrs. Mokane tilted her head as she handed back the small album. "Very nice. My son did not say you lived there. I thought you were from Hollywood." She shrugged her ample shoulders. "You do television and make movies, don't you?"

"Yes, but very few people involved in either live in Hollywood."

A silence followed, broken only by the sound of the turtle dove with its plaintive cry echoing, *work harder, work harder.*

Jonathan said, "While you two are getting acquainted, I'll get us some Cokes." He walked off.

Sela tried not to track his tall form around the tables—his stride so easy, so powerful—but her gaze kept following him while her own mind rushed along in its need to make connections, come up with answers. Why had he made sure she'd run into his mother, unless he still wanted her?

Mrs. Mokane said, "Cokes. So American."

Sela smiled. "He sounds British to me."

Mrs. Mokane shook her head, and the smile that had come so readily disappeared. "He sounds Shona."

Another silence followed. The tables around them were beginning to fill with tourists, the resonance and pitch of German and English blending.

"Your son and I are merely working partners," Sela said as a fly buzzed the table before landing.

Mrs. Mokane shook her head. "When he talks about you, he sounds like he did when he talked about Cana."

Sela changed her suppositions. Jonathan hadn't arranged the trip so she could meet his mother, but so his mother could meet her. "Cana was the girl who died?"

Mrs. Mokane's eyes narrowed. "He told you about her?"

"Just a little." Most, she had intuited.

Mrs. Mokane nodded, and her voice went flat. "He couldn't tell you all, because you couldn't understand all. How can an American know what we feel, what we have gone through?"

Sela overlooked the change in tone and tried to make her own voice conciliatory. "I agree. No one can ever really understand everything about the other person. Especially from one country to another. But we are all blacks. In that we are equal."

Mrs. Mokane shook her head. "Americans are not black. They are light as the sands of the Kalahari. We are black."

Sela wanted to run. It was the first time she'd ever been held accountable for her color. At home whites had excluded her, not other blacks. "I am sorry if I said something to offend you," Sela said, rising. "But, as I said, Jonathan and I are only co-workers, nothing else."

Mrs. Mokane touched Sela on the arm. "Please sit. We do not have to let Jonathan know we have said these things, but it is how things are. I wanted you to know. My son and I are all that is left in our family. We look out for one another."

"I am sure Jonathan can look out for himself." She sank back to the bench as she saw him coming back.

"And I am sure you can, too. You are a modern woman and, in many ways, I am, too. But men and woman are not alike, and in this matter you and I are closer than me and my son. You can get hurt. Not Jonathan. He would not want to hurt you, but . . ." She shrugged as he approached the table.

"No Coke, Mother, so I got us all orange."

Her laugh, so much like his, rang out. "He knows I love orange soda best of all."

Looking across the table to Sela, Jonathan kissed his mother's cheek, his hands on her shoulders.

Suddenly, without any warning, Sela found herself feeling extremely uneasy, as memories of his hands on her shoulders, his lips on hers, made vivid pictures in her mind. Abruptly, she got up. "I really must go. I'm still fighting jet lag, and maybe I can catch a nap before dinner."

"I hope to see you at the hotel restaurant tonight," Mrs. Mokane said. "My son will treat us, we can get better acquainted, and you can tell me all about America. Sometimes I am very proprietary, and for this I am sorry. Will you come, Miss Clay? I really want you to."

Sela looked from Jonathan to his mother. The woman had put her off, but now Mrs. Mokane's countenance showed mannerly consideration, as well as concern, and Jonathan's held even more. Hope and tenderness and passion stewed in a volatile mix barely concealed by his surface calm. If she said she really was too tired to be good company, would it all end here? Or would she and Jonathan continue working together, rigidly polite, and, when the picture was over, never see one another again? She didn't want to wait to find out. "It would be my pleasure," she said.

The night was dark, the moon playing hide and seek with the stars, rain spitting spasmodically. The restaurant was filled to capacity, and Sela hesitated in the doorway.

"Ms. Clay?" the white-jacketed maitre d' asked.

She nodded.

"This way."

A line of waiters moved out of the way as he led her to a booth where Jonathan and his mother waited, seated together on one side. Jonathan jumped to his feet.

She slid in opposite him, avoiding his touch like a cat avoiding the water. If his hand connected with hers she was sure it would unnerve her further, and today had been unnerving enough. He'd had her come to

Masvingo to meet his mother, and Sela didn't know whether to be angry or flattered.

The waiter handed her a menu.

"We've already ordered," Mrs. Mokane said. "The chicken with peri-peri sauce, sadza, corn, fruit. Traditional but good. But please feel free to order whatever you like." She glanced at Jonathan and chuckled, "inasmuch as he's paying."

"What you ordered sounds excellent," Sela said. "We have many family traditions regarding food and other things, some my grandmother doesn't let us forget."

"Your grandmother sounds very wise."

"She is," Jonathan said.

"But your parents do not always see eye to eye with your grandmother?"

"No," Sela said, taking a sip of water.

"Your grandmother is more attuned to the old ways, I surmise," Mrs. Mokane said.

"She talks about the rainbow and the big water, as if there was a pot of gold to be found if one could only find the rainbow."

"Ah yes, we all look for the rainbow, but we Shona have a lot of folk tales," Mrs. Mokane said. "Many concern the hare who is intelligent and quick and is usually the hero."

"The baboon is usually the villain or dunce and gets the worst of it," Jonathan added.

"Poor baboon. I really enjoyed watching the troops at Jonathan's camp. No other animals involved in the stories?"

Mrs. Mokane said, "I'm remembering one. It involves a group of sisters who are persuaded by smooth-talking young men to elope. Later, the men are transformed into lions and the foolish young women are only saved by their wiser younger brother." She paused as the waiter put down plates of cucumber salad. "The moral of the story is that a young woman must closely examine the family into which she marries, because she will have to live with them."

"I expect that goes both ways," Sela said.

Mrs. Mokane nodded. "Of course. A popular saying says that a son-in-law is like a fruit tree; one never finishes eating from it."

"The bride price," Sela said, tasting her salad, sure that Mrs. Mokane had told the story deliberately.

Mrs. Mokane shrugged slightly. "Some think a bride price should be done away with, now that we are a modern country. But the young people themselves cling to the practice. Apparently even women such as yourself find it flattering to know a man will pay such a large amount of money to her family for her hand in marriage. Educated women with important jobs come high. Once the *rutsambo*, the first part, is paid, it isn't long before the second part is due. In the old days, payment consisted of a hoe or some utilitarian object. Now, of course, it is money."

"I didn't realize there were two parts to the transaction," Sela said, toying with her water glass. She felt as if she had set herself up to be knocked down. Alone with Jonathan, she wouldn't have hesitated. On camera she would have known how to react, too, but this was Jonathan's mother.

"Oh, yes," Mrs. Mokane said, and smiled as if she were putting an end to the discussion, but Jonathan's gaze stayed upon Sela like a fire consuming a forest of acacia trees, whooshing up to race along the crown. So he has not given up on either me or the bride price, she thought, thrilled with the one, angry with the other.

For a while, neither Mokane said anything. Arguing cultural differences would get none of them anywhere, Sela knew, but she didn't like being put off. "Why the two payments?"

After a moment, Mrs. Mokane said, "After the *rut-sambo* payment, if the bride is infertile, the prospective groom can return her to her family and get his money back."

"*Prospective* groom?" Sela repeated. "And people say *America* is progressive."

"If she's fertile, he's obligated to pay the second part, and of course, marriage follows." Jonathan's smile was rueful. "It sounds more outrageous than it is."

Sela avoided meeting his eyes and, keeping her tone deliberately academic, said, "I think I'm beginning to see how this works. It looks as if the man has the advantage. What rights does the woman have?"

Mrs. Mokane nodded her head. "If the man is sterile, it is shameful but not disastrous. In the old days, he could discreetly arrange for someone else to impregnate the woman. The child that was born was considered his own. Of course, such customs aren't practiced now. A wife used to become her husband's property, but Prime Minister Mugabe passed a law that says a woman is a person all by herself, someone who has a right to some free choice about her destiny."

"Well, good for him," Sela said, hoping her tone wasn't brimming with the sarcasm she felt. "But that happened rather recently, didn't it?" she asked, her gaze including Jonathan. His persistence was getting to her. He sat there, looking so much a part of the modern world while all the time he was ready to carry her off like some cave man. Still, she felt something within herself that was ready to accept even that. Was it possible that she was more traditional than her outward appearance and career showed, or was it only that she was far from home and he sat opposite her, his gaze tangling with hers at times, his knee touching hers, his voice encompassing her in its lazy, deep-timbered rhythms? Yet when he smiled like that, as if he and she were a foregone conclusion, she wanted to deny all feelings of capitulation and run away as fast as possible.

Mrs. Mokane continued, "Of course, we're a very new country, Miss Clay, but we're moving rapidly into the modern world. In the remote villages, polygamy still occurs, but it's been outlawed, and people don't stay in bad marriages anymore, either. Divorce is quite as common as in your country. Every day, men divorce women who are unfaithful—or poor housewives, even."

"Or if they're married to someone who practices witchcraft," Jonathan said, laughter in his voice.

"He pretends to make a joke," his mother said. "It is true, some women think they do magic. But women have some rights now, too. If she can prove he's physically abusive, or if he fails to keep up his bride price payments, she can divorce him."

Drowning in information and the conflicting feelings bombarding her, Sela frowned. "I'd still say she gets the short end of the stick."

Mrs. Mokane smiled and patted her hand. "I told you we women had a lot in common. These men have to be reminded we won't take second-class status anymore." She raised her eyebrows at Jonathan and smiled at Sela. "I keep fighting uphill battles in the villages. Girls trained to cook, go to market, and tend babies wonder why they should learn science and literature. I don't suppose your little sister has any such problem."

"I told Mother about your parents' reaction to the bride price," Jonathan said.

Sela looked from him to his mother. *She's warning me about the big differences between our two countries and cultures, reminding both of us that the gulf between us is wider than an ocean.*

Mrs. Mokane said, "He came from America with his spirits so low, that I said: a woman who does this to a man who walks with his feet in two countries must have powerful spirits herself." She spooned into her dish of fruit. "Now, after I finish this slice of pineapple, I'm going to my room."

Within minutes, Mrs. Mokane was on her feet. "If you ever come to Victoria Falls, you must come see me, Miss Clay. My home is always open to Jonathan's friends."

"Thank you," Sela said.

"I'll see you to your room," he said.

His mother shook her head. "I travel all around the country by myself, and now you think I can't walk a few feet?"

He kissed her. "Goodnight, Mother."

"Goodnight, son. Miss Clay."

After the outside door closed behind her, Sela said, "It's time you told me all about Cana."

"It's not an easy story to tell, but I wasn't deliberately keeping it from you. I was young. New to war. It was one thing to practice battle with the men of my village. I had never tested my mettle against the enemy until the day I came upon her village. At first I didn't know anything had happened. I called out, but no one answered, and then I saw the bodies, lying between smoldering buildings. Men, women, children. They had been tortured, shot, hacked to pieces." He paused, looked past her to some vision in his head.

Sela nodded solemnly.

"I began burying the dead. When I was halfway through, Cana came down from the mahogany tree where she'd been hiding and helped me. We made a little ceremony for her family, and we put out the fires that still burned, and then we walked off into the forest."

His eyes had a far-away looked. "We were so very young. I had never been with a woman before. That night she slept in my arms, and the next and the next, and one night we became lovers. We were little more than children."

Sela shook her head. "I don't know what to say. How long did she . . . ?"

"Live? Almost a year. We were together constantly. One day I came back to our hut to find they had captured her. Tortured her and then killed her." He said the words dispassionately, but a haunted look lingered in his eyes.

Sela shuddered involuntarily. She felt inadequate to say anything. "I'm sorry," she whispered. Her gaze swept away from the table to the restaurant, where customers were leaving, waiters whispering now with one another. For a while neither she nor he said anything, but as the waiters glanced their way, she felt impelled to add, "All evening I felt like a child in school. As if this time was some kind of test I had to pass, and now I feel as if I've spent my life playing games while you . . ." She took a sip of coffee and glanced up from her cup to find Jonathan's gaze pressing upon her as if searching her soul. In an open-throated shirt and casual coat he appeared much as she had seen him before, but something about him was changed, and this she couldn't identify.

"You've just lived a different life," he said quietly. "I still want to marry you." He leaned closer. "I think you want to marry me, too."

She sighed. "Jonathan, I see obstacles rising higher than any mountain in Zimbabwe. What about your feelings, memories of Cana? I don't know if I could live with a ghost as well."

"I think we can find a way around the problems. And Cana is a memory, a person from another time, just as I am a different person now than I was then." He pulled a credit card from his wallet. "My mother liked you, too."

"She doesn't know me. I don't know her."

"I thought if we explained."

"I'm not sure . . ." She began to rise.

Jonathan put out a hand. "No, you don't get away that easily. I want you to understand how it was and how it can be. In the village now I would drink a beer and then quote poetry to you, and for the edification of anyone who wanted to listen, I'd sing your praises."

"Is that customary, too?"

"Damn customary. Every bit of it."

"And what would you say?"

"I'd say you're more beautiful than sunset at the Zambesi, more graceful than an impala, more fierce than a lion. Damn it all, Sela, you have me so confused, I don't know whether I want to kiss you or . . ."

"Kill me?"

"You said it. But it's only a phrase."

"And your customs are only traditions. But I'm not a woman who will walk meekly behind her mate."

"I know that."

"Then you know nothing can be settled so easily."

"So, we're at an impasse."

"Probably. Right now I'm going to bed."

"Before I've begun the poetry?"

She saw laughter in his eyes. Almost touching his hand, she let her eyes and lips tell him she'd go anywhere with him, do anything. But capitulation would prove nothing. "Yes, I'm leaving before you begin quoting rhymes."

"I'll walk you to your room."

"In case a lion or a hippo or an elephant waylays me?"

"No, in case Josh flew out here." His face was suddenly, wholly open, even though his eyes and his voice treated the words in a joking fashion.

So he was jealous of Josh. She smiled before getting

up, and she lowered her voice respectfully. "Josh is merely an old friend, and now an employer. But I want you to know how appreciative I was of your mother's explanations."

"I know."

"She seems like a very nice lady."

"She is." He rose.

While he settled the check, she went outside. The rain had stopped, but the moon was still skittering in and out behind the clouds. Without waiting for him, she took a route straight toward her room.

He caught up, halfway across the damp lawn.

"So what about what I said?"

"I think we should concentrate on doing the job we've been hired to do. Get the movie out of the way. Then we can sort out you and me. I want us to know one another as well as you and Cana knew one another."

"I want that, too."

She turned, looked up at him, saw the sculptured quality of his face, the firm line of his jaw, the tender obstinacy in his chin and mouth. "Yes," she said. Oh, yes, she wanted to lie in his arms in the jungle, know him intimately, sink into his embrace, enter his mind.

And then he kissed her, and his hands, his body, felt like she had fallen from a high, lofty place and landed in Paradise. She wanted more, so much more. But it seemed his lips had just touched hers when the touch was broken, he was saying goodnight and moving away from her. She was left with a tingling feeling that washed over her pleasantly as she went to sleep.

Still something nagged at her, remained unsolved, undisclosed, lurking like demons in her subconscious. In the middle of the night she woke with his mother's words in her mind.

Sela rose, pulled back the draperies and looked out.

The moon peeked from behind a cloud. Dimly, she could see the peacocks roosting in the trees, could see a troop of vervet monkeys swarming over the tables at the outside restaurant adjacent to the lawn. Did Jonathan consider her truly black? Or was she as different in her color as he was in his customs? It took a long time before she could finally put the problems from her mind and go back to sleep.

Thirteen

"It won't be easy," Jonathan said, standing by the Landrover he would drive from Kariba. "A two-hundred-kilometer trek through the bush is no lark." He'd made it every year since he'd started the camp, but each time was a new adventure, never without difficulty.

"So you've been telling me," Sela replied, as the other Landrovers and trucks making the trip jockeyed into place. "Why don't you just fly in?"

He explained that the small planes that could land in the jungle couldn't carry enough equipment to supply even a small work crew. Each year he had to take in everything that was needed to repair, restock and make the camp habitable. Electric generators, water pumps, bedding, fuel, food—the list got so long she began nodding before he finished. Her smile showed she'd made up her mind about him and was wanting to get on with the job, while still reminding him of their shaky relationship. He made sure his own smile was as perfunctory, friendly but distant. In America he had swirled through the preliminaries with the publishers, his ready confidence unimpaired. They had treated him with deference, wining and dining him like a visiting celebrity. He had looked forward eagerly to seeing Sela again, and thrilled when he looked down the corridor at the Kennedy Center and saw her standing there, surrounded by her family.

"I won't say another word," he said, only half facetiously.

"I will," Josh said, rushing up, a pith helmet on his head, long shorts and baggy T-shirt adding to the incongruity of feet thrust into stout boots. "You could wait, Sela, fly in with me later after they iron out the kinks."

Jonathan's jaw tightened as Josh walked from vehicle to vehicle, pulling unnecessarily on ropes, checking loads. When he winked at Sela, Jonathan looked away, envious of the years they'd known one another, and their easy teasing ways. Josh knew the shorthand words of America, he didn't.

Sela shook her head. "No thank you, I don't want to wait. I want to see the camp in its wildest state, not after Jonathan and his crew get it back in shape."

"If you get there," Josh said. "I mean, it's a zoo out there." He held up his hands defensively as Jonathan and the drivers looked at him. "Just kidding."

Jonathan said, "We make the trek every year and haven't lost a woman yet." He shrugged and attempted a light tone. "Of course none has ever made the trip."

The drivers laughed and Sela grinned.

Josh hugged Sela. "Don't forget, sweetheart. Get lots of pictures of lions tearing apart poor little defenseless antelopes or whatever."

"We'll do our best," she said, getting into the passenger seat.

"Only be careful," Josh said, finger to his mouth. "You'd make a tasty meal."

Jonathan turned the key in the ignition. "Josh, I guarantee she'll arrive in one piece."

Josh shook his head. "I feel as if I should break a

bottle of champagne over the hood before you start."
He leaned in, kissed Sela on the cheek.

"Save it for when the movie's finished," Jonathan growled and started the engine. What did Sela really think about Josh?

As the Landrover moved out, Josh kept pace, jogging alongside and looking across Sela to Jonathan. "Remember, radio back each day and, as soon as camp is set up again, I'll fly out."

Jonathan nodded, his lips tight.

"You've got it," Sela said and, as the Landrover began to outdistance Josh, her head swiveled until she was looking over her shoulder and waving until he was a speck on the horizon.

Annoyed, Jonathan tromped on the gas. Soon Josh was lost to sight. "You going to be okay without Mr. Boss Man?" Jonathan asked, wondering why he was letting it get to him. He threw a glance Sela's way. She was regarding him warily.

"I've told you, we're old friends. Anyway, that's how people act in Hollywood." She told him a story from college, something about Josh and the Dean that Jonathan didn't follow.

"Yeah, sure," he muttered, glad when the paved road disappeared, and the subsequent graveled one gave out quickly. The rest of the route hadn't been used since the previous year. Bouncing over the rough terrain, Sela would have little chance to regale him with stories about "brother" Josh.

"The easy part's over," Jonathan said, guiding the Landrover down a barely visible track that turned and twisted around mopane and acacia trees and through thick, high, elephant brush, the land a tumbled splendor of rocky hills and forests. Always it did his soul good to see it again, the beginning of the trip to the place he loved best, sweetening his mind, relaxing his body.

He didn't like thinking about Washington and that scene with her parents, but it came again, catching him off guard, just as he hadn't been prepared for the vast differences in their cultures. Yes, damn it, Sela had more in common with those Hollywood types than she did with him.

He tightened his grip on the steering wheel. Occasionally, he glimpsed giraffes in stilt-legged splendor, showing their long necks and heads above the grass as they munched their way through the treetops. They blended easily into the terrain, and it took a sharp eye to spot them, or any of the animals along the way. Pointing them out to Sela, he hoped to take pleasure in her smile, her look of awe, but her response was that of any animal lover, not a woman who had lain in his arms. Once a herd of zebras in the distance became silvery animals, the stripes disappearing in the bright light, and her voice grew hushed, and for a time she rested her hand on his arm, and he wanted to hold it there, pull it against his heart, let her feel the thunder in his veins. All for her.

At noon, he halted the safari, engines stopping all along the line, and he sat quietly, hearing the wind whistle through the grass. When it died he heard the rustle and quiet passage of a predator sneaking unseen a few yards away, its rank odor unmistakable. He glanced at Matui, who undoubtedly had heard and smelled it, too.

"Lion?"

"Probably."

And then came the sound of an engine and topping a rise, a Landrover appeared, hurtling down the draw at breakneck speed, Josh in the passenger seat. "I thought I shouldn't miss any of this," he cried, climbing out in a swirl of dust. "I can be observing the whole way. Getting a whole new angle." His hands formed a box he gazed through as if taking photographs.

Sela laughed and ran to welcome him. Jonathan shrugged philosophically, exchanged a look with Matui, and began helping the old man spread out a cold lunch on the hood of the lead vehicle. Heat was shimmering the day, but the clouds building up were beginning to filter the sun.

Josh took Sela's arm and stood with her, their backs to the rest of the group. Their voices came to Jonathan in a soft murmur, and he chided himself for the shaft of jealousy that shot through him. From the far side of the Landrover, he eyed her. In Harare, at the hotels, white women minced along on high heels, their tailbones tucked under—flat, uninteresting. But Sela had a high, well-rounded posterior like his mother and like Cana, and he feasted upon the sight, until she turned, drawn, no doubt, by the intensity of his gaze.

"Time to eat?" Her voice carried pleasantly.

Before Jonathan could answer, Josh said, "What's on the menu? I'm starved. Jonathan, old boy, you hit the road so early I missed my breakfast."

"Hot tea, bully beef and beans," Jonathan said shortly, not wanting to baby-sit another greenhorn, and unsure how Josh would act in the bush. The technicians and cameramen were already wandering off like it was a picnic site in the States. "Better tell your people to stay in sight of the vehicles," he advised.

"What? Oh, sure."

For the most part, they obeyed. Only Josh pushed at the boundaries, but, then, he was paying the way, Jonathan reminded himself, as Josh went into a monologue about the film.

Sela's T-shirt clung to her body and she looked washed clean, new, shiny, no makeup as she pulled at her shirt. Jonathan wanted to put his own hands over her breasts, warm them with the sudden heat he felt.

For a moment she met his look with one as frank as

his own. He wanted to kiss her, hold her, pour out his heart, but from up and down the line of vehicles people were calling to him, wanting to know what was wrong. "Nothing," he called and then, lowering his voice said, "Later," to her.

Jonathan eased the Landrover down a small bank, sliding half way. He forded a tiny gully and then braked to a sudden stop, the convoy behind him turning out to avoid banging into one another. A creek bed that usually was dry, the greenery clinging to the bottom reaching deep into the earth for moisture, was now a raging torrent. Water swirled between the banks, crested, foamed, showed white and ruffly where it slammed against rocks as it rushed downhill. On the banks, clouds of steam rose from the brush.

"What do we do, build a bridge?" Josh asked, getting out of his vehicle and coming over to Jonathan. "Can't be more than fifteen, sixteen feet wide."

"You can try, I wouldn't," Jonathan said, beginning to unpack the one tent and the few sleeping bags he carried in case of emergencies.

"It looks impossible to me," Sela said, "but how about fording farther down?"

"That's not possible, either. We wait a day or two until the water recedes. Then we build some kind of a road through, or we'll sink so deep in the mud we'll be lucky if the radio antenna sticks out."

"So what can we do now?" Sela asked.

"Be patient," Jonathan said, as he unrolled the tent, "and, at the moment, stay out of the way." He smiled at her to soften the words.

"Sor-ree," she drawled, and meandered over to where Josh stood watching the water.

Jonathan put up the center pole and let the canvas drape over it while he pounded in the tent stakes that drew the tent taut. He waited for Josh to ask where he'd found such an antique, heavy, canvas shelter, but Josh was lifting two collapsible director's chairs from the back of his Landrover.

"Here you are, my lady."

"Fantastic!" Sela cried. "You think of everything."

Jonathan mentally shook his head. How could a man with an ancient tent compete? Josh had a distinct edge. Sela understood his slang, his allusions to celebrities, his jokes. But she loves me, Jonathan thought, or at least he thought she did. Sometimes he imagined she looked at him with questions in her eyes, as if she, too, were puzzling over what had gone wrong between them. He took a deep breath. The air was stuffy inside the tent but, controlling his aversion to the enclosed space, he unrolled the five sleeping bags and draped a mosquito net from the center post. It barely covered two bags. He put his shaving kit on one of the bags, Sela's backpack on the one next to it. Ducking his head, he opened the tent flap and went back outside.

The clouds were mostly gone, and the sun was baking the land again. The heat felt good, and he stretched, unkinking his cramped muscles before he looked around. Most of the crew had lined up along the gully, shouting and spurring someone on in the water. Two of the Hollywood technicians were riding inner tubes down the swollen creek, their laughter infectious, the others all smiles as they watched Josh and Sela, like visiting royalty, lolled in their director's chairs.

"What the hell," Jonathan said, pushing to the edge to watch. The water was spinning the men and inner tubes like tops, then shooting them straight ahead through a narrow channel before twisting and turning again. A third of a kilometer or less, Jonathan knew the stream bed joined the river, but the thick brush made it impossible to see that far. After the "s" curves that were visible, the creek made a wide turn before rushing around a sand bar that jutted out into the stream. When they reached the large curve, the first man paddled desperately toward the sandbar, threw himself over a collection of small rocks and boulders, jumped out, and pulled the inner tube behind him. Then as the other man shot by, he reached out a hand and grabbed him, dragging him and the inner tube up onto the sandbar.

Everyone cheered as the two climbed the bank and strutted back up toward where everyone waited.

"Damn fools," Jonathan muttered as the two joined them on the high ground.

"It can't be too dangerous, can it?" Josh asked, his eyes glowing. "I mean, it's not more than six, eight feet deep, and I can see it's getting shallower all the time." He looked around. "Are there any crocodiles?"

Matui shook his head. "No crocodiles in rain water. They stay near the river. No way are they going to fight that crazy current."

"How was it?" Josh asked the men, who declared they were ready for a repeat.

"Man, it was some float trip."

Josh looked at Sela. "What do you say? Be like that white-water raft trip we took."

She shook her head. "I say you're crazy."

"You losing your nerve, Sela?"

She raised her eyebrows.

"I say, last one in's a rotten egg." He cocked his head at her.

"Rotten egg? Josh, you're reverting to childhood."

Jonathan wanted to grab her, hold her back.

Josh went to his Landrover, and rummaged through his overnight bag. "I got some cutoffs in here somewhere." He stepped around behind the vehicle, and, from his movements, it was obvious he was changing. "You're just chicken, Sela."

For a time, nothing was said, and Jonathan saw her

smile leave her face. Then suddenly she streaked past Jonathan and ran into the tent, and in a short time she emerged wearing a fluorescent bathing suit cut high on the sides and low in back and front, her figure a feast for all eyes. He couldn't believe she was really going to let Josh push her into such a crazy stunt.

"What's this you say about rotten eggs?" she asked innocently.

"Not a word," Josh said, grabbing one of the inner tubes and launching himself into the swirling water.

"Wait," Jonathan cried, but within seconds Sela was in behind Josh, draped over another inner tube, legs bobbing up, water whooshing over her belly, sliding up her chest, pinpointing her breasts.

Jonathan held his breath, shaken by the sight of her, frightened by her actions, berating himself because he hadn't acted fast enough to stop her.

Caught by the current, her inner tube was whisked down the curving gully.

Jonathan began running. "Come on," he shouted, racing along the bank before cutting a straight line through the brush and heading for the sandbar. If she missed it, there was no telling what she'd encounter below. These small streams changed configuration yearly, sand piling up, banks eroding. She could bang her head on a rock, be swept to the river. Anything could happen. The two men who had started the whole thing were not back in the river, but had remained strangely quiet while Josh had taunted Sela.

Jonathan ran faster, the ground blurring beneath his feet. Already she was out of sight. He threw himself down a bank, over a rock outcropping, and then leaped to the sandbar.

Looking upstream, he saw Josh shooting around the curve, Sela close behind him. Both were laughing, teasing one another and calling to the people running along the bank above them.

Matui cleared the rock outcropping and joined Jonathan. "You catch him," Jonathan said, wading into the water. "I'll get her." He had to save Sela.

And then Josh was at the turn, grabbing at the vegetation on the bank, trying desperately to slow down.

Matui held out a stout stick. Josh reached, missed, and then caught it and held on. Matui pulled him in.

Jonathan kept his gaze on the water. Sela, coming into the turn, was spun and then swept into the middle of the stream.

Holding his footing with difficulty, Jonathan reached for Sela, but the current grabbed the tube again and spun it out of reach.

With superhuman strength, Jonathan pushed against the water, pulled himself back to the sandbar and ran to its very tip. As Sela's inner tube hit the narrowest part of the gully, it was grabbed as if by a giant hand and sent ahead. Jonathan launched himself through the water, grabbed hold of the side, and tried to pull her back. But the current was too strong. As the water swirled the tube away, he clung to it. If she ran into difficulty, he wanted to be there.

"Hold on," Sela screamed, bending toward him.

The water roared in his ears, cold, deafening. His legs slammed into a rock, bounced off. He almost lost his hold before he let his legs float up, go with the current.

Around a bend the water swirled the tube around, Sela in the middle, he clinging to the outer edge.

For a while the banks were close, the water high and swift, and then all at once the banks opened up, the stream widened, and he, Sela, and the inner tube were dumped unceremoniously into six inches of water that trickled away to nothing.

"I'll be damned," he said, getting up, pulling himself

from the slime and mud, and holding out a hand for her.

Covered with ooze, Sela struggled to rise.

He grabbed her hand. It slid through his and she landed, sputtering up to her chin in mud. For a moment she stared up at him, startled, and then she started to laugh.

He joined in. After that, everything became a comic opera, with them both slipping and sliding, crawling on their knees toward the bank, laughing so much that Jonathan felt good clear through. Her body was slim and slick and covered with mud and oh so desirable.

"Some savior," she teased, putting a hand to her hair, in a mock flirtatious pose.

"Some savee," he retorted, putting his hand on her cheek and rubbing the spot before putting his mud-splattered lips on hers.

"Oooh," she giggled. "You taste of . . ." She held up a hand. "Let me see. Mud?"

"Something like that. But so do you, Ms. Clay."

"I dare you to kiss me again," she said, scooting away. "If you can catch me."

"Lady, you're on."

And then they were thrashing around in the mud, laughing and kissing and mock wrestling, touching and kissing until the voices from above stopped them.

"Damn, they *would* find us," Jonathan said, his eyes sober as they met hers.

"Maybe we can hide," she whispered. "Burrow into the mud, never come back."

He looked around, willing there to be a water hole where they could wash, kiss, make love and get past the awkwardness of all that had separated them. But already the others were looking down from above.

With all the dignity he could muster, Jonathan climbed the hill, Sela in step with him.

"Boss, you look pretty bad," Matui said, his old eyes twinkling.

"I didn't figure I looked good," Jonathan said. But no matter the mud, Sela looked fresh, and so gorgeous he wanted to lift her up in his arms and carry her the rest of the way in. So he did.

She whooped with laughter, and the little band of drivers and film makers parted to let them through, and then trailed them, everyone laughing and talking.

So much for Josh, Jonathan thought, seeing the wet but clean producer/director shake his head.

"Winning comes in different guises, and sometimes you have to lose first," Matui said, his voice pitched for Jonathan's ears alone.

Jonathan nodded, as he set Sela on her feet. She was smiling happily, and that was the most important thing of all.

He looked around at the others. "Tomorrow, with luck, we'll make it to my camp."

"Hip, hip, hooray!" the Hollywood clique shouted.

Jonathan didn't say that there was no telling what they'd find. The rainy season and the animals would have taken their toll on the camp, thatched roofs leaking, wall collapsing, the picnic tables and benches overturned. But if they were to film lions on the kill, there'd be little time to make things ship-shape before going out into the bush again. The camp wouldn't be the refuge they anticipated, but he'd be damned if he'd say so now. He'd just make sure Sela was near him at all times. The next few weeks might be the most dangerous she'd ever experienced.

Fourteen

That evening after their mutual baptism by mud, a new sense of camaraderie sprang up between Sela and Jonathan. *We treat one another with respect,* she thought, recognizing the underlying passion that smoldered regardless of anything either said or did. Even though his mother's "sands of the Kalahari" line stayed with Sela, she felt very comfortable with and about Jonathan. He led the conversation around the campfire, laughing often and talking easily. He seemed more like the man who had charmed her when she'd first gone to his camp—not like the man who had foundered in her parents' living room and who had seemed glum and unapproachable later.

Everyone retired early, hoping to get an early start in the morning. In the tent, despite the Deet she had wiped liberally on her skin, mosquitoes drove her under Jonathan's mosquito netting. Although he had draped the netting over her sleeping bag, too, she had moved her bag far enough away so that the netting didn't cover her properly. She made the move closer to him noisily, aware of Josh and Matui and a cameraman stretched out in sleeping bags nearby. Still, under the netting, an aura of intimacy shut out the others and sent shivers of pleasure shooting through her at Jonathan's physical presence. She was aware when he slept and when he was awake, and knew he was as aware of her sleep patterns, too.

Once, a wuffing sound came from nearby, and she knew in an instant that a lion prowled the makeshift camp. If there was one, wouldn't there be more? She pictured them slinking around on the other side of the canvas, heads turned in a listening attitude, picking up Josh's snores, Matui's snorts, her perfume. Would she be done in because of her taste for pricey scents, the new Samsara cologne she'd splashed liberally over her body after the mud bath? She scooted closer to Jonathan's sleeping bag until his body, firm and reassuring, stopped further movement.

"It's all right." He whispered the words into her hair, and she felt her scalp prickle with pleasure that sent butterfly touches down her neck, over her shoulders, through her breasts.

A little while later, a bang and clatter woke everyone. Sela jumped.

Jonathan put his hand on her shoulder. "Something bumped into some of the gear we left sitting around. Probably scared it more than us."

But he didn't remove his hand, and she didn't turn away, but put her own over it, drawing upon his quiet strength.

Matui said from near the front of the tent, *"Shumba."*

"What is a *shumba?"* Josh asked.

"Lion," Sela interpreted, glad her concern was justified.

"Oh, great." Josh shot to a sitting position, his silhouette a vague outline. "Just when I was feeling the need to answer a call of nature."

Everyone laughed, the tension broken. Someone flashed a light. Sela rolled away from Jonathan.

Several minutes later, a growl and then a roar came from a distance.

Jonathan said, "They're probably a good kilometer away by now. I think you're safe, Josh."

Again, laughter.

Sela closed her eyes, drifted off. In her sleep, lions stalked her, and once again Jonathan saved her. In the morning, she woke in the circle of his arm. How long had she slept that way? Vaguely, she remembered once exchanging a lazy, half-asleep kiss. Now her back was to him, but his arm was around her, his breath on her neck. She restrained herself from turning over to look into his eyes.

Daylight streamed through the open tent flaps, giving her a pie-slice view of outside. Beyond Matui, who poured coffee from thermos mugs into Styrofoam cups, sunlight settled like molten gold over the brush. No water rushed down the creek bed.

Later, eating biscuits and drinking coffee, she watched the men fill the creek bed with branches and logs. With the fill forming a cushion, Jonathan assured her that the remaining few inches of water standing in the bottom offered no problem for the all-terrain vehicles. But the perpendicular bank on the other side posed a real problem. With shovels, they dug it down so that it offered a gradual slope out.

Smiling as he issued orders, Jonathan seemed to thrive on the adversity, joking with Josh, and looking at her in a way that said, "we're buddies and more." But his eyes also said he wouldn't push it now. Instead, they said, we will live in the day, take each thing as it comes.

The new relationship freed her, allowing her to bury personal misgivings behind the chores of the moment. She taped a description of the place for a documentary Josh would do about the making of the film. Once more, she felt in charge of herself and her life, not reacting to Jonathan like a spoiled child or an angry adversary, or even as an American who had to defend everything American. Living in the moment, she once more became aware of the jungle humming around her, the birds singing, the animals grazing, and of Jonathan moving like a god in a garden of eden.

The garden grew even more lush as the convoy progressed to the camp—acacia, mopane, and mahogany trees towering, spreading out, offering shade to waterbuck, kudu, and innumerable elephants. Once Jonathan pointed out a duiker, an animal that used to be extremely numerous, but was not seen very often anymore. There were less than thirty kilometers to go, and good moods proliferated. Everyone laughed, joked, and called out animal sightings—a dik-dik, two wart hogs, and numerous impala.

Again, Sela rode with Jonathan, both commenting about everything they saw. The sky seemed alive with birds. A whir of wings and a pair of Egyptian geese and a covey of lilac-breasted rollers fanned the air. But, a short time later, a yellow hornbill sitting quietly by the faint track had everyone taking pictures, amazed at the bird's seeming docility.

Sela perched on the edge of the seat as Jonathan drove by the baobab tree. "I feel as if I were coming home," she said, needing to be entirely honest, as if anything less would cheapen them both.

Jonathan's smile bathed her in warmth, and she knew that her turbulent emotions were tame next to the deep emotions the camp engendered in him.

"What about Sheba and her family?" she said, the words matter-of-fact, but her heart pounding rapidly as she spoke. It was the first time she'd alluded to the official culling of the elephant herds, the first wedge in their relationship.

"Last I heard, they were fine."

So much said in so few words.

The grass, high and green, rippled—unlike the low, spiky, brown and tan foliage of months ago. "Do you think the elephants will still be in camp?"

Jonathan peered ahead with concern. "Better there than on the way in. Each time I go around a curve, I wonder if we're going to slam into one." He geared down. "It's a balancing act. If I go too slow, I'll bog down in the swampy areas."

"Everything's beautiful," she said, staring at the impenetrable wall of grass. "Aren't those water lilies? And look at all those bird nests! I don't think I've ever heard so many insects either. It's a little intimidating."

"The season is ripe for bugs and that sort of thing."

Snakes, spiders, scorpions: all the things she hadn't seen before. "Look," she cried as two fluffy, chocolate brown buffalo calves suddenly appeared in the track.

Jonathan braked and spun the wheel to avoid hitting them.

The animals hopped out of the way.

Sela watched them disappear. "They're almost cute," she said, listening to them crash through the brush.

Jonathan laughed and wrestled the Landrover back onto the track. "That's the first time I've heard Cape Buffalo called cute, even when young."

A short time later he touched Sela's shoulder and drew her attention to a roof peeking through the trees. "We're almost at camp."

She tried to see more, but trees intervened. A short time later the banks of the Zambesi River showed to the right of the track, and a crocodile slid into the fast moving water. There was a ripple and then two eyes broke the surface.

A frown touched Jonathan's face. "About this time, I begin to wonder what I'll find in camp."

"What do you mean?"

"For one thing, the river could have changed course,

cut off a couple of chalets. Each season the camp's different. I wonder how different it will be this time."

"It's going to be the same as I remember it," Sela said, needing the camp, Lobengula, to remain unchanged. It was the unspoiled paradise, the place where time stood still, the treasure in her mind.

He shook his head. "Lobengula's like life, always changing."

And then tall trees overshadowed her, and a sea of grass, exquisite in its freshness, stretched as far as she could see. Mint-green foliage and shrubs in the bright sunlight became forest green under the trees, and viridian along the riverbanks. Newly washed. Pristine. A splash of color, momentarily blinding, came from the leaves of the deciduous trees beginning to change color, scarlet and russet touches pasted like jewels upon the wide expanse of green. "It's beautiful."

"Yes," he said, and put his hand over hers. "And deadly. In the spring it's impossible to see what's out there."

He took his hand away from hers, but the feel of his touch remained. She craned her neck as he pulled up near the kitchen and the outside eating area beneath the trees. Branches and twigs and grass covered the tables, and the wood looked weathered and old.

Jonathan got out, and Sela followed as the other Landrovers and trucks lined up, everyone quiet as they got down, looks of wonder and curiosity on their faces. We're like children not knowing what to do, Sela thought, seeing everyone's gaze go to Jonathan.

"Watch your step. The rules of safari are still in effect, but even more so during the rainy season. With luck we'll be able to use the chalets tonight," he explained, directing the kitchen crew who were unloading supplies.

"Good," Josh said, moving gingerly around, framing

views through his hands. "Whenever you're ready," he said to Sela, "we can begin filming for the documentary."

With a pocket comb and mirror, she fixed her hair and, then, with a cameraman following, she took the trail Matui was clearing toward the chalet she'd stayed in before. Where Matui's path intersected the elephant trail, she paused to narrate. "Elephants have big, cushioned feet that carry their great weight almost noiselessly." She indicated an indentation in the sand. As she spoke, the camera came in close to capture the print with her foot close by for comparison.

She paused, and looked in both directions, and then she spied Sheba and Bump, Madonna, Sting, and the others coming down the trail from the direction of Jonathan's house. A feeling of exaltation raced through her. Jonathan's supposition was right; they hadn't been culled. "We're being welcomed back," she called, her voice gleeful, her smile spontaneous.

The camera caught her expression, and the cameraman put thumb to forefinger. Smiling eagerly, she commented about each elephant before she went on to the chalet.

Standing in front, she looked out across the dry creek bed. Pools of water stood here and there, and the sand looked damp and unappealing.

"It's been several months since this was used," she reminded herself and the eventual audience as she unlatched the door to the chalet. "As I said before, the Zimbabwe winter is our summer." Moving aside, she gave the camera time to pan. Inside, under the thatch, it was dim and cool, but leaves had collected in the bedroom. The bed had been stripped, the mattress was gone, and a drift of sand covered the dresser and shelves. In the adjacent bathroom, a damp earth smell, not unpleasant, fed her nostrils, and she said, "A broom, a little elbow grease, and this place will look as good as new." She signaled the end of the session. After the room was cleaned and refurbished, she'd film again.

Frogs seemed to have taken up permanent residence in the bathroom, and she put out her finger and moved one aside as she gazed back to the bedroom. Spiderwebs festooned the corners and hung over the door.

As she turned to leave the bathroom, a long, green snake glided out from the shower stall and slithered toward her, its head up and its yellow eyes alert.

She cleared the bedroom in three steps and was outside before she stopped shaking. Standing next to the termite mound at the edge of the dry water course, she shook her head in retrospect. She'd let a nonpoisonous snake frighten her.

"You can stay in my place," Jonathan said later, hearing the story from the cameraman.

Sela liked that no one questioned her adamant dislike of snakes. Off the forest floor, Jonathan's house was more closed to the elements, safer in all respects. Josh had already stashed much of his equipment inside and would be bunking on the balcony.

"I feel ridiculous," she confided. The snake was harmless. Still, she felt better two hours later, when the grass had been trimmed in camp.

"Come on, take you over to my place now," Jonathan said, leading her to one of the Landrovers.

The baboons met them, their voices calling angrily as Jonathan and Sela climbed the ladder to the tree house.

"Once they got into the kitchen and created havoc with the pots and pans while we were gone," Jonathan said, going ahead to check out each room.

At the far end of his house, a shutter had come undone and was flapping open, hanging by one screw. The mosquito netting covering the window was broken.

Old magazines and books were knocked over, and paper fluttered like confetti in the breeze. "The baboons entered while I was gone." Jonathan said taking the shutter down. "Luckily, they weren't able to come into the main part of the house." He shut the door and dropped her luggage on his bed. "You can use this until the chalets are snake proofed."

"I don't want to put you out."

Laughter in his eyes, he looked straight at her and shaking his head said, "Who says you're putting me out?"

For a time, she met his teasing gaze head-on. Maybe this was what it was really like—living in the moment, not being so serious about everything said. Her own smile was as light-hearted as his, and she said easily, "Not me. You're like one of those ten-ton elephants. I'm not about to argue."

"You mean I'm that formidable? Or I sleep where I want?"

For another moment, she looked into his eyes, and she saw so many things there that she looked aside again, found an easy smile. "I don't know about somebody who bathes in mud. Anyway, I think it's time to get on with our job. Lions, wasn't it?"

He kissed her cheek. "You make a good boss, keep the help on target. If we're going to film lion like Josh wants, you're right, we'd better get going." Across the dry riverbed a rocky escarpment rose, with boulders strewn indiscriminately. A good place for lion. They'd look there.

That night, Jonathan joined Josh on the balcony, and Sela used the bedroom. Still, the sounds of the jungle, the rustling of leaves, the movement of baboons, the call of the birds, woke her. She lay awhile savoring the moment, then jumped from bed, dressed quickly, and called out, "Hey you lazy-bones, day's half over!"

Jonathan's voice came from the kitchen.
She joined him.
"Brother Josh is still sleeping," he said handing her a cup of coffee.
She tried not to smile. So, he was still jealous.
Matui had a lunch packed for them, and after gulping some toast with marmalade, Sela set off with Jonathan in the Landrover. Dawn burst gloriously, sunbursts impaling the sky, showing a clear blue patch with no sign of a cloud.
"It makes me feel reverent," she murmured.
Jonathan nodded and smiled as he drove sedately through camp.
With the grass trimmed, the place was beginning to resemble the memories she had so carefully husbanded. She stared back at it as they moved toward the dry riverbed.
Abruptly, Jonathan plunged the Landrover down the embankment.
"Hey, you could have warned me," Sela cried, holding on. But the sudden movement actually made her feel good, as if she were getting on with the job. Once past the low spots and around rocks he maneuvered. Only traces of water remained, dull and lifeless looking. He gunned the Rover up the bank on the other side.
Sela hung on this time. Even so, she slid down the seat into him, pulled herself back, and a little later repeated the procedure. Each time he grinned, as if to ask, was that on purpose? Above her, two plus kilometers from camp, a large ridge of rocks and rock outcropping overshadowed the sand, the trees, and the rippling grassland that extended to the river.
"Africa," she murmured.
"Zimbabwe," he corrected.
They both laughed.
Fifteen minutes later, closer to the ridge, Jonathan

braked, shifted to neutral, and trained his binoculars on the ridge.

"See anything?"

"No, but the rock provides caves as well as a good lookout. We should find lion nearby."

Shortly afterward, he found their spoor—distinctive markings in the sand. Larger than a leopard's, the lion tracks dug deeper into the sand.

A few minutes later, in the shade of a tree, not far from the dry riverbed where rock and sand kept the grass to a minimum, Sela spotted a pride of lions stretched out. "Look," she whispered, pointing, lowering her binoculars.

Jonathan stopped the Landrover near a mopane tree approximately 20 meters away, and unobserved by the pride, he and Sela watched through field glasses.

Four grown lionesses—their coats vivid as spun gold against the silvery rock behind them—two half-grown lions, and four young cubs shared the shade. The cubs crawled up and over the mother, rolling onto their backs, batting with their paws at her switching tail.

"She's extremely patient," Sela whispered. Last night she had been dead to the world, but she'd been aware when she woke that she was sleeping in Jonathan's bed, on his sheets. His belongings surrounded her, now his eyes held her.

"Like all mothers, I suppose," Jonathan said, a touch of reverence in his tone.

"But not all women?" she teased him to lighten the moment.

"I didn't say that."

A fly buzzed around her head, and Sela ducked to avoid it. Her hair brushed along Jonathan's left shoulder and touched his cheek.

He smiled at her. "My mother liked you."

"I liked her, too," she said, not knowing how true

that was. She had respected her, but she hadn't quite trusted her. Was his mother jealous of any woman who wanted her son? It was hard to tell. She felt relieved that Jonathan started the Landrover again and so there was no need to extend the conversation. She didn't want to upset the gentle balance they had achieved.

"I want to get closer, habituate them to the vehicle and us in it. Then, when we come out at night, they'll be used to us."

"I hope," she said, as he moved slowly closer and stopped again. This time, she observed almost full grown lions stand on their hind legs, reach up and sharpen their claws on trees.

"They can climb that way," Jonathan whispered. "Not that they do it very often, but they have the ability."

Inadvertently, Sela shivered.

Three times he moved the vehicle closer, and each time the pride beneath the tree became more alert, their ears pricked, their head up. Now, the adults watched them at all times, their large eyes turned in the Landrover's direction.

"What if I got out?" Sela breathed the words.

"They have very acute hearing and sight," Jonathan said. "They'd see you as a vulnerable, breathing, living animal who's intruding on their territory." He grinned. "Shall I wait for you?"

"I'm not going anywhere, thank you." She edged closer to him.

He winked and hugged her before he drove closer, not stopping until the pride was less than ten meters away. When he shut off the motor, Sela felt exposed. The jungle hummed and rustled around them.

Near the pride, but not quite with them, a lion with a black mane turned its head. "Feisty!" Sela said.

"Yes. How did you know?"

"I remembered that round black mark on his shoulder."

Jonathan put a finger to his lips as the lionesses rose, the half-grown lions growled and retreated a few steps, the cubs quit their tumbling, and all faced the Landrover. Their rank smell carried on the wind's current.

Sela held her breath.

"Don't move," Jonathan said, putting his hand on Sela's knee. "We're being watched from more than one direction."

And then Sela spotted the others. A huge-maned lion, partially hidden by scrub grass, lay on a ledge above ground level and, below him and to the right, a long line of semi-grown lions and full-grown lionesses and a few year-old cubs filed from between two sentinel rocks in the escarpment. Flowing like a river of golden flesh, they moved silently around and past the Landrover, so close that Sela could have leaned out and touched them before they disappeared into the brush fronting the river.

"My God," she breathed, a life-and-death scenario moving through her mind. "I'd hate to run out of gas out here." Her gaze tangled with Jonathan's, losing itself somewhere in the depth of his irises.

"The baptism continues," Jonathan said. "Africa is giving you the full treatment." He leaned toward her, his gaze reading her face.

She looked away, aware of him resting his arms on the wheel, his gaze still on her. The world had ceased to exist; only the animals, Jonathan and she were real.

"At times like this, I don't feel a bit different from you," she whispered. "I feel as if I'm in your skin."

"I never thought you were different. You did. I feel you here." He touched his chest.

She looked away, stunned by the revelation, not wanting to answer it.

As he started the engine, the pride beneath the tree tensed: alert, watching.

"I expect they get a whiff of petrol and are confused," he said, turning the wheel gently so the car didn't slide on the sandy hill.

A half hour later, they were back at the dry riverbed again.

"Is it all right to breathe now?"

He put his hand over hers. She felt the touch stronger than a kiss.

That night she slept like she was drugged, not even hearing the rain that drummed like an anthem on the tin roof.

"What happened to the baboons?" she asked in the morning because she didn't hear their angry voices. The sun had come out, pulling moisture from the leaves, drying up the water holes again.

"Matui and the others drove them off. Momentarily, anyway. They don't give up easily. Neither does the rain, but I have a notion that's it for the year."

"I hope so," she said. It was easier to see lions when the grass yellowed and disappeared.

Each day, Sela and Jonathan went back to where they'd spotted the pride, and each day the animals paid them less attention. They were almost ready for a camera crew.

But first, at Josh's direction, they filmed background shots in other locations. One whole, stuffy day, they sat with him and a cameraman and all his equipment in a small tin-and-brush hide and photographed the wallow nearby.

The hot air in the ersatz house grew thick and close with tension. If they betrayed their hiding place the buffalo could stampede, knock it over, and stomp them to death.

Sela hunched in the circle of Jonathan's arms, feeling his every movement. Unknown to the others, who pressed their eyes to the peep holes, when she tensed, Jonathan's hand went gently to her mouth. Once he kissed her neck and let his hand graze her breast.

A searing need shot through her. She knew that if Josh wasn't going to be there, she would go to the balcony that night, and give herself to Jonathan. She imagined him pressing hard against her, his hand moving up her thigh and against her groin. She almost moaned with pleasure. In Washington, their coming together had been natural, without complications. Now it was a dream remembered.

Josh invariably extended the evening, talking about this and that as he walked back and forth, safari shirt flapping over spandex shorts. Once he propositioned her—straight out, no subterfuge.

"Josh, damn it, you've got more lust in your little finger than most people have in their minds. I'm not interested."

"You wound me," he said.

She knew better. Josh was always semi-serious in his personal relationships, lustful in a playful, easily dismissed way. Jonathan's interest in her had to be more than raw desire.

That night, she and Jonathan made their first foray after dark. Leaving camp, their headlights pinpointed an elephant tearing at foliage, a waterbuck poised for flight. When they came to lion country, the headlights caught the pride crossing the grassland. Jonathan switched on a flashlight and shone it along the line of prowling predators. Their eyes reflected the light like glass; their ears pricked, listening.

With a tense, alert feeling racing through her, Sela

counted thirty lions. She felt her pulse throb like dynamite ready to blast off. She stared, hollow-eyed, into the dark all night.

On the second night, she fell asleep in the bright moonlight, her head on Jonathan's shoulder.

"You could stretch out," he whispered.

With her knees bent, she could almost fit on the seat if she put her head in his lap. "I should watch."

"Suit yourself."

She let her head find his shoulder.

In the moonlight, she saw him smile.

On the third night, Jonathan switched on a spotlight, flooding the adjacent area with light. Everywhere, eyes looked back. Hyenas, jackals, elephants, waterbuck, lions, and more lions.

"I feel safer without the light," Sela confided. "Maybe ignorance is bliss." Still, sleep sanded her eyes. She dozed and jerked awake several times before she gave in to the impulse.

Facing Jonathan, she slept chest to chest, curled up on the seat, his arms around her, his gaze finding hers whenever she opened her eyes.

"Aren't you ever going to sleep?" she murmured, feeling his heart beat beneath her cheek. Around and out from the Landrover, animal eyes melted in and out of the dark.

"Someone has to watch."

"We could take turns." His mouth was so close she could see its shadowy outline. She lifted her head slightly, and touched her lips to Jonathan's before he knew she was going to do it. His eyes crinkled and he tightened his arms around her.

A lion roared.

Pushing bolt upright, away from Jonathan, Sela peered into the dark.

Jonathan chuckled. "He's a long way off."

"He sounded close, and angry."

"He was calling for his mate." His hands urged her back into his arms.

According to her watch, dawn wasn't far off. Shaking her head, she moved to her side of the seat, opened her backpack, and took out her makeup bag. Her reflection stared palely back from her pocket mirror. She combed her hair and then carefully put on lipstick.

He watched her. "Why do women do that?"

"What?"

"Put on lipstick in the middle of the night."

She shrugged. "I could point out that it's dawn and women put on their faces in the morning. Truthfully, it's a habit, I suppose. At least that's as good a reason as any." She'd never tell him it was to impress him, but whenever she was near him she found herself reacting in ways that surprised even her.

"Lately my habit is thinking of you."

His voice sounded far-off and dreamy. She looked toward him and saw that he wasn't looking at her, but at some vision in his head.

"Each day I come into my room, and I see you in my bed, and I think I'd like you there always." He looked her way.

"Shhh, we promised not to discuss anything personal until the picture is done."

"I don't recall promising anything."

"It was implied."

"Perhaps."

She poured coffee into a thermos top. "Want some?"

"Colombian?"

"You fussy?"

"I heard someone say Colombian in America. Just trying to show my bloody flexibility." He shifted his long legs.

"That what they call it?"

Taking the thermos top from her, he set it down, folded her into his arms, and kissed her thoroughly.

He didn't stop, even though she knew he heard the panicky sound of an animal rushing through the brush, hoofbeats pounding, twigs snapping, growls, a strangled cry, and then the horrible silence of death.

But kisses meant life, she mused, as the lions jousted for position at the feast. As they tore into the fallen prey, Jonathan's kisses became incredibly gentle, his hands touching her back and her breasts lightly.

"I think it was a zebra," she said, looking past his shoulders as the moon came out from behind a cloud.

He didn't answer, his lips finding pleasure spots on her shoulders, her neck, until she realized it was his way of reassuring her, trying to take her mind from the killing taking place so close to them.

"Keep it up, and you'll be as impetuous as me," she whispered into the warm spot between his neck and his shoulder, grateful to him for diverting her attention at least partially.

When a lion roared close by, shaking the Landrover with its reverberations, Sela pressed closer to Jonathan, liking the bulk of his body between her and the lions gathering in the near dawn. "Do you think they ever really accept the Landrover and the lights?" she whispered.

"It's been proven."

"That's comforting." But his arms were more so.

Every night that week, she alternately dozed in the circle of his arms and sat close as Jonathan moved the Landrover in conjunction with the lions. Mostly, in the silvery moonlight, the pride rested, gliding smoothly over the savanna only when dark ruled the night.

Once while the pride marched solemnly toward the river, Jonathan touched her arm. "Impala," he whispered, pointing to a herd twenty meters away watching the lions approach, lit by Jonathan's spotlight.

The swift, slim impala, who always delighted Sela with their leaps and graceful movements, were frozen in place watching. Suddenly, the lions raced toward them. Startled, the impala fled, their hoofs hardly touching the ground as they bounded away.

A yearling hesitated, then hurried after the herd.

For a moment it seemed as if it would gain the safety of the older animals. But the lions ran it down, one lion dogging it while the others circled and drove a wedge between the yearling and the mature impala of the herd. They forced the youngster into ever tighter circles. Then a lioness pounced, grabbed it with teeth and claws and bowled it over. The impala's slim elegant legs pawed the air.

Soon, a feeding frenzy began.

Sela looked away.

"I think that tomorrow we will bring a cameraman out here with us," Jonathan said, taking her hand, squeezing it reassuringly. "We'll go straight to the riverbank and wait. Film the animals as they arrive."

But the next day when they rose from a late sleep, the camp was empty—no one in sight—and all the vehicles were gone except the Landrover Josh had rented.

"I guess we take that," Jonathan said. "You can do an audio tape anyway, and I can get some still pictures for Josh." As the cook packed a lunch, he asked, "You sure you don't know where they went?"

The woman shrugged. "They leave early. That's all I know." She wasn't really interested.

"I hope brother Josh's Landrover's in good condition," Jonathan said as they climbed in.

Soon they were jostling down the bank and over the dry creek bed. Heat shimmered, and dust funneled up behind the vehicle as they circled the water holes which were only damp spots now.

"I'm beginning to think life is you and me and a wilderness adventure," Sela said. She was beginning to recognize different lions. "There's Short Tail," she pointed out as Jonathan drove into the meadow that the lions crossed on their way to the river.

"And Claw Back, you can't forget her."

"And Papa Lion," Sela said.

"And what was it you called that cub?"

"Playbaby."

They laughed in concert.

It was the last laugh they had that day. Suddenly the Landrover lurched to the side. Jonathan fought the wheel and brought the vehicle to a stop.

"What is it?"

"I think we have a flat tire."

"Thank goodness that's all. Is it safe to get out and change it?"

"The way they gorged last night, they're too full to move."

She made a face. "Even if they see us?"

"Anything comes around, you just pull out the gun and shoot 'em."

"Jonathan, I'm not a gun person. On my show I talked animal husbandry or 'see the sweet babies at the zoo,' not hunting, for heaven's sake."

"Okay, we're a good kilometer from the den. No problem."

But there was no spare. And no radio.

"What a damn fucking deal!" Jonathan said, hitting the steering wheel with his fists.

"You sound really American, if that means anything."

"Not at this bloody moment. Damn! Everyone knows the unwritten rule: after using a vehicle you leave it full of petrol and in running order. That means a working spare tire."

"Maybe Josh didn't realize."

"Then he's an idiot."

"What'll we do?" she asked, looking toward the escarpment.

"I'll walk back, and that's not American at all. Wouldn't an American get a helicopter to rescue us? Some damn bloody Rambo action or something like that." He slammed a hand against the wheel and got out. "I'll go get help."

"And let me wait here alone? No, thank you." She scooted across the seat after him.

"You want to walk back with me?"

"No." She cried emphatically, thinking of the lions, and the animals hunkered and slithering near the almost dry riverbed.

He looked at her closely. "The second 'no' sounded serious."

"It was. I'm remembering that herd of buffalo we passed on the way in."

"You really would be safer if you waited here. You'd be all right in the vehicle. Uncomfortable, of course, but safe."

She nodded. "I suppose I have no choice. Of course you could wait with me. The others will be back in camp soon."

"And expect us to be out here all night."

"I was hoping you wouldn't think of that." Feeling vulnerable and a little irritable, she lifted her hair from her neck and stuck out her lip in a mock gesture of anger. "You sure there's no other way?"

He looked thoughtful. "We have another option. There's an animal-viewing platform in a tree overlooking a draw. I quit using it when a tourist fell, climbing the ladder. But I left a radio rigged to the tree. If it's still operable, I can call camp."

"How far would we have to walk?"

"Who said we?"

"I'm not staying here alone."

He shrugged. "It's not as far as camp."

Anything was better than another cramped night in the Rover, she thought.

"You're serious about not staying here?"

"Lead on, my legs are beginning to atrophy from no use. Anyway, I'm betting the local buffalo herd are all behind us."

"I think you might be right." He slung the rifle over one shoulder, put on an ammo vest, hung the canteen from his belt, and handed the lunch to Sela.

"Oh, hell," she said, as he started off. "Another safari. You didn't tell me the viewing platform was away from camp."

"You didn't ask," he said, winking at her.

He's trying to reassure me, she thought, but she was too concerned to retort or wink back. Glancing up at the escarpment to the caves where she'd watched lions through her binoculars, she wondered how many pairs of eyes observed her sudden, jerky passage through the grass.

Fifteen

A ridge, slightly higher than the surrounding territory, rose above the slope to the river. Jonathan led a zigzag course toward it. From the high ground, he paused to check over the land, see what obstacles, if any, were in the way. As he swept the area with field glasses, Sela looked through hers. They'd been walking for more than an hour, stopping often to reconnoiter, check the land.

Two separate elephant herds browsed between them and the curve of the river where Jonathan told her he had built the viewing platform. If they stayed on the ridge, they'd circumvent both herds. Except for a stand of tawny color halfway up the escarpment, the lions weren't visible. Neither were any buffalo.

The air was still, the day hot. Flies buzzed, and a myriad of small gnat-like creatures clung to Sela's dampened skin.

She stayed in Jonathan's footsteps as he set out again, maintaining a steady pace.

"I'm glad to be moving," she said. "I was beginning to feel older than Grandma Minnie, all that sitting. Anyway, as you know, I'm used to running." She didn't know why she reminded him. Maybe because the predicament they were in was beginning to bother her more than a little.

"You're not used to running in this kind of heat," he said.

"You don't know Washington's summers. The humidity's bad. In the old days we used to sleep on the roofs." She glanced over her shoulder. "You think the lions are investigating the Landrover?"

"They're probably sleeping."

"Except for those trailing us."

He whirled around, slapping the rifle to his shoulder.

"Just kidding."

He shook his head, a stern, no-nonsense look making hard planes in his face. "Don't do that again. I could have shot you."

"You mean there could be lions following?"

"At this time of day, they're usually napping."

Usually. Involuntarily, she glanced back. The sun was high overhead now and not a blade of grass stirred. No shadows marred the land. She wiped sweat from her brow and checked her battery operated, water-and-shock-proof watch. Fatigue was weighing heavily on her shoulders, and she longed for uninterrupted sleep, with her legs stretched out, her head level. "Will we be there soon?" She glanced at her watch. Close to nine.

"Depends," he said, slowing his steps. Leaning over, he studied the ground at his feet. Suddenly, he shifted direction, went off at an angle.

She glanced at the prints in the dirt: pad marks with four toes, almost five inches overall. She hurried to catch up and tap him on the back. "Was that lion spoor?"

He nodded, and skirted a tangle of branches and a downed tree host to big, stinging ants.

"Damn, you're talkative. How old were the tracks?"

"Not very."

"Jonathan, level with me, or I'll sock you in the back,

and I've got a mean fist." She knocked an ant from her leg.

"Hours probably."

"Were they made this morning?"

"More recent. They probably went to the river."

"They?"

"I think there were three. The spoor is too old for real concern. Still, I'd rather detour."

"And I'd rather you'd told me immediately. Those kind of delayed sentences—'hey, there's a lion in your bed, Mama Bear,' aren't the kind of stories I like." Irritation was growing in her, at him, at Josh, at all the things said and unsaid.

"What are you talking about?"

"Fairy Tales. Communication. The Three Bears. Take your choice." Was he being deliberately obtuse? "Don't you know the Three Bears?" Anything to keep her mind from the lions.

He stopped abruptly, faced her, and said through clenched teeth, "One of the rules in the bush. Keep your mouth shut."

For an instant his gaze met hers, and she read concern in the depths of his eyes, so staggering she wanted to vault into his arms, nestle safely against his chest. She skittered a look past him and waited until she could control her voice and inject a light touch into a moment that frightened her more than she'd ever admit. "My lips are sealed." She made a zippering motion and was relieved when he smiled.

He led on; she followed closely. No animals, no animal sounds, only the constant background murmur of the doves announced the presence of any other life.

Stopping often, always alert and aware, they arrived at the tree at noon. Big, sprawling, with branches bigger than most trunks, it was the kind of tree she would have loved while growing up. Except for the ladder, the platform was practically invisible from below, hidden by thick foliage.

"You first," Jonathan said.

Despite two broken rungs, Sela scrambled up without much difficulty. Jonathan was close behind her, boosting her over the top.

She walked warily, making sure that the flooring was secure. A few leaves crunched underfoot, but nothing else gave. She looked out. The tree hugged the edge of a dry creek. From the platform, which surrounded the trunk, much of the savanna and a bit of the narrow dry creek bed was visible, its strip of sand bright in the waning light. For the first time in hours she let her shoulders sag, her breath come easy.

Jonathan checked the branches above before he opened the tin box nailed to the trunk.

He's looking for leopard, Sela thought, deliberately not saying anything. As he checked through the supplies in the box, she made mental notes of the contents: matches, a first aid kit, canned foods and an opener, blankets, a jar of water.

"How long has this stuff been here?"

"Some of it a year. You hungry? I could open the cans, or we can start on the lunch you brought."

Her stomach had begun to growl. "I'll go for the lunch." She took out an apple, offered him one.

He shook his head and went to the railing.

"You look bothered. What is it?"

"Some damn poacher stole the radio. Or, at least it's gone."

We're stuck, she thought gazing around, surprised that the news didn't devastate her, but that she felt an edge of relief that they didn't have to go back through the grass again for awhile. "What do we do now?"

"Stay here until daylight."

As soon as he said the words, they took on a life of

their own, conjuring up images: lions prowling below, she in Jonathan's arms, safe, warm, loved. She looked away from his swift gaze.

"At least it'll be more comfortable than the Rover," he said uncorking the water bottle and sipping.

She pressed her back against the tree's trunk and watched below, conscious of him taking blankets from the box, shaking them, hanging them to air on the railing.

The slice of the forest below seemed benign; no animals were intruding. In the far distance, a herd of twenty or thirty peaceful pachyderms crossed the dry watercourse. Then, suddenly, a crashing nearby made her run to the railing. Two cape buffalo thundered into the clearing below the tree. "I'm glad I'm up here," she whispered.

"I'm glad you are, too," Jonathan said, coming to stand next to her. "You mentioned the Three Bears, earlier. The British had us read it in school. It had no relevance. No bears in Zimbabwe."

"Actually, I had trouble relating to Goldilocks."

His arms went around her. "I always thought blue eyes were too pale."

Love in the wild, she thought, before his lips touched hers. She could hear the buffalo rooting around below, hear the insects and birds in a duo. Then he released her and took his time looking below. When his voice came it was to question: what had she been like as a girl? Where had she gone to school, what had been her dreams?

She talked, slowly, truthfully, and for hours the quiet hum of the jungle with background orchestration.

Dusk brought other sounds, and when Jonathan put his arms around her again, she thought: tomorrow, this will be an interlude only. But no matter, with all the words exchanged, could she really manage that she wondered as her breasts were pressed against his chest. She heard the quickening of his breath, felt the thumping of his heart moving in a rhythm with her own. The moment was all that counted and all those misunderstandings could be forgotten, drowned in a sea of need.

He played his hands up and down her back, over her shoulders, his fingers on her neck, beneath her hair, molding her head. His hands touching chin, mouth, cheeks, eyes, delicately, as if memorizing each feature.

Slowly, he lowered his head, and when his lips touched hers, a frenzy of longing ripped through her. She had lived with too much denial, and, now, too much time had elapsed between real embraces. She wanted more. Much more. She was the first woman on earth, and he her man, and who cared what would happen tomorrow?

The light was going now, a lone ray from the sun touching the edge of the platform, turning the forest beyond it to shadowy outlines.

"Just a moment," she said, pushing gently away. She undid her shirt, her belt, her shorts, and stepped out of them, discarded them. She stood proud, tall, smiling, knowing her white cotton underclothes, bought specifically to wear in the African wilds, contrasted beautifully with her brown skin.

His hands found the fastening for her bra. She slipped out of her panties, moving easily, without embarrassment, wanting him to see her, admire her.

Looking as if he would never do anything but smile for the rest of his life, he spread one of the blankets on the platform and gestured toward it as he rapidly threw off his own clothing.

A chorus of movement, spontaneous but as if orchestrated, followed, and she watched each action as he smoothed the blanket and made a proper nest for them. She delighted in the play of his muscles, the hard frankness of his desire. Settling slowly to the blanket, she felt like a temptress and a virgin all in one.

Like a giant, he stood above her, smiling, self-satisfied.

She stretched, letting him see her body in its female glory.

He smiled and lay beside her.

She reached for him, wanting to have her hands on his skin. His body gleamed as if polished, a statue come to life, pulsing with desire. When his mouth fastened over hers, the tip of his tongue touching her lips and then withdrawing, she pulled him back.

"We have all night," he whispered.

She laughed, her need announced, delayed.

His own laughter followed, so rich, so sure, that she wanted to wallow in it like the buffalo had wallowed in the mire. Sitting up, then kneeling, she faced him. Rubbing her breasts up and down his chest, she pressed him down to the blanket, leaned over him, and dropped kisses along the ridge of his jaw, his chest, his thighs.

He groaned and, laughing, pushed her gently down so that she was lying on her back again, while his mouth forged a similar trail over her body.

The conflagration within her built, instant by instant, flames burning bright and clear, an exquisite desire shooting through her body, shutting out everything but the need for him. An ant, which had probably been on her clothes, raced along her arm. She squashed it without interrupting the moment.

Jonathan bent his head, kissed her breasts, sucking and teasing them until all thought left her mind and nothing but feeling remained. When he moved on, she knew she would explode with desire. She reached for him, drew him so close it was difficult to tell where one body ended and the other began. "Yes, yes," she cried.

As much as she needed food, air, and water, she needed him.

His hands moved upon her, released her, teased her, moved away. Her whole body tingled. She cried out, "Don't stop!"

The fire consumed her when he entered her. She nipped his shoulder, clung tight, rode with him to a place where nothing mattered but their need for each other.

Afterward, she lay in the circle of his arm, the night unwinding around her, showing its true shape.

Love was all. Or was it? She felt sated but wanting. For what? Commitment?

She sighed, kissed his chest, heard his chuckle. Saw the shape of the platform take form. God, anyone, anything could come up that ladder. Don't think about that; you're safe with Jonathan.

He played with her hair. Kissed her cheek, and slowly, ever so agonizingly slowly, he made love to her again.

This time she let him lead. She thought she had never been so happy.

"What was the name of that man you were engaged to?" he asked while they lay facing one another, legs twined, lips a breath apart.

"Frank."

"Did he ever make you feel like that?"

"No." And then, more emphatically. "No."

He laughed.

And then she said the words that had been clogging her throat from the first. "Was it like that with you and Cana?"

He said nothing for the longest time, and she thought: in one second, I'll sock him one. Then he said, going up on an elbow and looking down on her, "No."

His features were lost in the dark. Was he smiling?

Angry? She knew she had to be content with the one word.

And then he said, "Cana was a whole other time."

"So was Frank."

It was his turn to sigh.

"Truth time," she said, wishing she smoked. It would help bridge the awkwardness of what she would say. "When I first saw you, I didn't like you."

"I didn't like you, either. Stuck-up rich American."

"So we're even." She snuggled closer. Heard a twig break below. Then another. She shivered.

"Here." Jonathan put the other blanket over her before he got up and pulled the ladder up to the platform.

"But some animals climb trees," she said.

"Shhh, don't be so blooming negative."

"I never thought I was negative. I . . ." But he was kissing her again, and exhaustion was nagging at her. Before another thought could be completed, sleep claimed her.

She woke as black night lightened to gray day, knowing she and Jonathan had come together again. Oh, had they! She felt exceedingly aware of her body and his, a tingling zooming through her, feeding nerve ends, heightening her consciousness of her body and his.

For a while in the gunmetal sheen of dawn, she watched him, the lines of his face softened in deep sleep. Then, slipping out from beneath the blanket, she got up. She wanted to greet the day with a shout, tell the world of her love. Instead, she put on her clothes, the shorts and shirt chilly, the socks holding the shape of her feet from yesterday.

At the railing, she looked below, saw nothing but the foliage she'd seen last night. From behind her Jonathan stirred. When she glanced around he was buttoning his shirt, tucking it into his walking shorts. The intimate details of togetherness, she thought, grinning.

He dampened his handkerchief from the thermos, wiped his face and hands.

"My grandmother would approve," she said.

"Another day out here, and she wouldn't. We would have to save all water for drinking," he said, portioning out their meager breakfast of canned tomatoes and one quarter cup of water each. "I'm going back to camp for help. I think you should wait here."

"Okay."

Nodding at her, he set out before she had her wits together. Standing at the rail, looking down, she found her wits in a hurry when she watched him lean over and examine the ground. "What is it?" she called, and when he didn't answer, she demanded, "Lion spoor?" His frown deepened, but he said nothing, and that wasn't like him. It had to be lion. She half-slid, half-backed down the ladder. "I'm going with you. Lions do climb trees, you said so yourself. And what are they hanging around here for? American meat?"

"I really think you should wait here."

"I hate waiting. I'm going."

"Lady, you can be difficult." But he said the last word so that it sounded as if he'd given her a compliment.

She grinned. "Impetuous has a better ring." Beneath the tree she saw so many lion tracks that her mouth fell open and her stomach felt heavy as molten lead. She would not wait in the jungle alone.

"Then hurry up, we can't waste any time."

Later Sela saw where the pride had brought down a large animal.

"Waterbuck," Jonathan pointed out the remains.

She saw where they'd dragged the carcass, saw the carrion birds picking at the few bones left.

"Do you suppose they're long gone?" Sela asked, her

voice dropping so low she wondered how he heard her, but he did, his breath warm on her cheek.

"Probably. If they had a successful hunt. Even if they're not gone, if they spot us and are full, they will ignore us," Jonathan's voice reassured her. "Come on, unless you'd rather wait here." He grinned.

"I don't want to *wait* anywhere."

"I'll drop you at the Rover."

She shook her head. "I'm going the whole way." The Landrover had sat there too long with no one in it. The baboons could have overrun it by now. If so, the lions would be next. Anyway, last night she and Jonathan had crossed a line, and neither could go back. This had been more than sex, and she knew it as well as he did. For an instant he smiled at her with his eyes and then there in the rustling, sighing jungle, he kissed her.

His clothes were dirty. Hers smelled of sex and perspiration. Her hair had gone frizzy; his looked tousled.

"Once we get back to civilization we have to talk," she said.

"I've been thinking. We can commute," he said. "America to Zimbabwe."

"It would make all the papers and probably Guinness's World Record. Three days here, two traveling, and two in the U.S."

He grinned and moved out again. "Stay close."

Again he followed the ridge, and once she glimpsed movement under the trees near the Zambesi River, but it was nothing she could identify. "It would be some schedule," she said when he paused to look over the land. "Unless you'd prefer three in Washington, two here." She detoured around a rock. "Or we could do it by weeks." She glanced ahead.

Jonathan motioned for her to be quiet. His arm went in an arc. Looking off to the left, she saw a line of lionesses moving stealthily through the brush. If they continued on the same route, they would intersect with the ridge where she and Jonathan were walking.

"Instead of going straight to camp, we'll head for the Landrover first. With luck we'll be in the brush by the time they hit the ridge and they won't see us," Jonathan whispered, setting off so rapidly she had to run to catch up.

She almost ran him down.

"Quiet," he warned.

She looked back, saw the lioness she'd called Scarback standing on the ridge. For a moment the scarred animal met her gaze, and then disappeared into the thicket. Sela shivered.

"No matter what, at all times stick like a burr to me." Jonathan breathed the words into her ear.

She nodded. "I'll stick better than Elmer's glue."

Jonathan moved slowly now, stepping softly, carefully. She duplicated his movements, making sure not to step on any branches and break the silence that was holding its secrets so stubbornly. The moment seemed unreal, otherworldly. She was glad Jonathan had the rifle. He'd said earlier that it would stop elephants in their tracks. But if she remembered right, he said it needed loading.

If he paused now to drop in, pump in bullets, whatever he did, would the sounds alert the lions? A sliding of a bolt, a breaking of a breech, a sound of metal against metal? Damn, she wished she'd taken a class in weapon awareness . . . but naturally, he wouldn't carry an unloaded gun.

Oh, hell, think of other things. Where were Josh and his camera when she needed them? Talk about ratings. This would push Oprah from the air, make Bowles take back every single stupid thing he'd ever said or done.

She tapped Jonathan on the shoulder. "Slow down."

If she fell, this could be the end of it all, the night of glory followed by . . .

Jonathan stopped so abruptly that she ran into him. As she opened her mouth, his hand went over it.

To the right, through the waving elephant grass, not more than forty meters away, two lions moved, in step with them. Pacing them?

"They've outflanked us," Jonathan said, pulling a handgun from his jacket. "Better take this. Up close, it might help."

Her heart hammering in her ears, she muttered, "Thanks a lot."

He handed it to her, safety off. "Just don't shoot me."

She held it gingerly, a "this isn't real" feeling humming through her mind, her heart thundering so loudly, that she had trouble hearing anything else.

"Come on. We're almost to the Landrover."

"Thank God," she cried, knowing instantly that she'd spoken too loudly. Through the waving grass to her right, closer than before, she caught a glimpse of tawny yellow, a blur that was gone as soon as she saw it. She was imagining things, had to be.

Ahead of Jonathan, the grass gave out. A sandy stretch, a gravel bed, and then the Landrover.

Twenty feet, she estimated.

Would the lions follow them into the vehicle?

"You go first; I'll cover you," Jonathan said.

She began to move, jerky, fast.

"Slow down. If you run, they'll nab you. When you get in, start the engine. Understand?"

She nodded, the words running like a roundelay through her mind. Move slowly, slowly. For a second, her feet wouldn't obey, and then she was overwhelmingly aware of them taking a step, and then another, Jonathan backing behind her, in step. She kept her gaze on the Landrover's door, imagined herself opening it, throwing herself in.

And then she became aware of a rancid, rank odor, and she saw, lying against the Landrover's front wheel, the large-maned lion she had jokingly called Papa. As it opened its mouth to roar, she screamed, terror striking like a knife severing her veins. Running now, away from the Landrover, away from the lion. Had to get away. But others were coming from the grass, large lethal golden animals, from both right and left, and she could think of nothing to do but run. She'd hide among the quivering blades of grass, sink into a ball, curl up and hope they wouldn't see her.

But Jonathan was shooting, and over her shoulder Sela saw the big lion falling, the lioness on the right going over in a heap, the ones behind her turning, running back toward the trees, out of sight.

She began to collapse, her muscles feeling as if they would not support her.

Jonathan turned toward her. "You all right?"

Shaking, she managed to nod. Behind him the downed lions twitched in the final throes of death, blood foaming, flies already settling.

Jonathan moved toward her.

And then she saw the two lionesses who had been stalking them from the right. A blur of color, they streaked toward Sela. She turned, poised as if on a starting block.

"Stand still," Jonathan shouted.

The lion in the lead ran full out, the other followed slightly behind.

Sela's scream tore from her throat. Jonathan whirled, ripped off a shot that clicked on a dead chamber. "Damn," he cried frantically reloading.

As he fumbled with bullets, the lion in the lead sprang.

Pushing back the shaking emptiness that clawed at her stomach, Sela stepped up next to Jonathan and, as the lioness opened her jaws, she lifted the handgun with both hands and fired.

The bullet exploded into soft tissue and brains, spattered bits of flesh and hair, but still the lion came, a blur of sun-drenched color carried forward by momentum. Stunned, Sela pulled the trigger again and again unable to stop even when the lioness collapsed at her feet. Vaguely, she was aware that Jonathan had shot the other one with the rifle, blasted it from the ground, dropping it immediately. *Deadly clumps of flesh and bones and golden hair,* she thought, the words a poetic litany pushing at her brain.

Bile rose in her mouth. She leaned over, let it flow.

Jonathan handed her a clean olive-green handkerchief.

In her wretchedness, she didn't want him to see her. She turned away.

After a while, above the hot putrid smells and the buzzing of the jungle, his voice came calm and clear. "Did I ever tell you I loved you?"

Wiping her mouth, she turned to meet his gaze. Aware of the great blood-frothed carcasses behind him, she shook her head.

"I think you love me, too."

"How do you know?" she asked, seeing at once the benign looking grass, the graceful trees, the sky a blue bowl above. Yes, yes, she loved him.

He shrugged. "For one thing, you saved my life."

The enormity of what had happened hit her again. She fought back tears, managed a half-smile. "I didn't want to walk back to camp alone."

"Hell, no way I'm going to walk," he said, laughter and incredulity and amazement sounding all at once.

"Lady, no matter what Josh thinks about his vehicle, we're riding in on the rim."

She laughed and ran into his arms. They felt very strong and very good, and after all that had happened and all that was yet to be, that was what counted.

Sixteen

We're limping back to camp Sela thought, as the Landrover bumped along. She sat close to Jonathan, her hand in his. Once in a while, he said something about the route, made note of some animal along the way. Mostly he said nothing. Neither did she. A strange lassitude was gripping her, while she sensed anger festering and growing within him. It was evident in the firmness of his jaw, the no-nonsense tilt to his head, the grim line of his mouth.

At Jonathan's house, they took turns using the shower. Again, neither one said much as they padded around, nude, towel-draped, hair wet, although his eyes accorded her praise which she accepted, and returned in full measure. The somnolence of afternoon gripped the camp, animals and people resting, the sun slanting shadows everywhere.

Neither Sela nor Jonathan had a need for speech. She felt closer to him than she'd ever been to anyone; she knew what he must be thinking, feeling. The gap between their countries and their cultures, their differences had to be possible to leap. She'd think of how later. Resting her head against his chest, she listened to his heart beat. *A hammer blow,* she thought, aware of the incongruity, for he held her gently, tenderly as they swayed to a rhythm they both heard.

"I suppose we'd better let people know we're back." His voice was honey, but his mouth still formed that grim line. She supposed she knew why.

"I suppose we have to." Reluctantly, she preceded him down the ladder to the waiting Landrover.

The drive to the camp proper seemed shorter than it had ever been before. In the dappled sunlight of the dining area, Josh stood shaking his head when they drove up. "What in the hell were you doing, riding on the rim?"

Without saying a word, Jonathan walked up to him and punched him in the nose.

Josh crumpled like stale bread, his arms and legs flying in all directions like crumbs falling. As he picked himself up from the ground, Jonathan's voice, low, firm, and deadly, lashed him for taking off with all the vehicles, leaving only the rented one. "You bloody ass, you sent us into the bush without a spare tire and no radio."

Josh, who had waged the wars of Hollywood and emerged victorious, pressed a handkerchief to his nose and wondered aloud how Jonathan, who had presumably grown up in the bush, hadn't checked those things for himself. After all, he was the guide, the authority.

Matui pressed a cloth to the blood. "It's going to be all right," he assured Josh.

Josh grinned. "My god, the things I do for art. It could have been broken." He took the cloth away, probed gently.

Jonathan said, "You're bloody fault for acting like an idiot."

Sela turned aside. The fight had a touch of unreality. Reality was still the high grass, the lions. Pulling herself into the present, she reminded everyone that they had a movie to make and blame putting—while admittedly alleviating stress—did nothing to complete the film. In a few words, she told about the flat tire and the lions.

Matui shook his head and muttered about Shumba.

Others questioned, their voices excited.

Jonathan answered briefly, shrugging away his part in it, saying Sela had saved the day. "She shot a lion."

"You really shoot a lion?" one of the cameramen asked, and everyone turned to look at her.

The enormity of what had happened swept through her again. "Yes."

Josh's eyes grew big. "No kidding? Lions actually attacked you? Sela, you all right?" He moved toward her.

"I'm fine."

Eyes gleaming, he pestered her and Jonathan for details.

His unfeigned interest proved better than a fist to the nose for relieving the tension that held them. Slowly Jonathan began to explain how things had really happened, and then Sela was speaking, the two of them tripping over one another's words, telling, remembering, reliving.

The crew hung on their tale, and Sela moved like a queen between Jonathan and Josh, getting a cup of coffee, wolfing down biscuits, feeling suddenly overwhelmed with hunger. Words about the lions soared, tripped, and soared again. Trying to get the details right, it seemed as if she was peering through the wrong end of a telescope; everything was slightly off focus. Had she told Jonathan she loved him? That was the important part, and she had no memory of it.

When two cape buffalo appeared in the dry riverbed, hardly anyone paid attention. Josh paced excitedly. "I never thought the lions around here would be that ferocious."

Jonathan shrugged. "They had no choice. We were

encroaching on their territory. And I expect they were still hungry." The anger had left his voice.

Matui and the others, who had watched critically, as if measuring the severity of the situation and pondering when and if to intercede, crowded around now, asking questions.

Jonathan gave more and more details, but Sela found it impossible to speak on and on in an emotionless way. She still felt the terror, the horror, the feeling of death that had stalked her. It was too soon, too personal, and belonged to her and Jonathan. Later, she knew she would whisper it all to him, let him kiss away the lingering fear.

Now Josh was viewing their experience from a movie director's perspective. "I never have such deliciously scary things happen to me." He touched his nose. "I can't even get a good nosebleed." He grinned.

The others laughed; Jonathan almost smiled. It was impossible to stay angry with Josh when he became so enthusiastic, jumping around, laying out possible scenes, pressing people into play as extras. "Maybe I could get Denzel Washington!" he cried. "What box office. Mr. Sex Appeal himself and lions on the prowl." He mimed a lion attacking, Washington shooting. Everyone laughed except Jonathan.

Sela exchanged glances with him, and for a while it was as if she were inside his skin. His eyes seemed to say: this is something we have to get used to. No one else will ever really understand, and because they feel awed, they will make light of our experience.

Josh smoothed the fake snakeskin band on his hat, a producer once more in charge. "Seriously, the lion segment would make a great documentary." He headed toward the closest canvas chair, but Jonathan got there first.

Josh hesitated and then, with a shrug, took another

seat. "In the meantime, Jonathan," he said, pulling the chair away from the direct sun, "will you show me a location I can use as an establishing background shot for the heroine? One pretty enough to use throughout the film?"

As the talk of lions ended, the crew drifted off to their chalets. Listening to Jonathan unwind, the afternoon became anticlimactic to Sela. She tuned out as his and Josh's low-pitched murmurs maintained a congenial ring.

Enormously aware of her fatigue, the clean soap smell of her skin, and the crisp folds of her newly laundered shorts, Sela curled up on a lounge chair in the shade. Jonathan and Josh's talk drifted by, backed by the soft murmur of the kitchen staff. She almost went to sleep. Then Jonathan spoke her name, and her mind and body became instantly alert. In a soft voice, one full of awe, he recounted to Josh how she had shot the lion.

A tide of feeling raced through her. His voice held deep respect and something more, a tender protectiveness that outweighed his earlier passionate declarations. He truly loves me, she thought, knowing with finality now that she loved him, not with the school-girl crush she had felt for him in the beginning, not with the sophisticated competitiveness she had known later, but with a givingness that wanted to surmount obstacles. And she knew she had felt this way for a long time.

Troublesome thoughts followed. Could they really overcome the difficulties surrounding the differences between their cultures? The distances were vast, the differences between cultures alarmingly complex. As Jonathan spoke to Matui in Shona, Sela was reminded of her previous misgivings. Perhaps women who chose the safe mate were right. Class to class, race to race.

Hearing her name and the word for lion repeated in close juxtaposition, she straightened, pricked her ears.

Josh's rapid speech slowed, and he said. "It took a lot of guts for Sela to do what she did."

"She has what it takes," Jonathan said.

"Yes," Josh agreed. "I saw that in college. I was never surprised by her success. I kick myself for not following up on my advantage then."

A pregnant silence followed, and Sela looked out at them from beneath the fringes of her lashes.

Jonathan was sitting with his legs stretched out in front of him, his arms on the armrests of his captain's chair. "You know you don't have a chance." Jonathan spoke with confidence, but no sign of braggadocio.

For a while, no human vocal chords added to the afternoon hum. Then Josh said softly, "Hey, man, she speaks my language."

Jonathan's fingers tightened on the armrest. "I don't think so." His voice held a challenge.

Sela closed her eyes before either man realized she was awake. Her parents would be thrilled with Josh, a moviemaker and fast-talking American. They knew all about him, understood when he mentioned basketball stars and movie goddesses.

"I think anyone who tries to come between Sela and me gets squashed," Jonathan said. "I plan to work with her, be with her."

Sela imagined Josh doing another of his face-saving gestures, and his voice when it came had a neutral ring. "No matter; we finish here and then we go to Vic Falls next week. A guy who knows how to order wine can really shine someplace like that." He laughed, making light of the words that fell like overripe fruit from a burgeoning tree.

Victoria Falls. She tried to remember the schedule exactly, but Jonathan's image kept intruding. He had never said he wanted to marry her, except on his terms. Could she handle that?

She dozed, felt the sun lap at her face. Drowsily, she moved her chair deeper into the shade, closer to the trail.

Jonathan and Josh's voices hummed on, backed up by the soft whisper of the African afternoon. All action seemed held in abeyance, at rest.

She slept deeply and woke dreaming that the lions were grouping again, surrounding her. Perspiration stood on her forehead, dripped from her nose. She moved restlessly, pushing away the dream and the remembered fear, and looked out through half-asleep eyes. A shadow had cut off the sun that had touched the edge of her chair. She opened her eyes wide.

Baggy gray skin hanging in folds, a towering elephant leaned over her, examining her. Its big ears flapped to cool itself.

Sela started to sit up. Sheba! For a moment she met the elephant's gaze straight on and then startled, she glanced away before looking back. She imagined she read—if not kindness, perhaps tolerance—in the steady regard Sheba gave her, and an underlying understanding of the mutuality of their being. Sheba shifted, her big feet coming within an inch of Sela's chair, and concern pressed its full weight on Sela's chest. Her chair protruded into the path Sheba routinely trod.

"Don't move," Jonathan murmured, his voice low, reassuring.

She sank back into herself, not really alarmed. Hadn't she survived the lions? Through half-closed eyes, she saw Sheba's trunk swing close. She felt her chair nudged, felt it move back closer to the tree, and knew it would have tipped over if the tree hadn't held it upright.

Balanced there, Sela watched, too enthralled to move farther out of the way.

The matriarch looked back over her shoulder to the

other elephants coming along the trail, as if communicating with them before she moved with majesty along the path between the chalets. Bump followed her into view, a baby in need of guidance, his walk awkward, his attitude playful. He, too, paused at Sela's chair and, without thinking, she stuck out her hand, palm up. He sniffed it with his trunk and then moved on. The others in the herd followed him in line, all swinging their heads to look for a second at Sela.

As the last of the herd passed, she regained her balance, sat up, and watched them make their slow way through camp, tearing at tasty branches of leaves, wielding their trunks delicately. Belatedly, she realized that Josh was filming, that Jonathan was smiling and shaking his head.

When the last elephant disappeared down the trail, Josh said, "I think we just saw the true king of the beasts, and I got every damn minute of it on film."

"Sheba's a queen who rules the roost around here," Sela said, getting up. She wanted to run to Jonathan, throw herself in his arms, exclaim excitedly over what had happened. She contented herself with basking in the warmth of his smile.

Josh shook his head. "No, Sela. You're the leader, the lynchpin, the ruler. Ms. Ultimate."

As he and everyone within hearing laughed, Sela managed a faint smile. She had never felt so close to nature. "You're just jealous," she said.

"Face it, sweetheart, wildlife is just naturally attracted to you." Josh beckoned and did a little dance. "Come on, tell me, how did it feel when you were out there with the lions breathing down your neck?"

"Josh, don't be a bigger ass than you are," Jonathan said. "Keep your mouth shut, and I'll give you and Sela a lift to my house so you can get your things." The chalets were all in order again, and both would be moving out.

Josh said, "Okay, so I've got foot-in-mouth disease. Part of the Hollywood persona. Ain't that so, Sela?" But he managed a discreet silence on the way to Jonathan's.

Sela felt grateful. She needed time to think, to plan where this sudden closeness to Jonathan would lead. Josh's clowning didn't help, but he had made it clear more than once his interest in her. The option was always there. Yet the option seemed less viable as Jonathan began to talk about how well he and she worked together. "I'm thinking we should not call a stop after this movie."

She agreed, not sure what he meant.

Entering Jonathan's house, she didn't see the baboon faces pressed to the screen between the thatch and the wooden uprights until she heard Josh's angry cry. She almost jumped before she realized what had happened. The animals had overrun the balcony, scattering Josh's clothes and papers and tearing his sleeping bag apart.

"Damn animals," he cried, chasing them down the deck, and running after those who went in the opposite direction. But there were too many, and the largest stood his ground, defying him, teeth bared. Josh backed to the door and retreated inside.

Jonathan laughed. "I think they just wanted to remind you of Hollywood. I heard it was a zoo out there."

For once, Josh never said a word.

Sela felt a sudden urge to laugh but, with difficulty, she restrained the impulse. Josh would be hurt worse than when Jonathan had hit him, and she really didn't want to crush his ego any more. She glanced at Jonathan, who was watching Josh with concern, and she knew he was thinking some of the same things. But each man in their own way had challenged the other. Of that she was sure.

* * *

That evening Sela sat in a folding chair outside her chalet, listened to the hippos munch grass, and watched them draw inexorably closer. They lumbered away from the river, climbed the bank in front of her chalet and stared at her. When they passed the termite mound at the edge of the bank, she pulled her chair inside the chalet, propped open the door and watched night descend.

"Sometimes it's my favorite time of day," Jonathan said, coming around the corner of the thatched roof hut. He propped his rifle close by, pulled the other chair close to hers.

He had shaved and it had brought out the masculine angles of his cheeks. She said, her voice scratching her throat, "At home we have twilight. Slowly we go from day to night. We don't rush like a bad movie."

"You're worried."

She nodded.

He put his hand over hers. "About us?"

What else, she thought, feeling his touch to her core. "I'm beginning to think my parents were right. Too many things separate Americans from Africa and Africans. Josh may be a clown, but he's no fool. We do speak the same language. You and I don't."

"I think we can learn."

"That's not what our families think."

"Then it's up to us to prove them wrong."

"You make it sound easy."

"No, it will be hard. But maybe if your family came out here, saw how it is, they wouldn't be so hard on us. Maybe, too, I want them to see me in my element." He added a somewhat sheepish grin.

"I think you want their approval," she said, the idea

seeming so wonderful and so foreign that it flabbergasted her.

"It would be better for our children if it were so," he said, simply.

"Children?" The thought reached her core and sent shafts of desire zipping through her, for him, for them. "Two, maybe."

"If it's one of each."

"You see, already we're differing. Two, total. I won't budge an inch on that." She put her hand in his. Always, she had thought in terms of a career. Too many women had floundered in relationships they had depended upon. Her parents were the exception, and now she felt a need to emulate them.

He laughed, twined his fingers with hers. "Whatever you say."

She stared at him. The room behind him was lost in shadow, and his face was unclear. Leaning close, she got caught up in the wonder of his sable eyes, the love shining so brightly. Jumping up, she tripped over his shoes and plopped down suddenly on his lap. Laughing, she kissed him.

"Oh, Sela," he murmured, and she felt his urgency, his need, and it met her own. They had faced death together and won. Anything else was forgotten. They were survivors with survivors' needs.

With a wantonness she hadn't realized could be in her, she unbuttoned her blouse and displayed her breasts. She didn't hear or see when the hippos rounded the termite mound. But Jonathan evidently did for he lifted her in his arms, closed the door, and carried her toward the bed.

The future began to have possibilities, to grow clear in her mind. She would send for her family tomorrow. Her mother would say, "All that money for a trip." Her father would say, "I'd feel better paying my own way."

But her Grandma Minnie would understand, and she'd begin packing immediately.

Two weeks later, Jonathan watched Sela stroll the manicured grounds of the Victoria Falls Hotel, her family with her. A gut-wrenching need to hold on to her, to keep her with him always, gripped him. She looked like the rich British who still frequented the hotel—her white tennis dress and walking shoes, her forthright gaze—but her diction shouted American, outsider. Yet how could someone who had lain in his arms, arched her body beneath his, be an outsider? He loved to watch her, knowing that under her proper stroll lay a capricious charmer and a woman who had stood toe-to-toe with him in the wilds and survived. He glanced past the final gleaming white verandah, the last outside terrace with its umbrella-shaded tables, beyond the swimming pool and the walkways, to a mist that rose in the distance. Climbing the blue bowl of the sky, the cloudy haze spread out like steam from a cooking pot, drifting high and wide, ethereal. In Shona, they called it the *guti,* and it came from Victoria Falls, a mile away.

"Doesn't seem possible," Mrs. Clay said, her gaze not quite meeting his. Her ample curves were controlled by underclothes, he supposed, and covered with expensive linen, also like the British. Sometimes he imagined the Americans were actual clones, but then someone like Josh came along, or, of course, his Sela, and he knew he was wrong.

Still, all the Clays seemed a little distant, not sure what he was doing with their Sela, their words and manners correct but hardly bursting with warmth. He felt like an interloper.

The next day he stood to the back of the Clay family group while they viewed the first cascade at Victoria

Falls. Volumes and volumes of water tumbled over the edge in a torrent so wide that they had reluctantly walked more than a kilometer to view the whole immense expanse. No one had said much of anything during the walk, and Jonathan wondered if they had expected extravagant Walt Disney touches, too.

As they watched in the gunmetal pre-dawn, the mist settling on them like rain, everyone shivered except Sela's grandmother who shook her head and cried, "Cold? Why should I be cold? I'm in Africa."

Full of nervous energy, her eyes darted around, and she moved like a woman much younger than her years. Jonathan felt the affinity that stretched between them renew itself.

"The others will try to play it cool," Sela had explained earlier, "so don't be disappointed by their response." Jonathan had trouble understanding her words or her family's actions, and so he said little, but stood back and watched, not answering when Mr. Clay talked about Niagara or Nefari spoke of the Grand Canyon.

"So what do you think?" Sela urged, leaning toward her mother.

"It's very nice," Mrs. Clay said, smiling over her shoulder at Jonathan.

Sela persisted. "What do you really think? Isn't it magnificent?"

"I'm studying on it," she said, tilting her head to one side and then the other.

Maybe it wasn't the best idea, bringing them out here, Sela's glance said, and Jonathan looked away, wondering what would impress them if Victoria Falls didn't. In the brush he knew how to act and react, but now he couldn't think what to say or do. He waited for them to give him a clue.

Then the sun rose, its rays shooting into the sky, bisecting the mist, a rainbow forming suddenly, abruptly.

Shimmering, vibrant bands of color moved above the roaring water. The ribbons of brilliance swept in an arc from the bottom of the falls to high above, where they faded into the mist. Touching the heavens, they dissipated gently, disappearing into the ether.

"For land's sake, just like Grandma always said," Sela's mother cried, squeezing her husband's arm. "Sam, look at that."

"I thought it was just some kind of story," Sela's father added, hooking sunglasses to his regular spectacles.

"Look!" Nefari cried, running along the rim of the canyon facing the falls. "There's another rainbow farther on."

This one was wider, bigger, brighter, all the vivid bands rising from the water to arch above it, encompassing every shade and hue imaginable.

Grandma Minnie, a beatific expression on her face, cried. "Praise be. Oh, Lord, praise be."

"Amen," Mrs. Clay whispered.

Nefari began to give a scientific explanation of rainbows.

Grandma Minnie shook her head. "Child, will you shut up? We're home, don't you see? We've found the place."

Nefari stood with her mouth hanging open and no sound coming out. Everyone laughed.

"It's just like they say," Grandma Minnie said. "Oh, Lord, it surely is. We're home." Then she turned away, and Jonathan saw her bony shoulders moving as she cried silently. Sela rushed to her and, with the mist falling around them like rain, plastering their clothes and their hair to their bodies, the two women stood hugging one another, the water that thundered behind them snatching their words away as they spoke.

"Oh, Grandma, do you think it's really true?" Sela shouted, her face open, ready to believe, as Grandma

Minnie moved back away from the edge, leaning now on Sela.

"Course it is." She blinked away tears. "I just never thought I'd see it."

"So maybe we're Shona," Nefari cried, going from one to another and hugging them. "American Shona."

"Thank you," Grandma Minnie said to Jonathan. "Thank you for this. Now, mister Mokane, where we going next?"

"I have an idea," he said, leading them out of the park to where he'd left his rented van. Flags fluttered and posters proclaimed a variety of sales goods. Food and souvenir vendors looked up from their stands, interested, no doubt, in the strangers, but no one called out or stopped them as he hurried them to his car.

He drove through the small town, Sela at his side, the others in the seats behind them. The day's heat seemed coiled and waiting when they got in. They all rolled down their windows, and Mrs. Clay and Grandma Minnie fanned themselves with their hands. Past restaurants, a bookstore, and a memento shop, he kept up a running commentary, explaining who owned what. No one said much in return, but he noticed them looking, creases of interest in their foreheads.

In a residential district toward the outskirts of town he pulled up in front of a small house. "My mother lives here."

He saw the look of surprise on Sela's face and he wanted to say, what did you expect, that the two families would never get together?

The small frame house hunkered among a riot of jacaranda trees. Square, Jonathan summed up in his mind as the Clay family filed out at the roadside. No curb, he added watching Sela and her parents for reactions. They looked like Josh: wraparound sunglasses, cruise clothes. So very much American.

Across the hard-packed dirt yard, his mother greeted them at the front door. She wore a dignified smile, and gave polite words of welcome as she came out to the stoop. Next to Mrs. Clay, who hid her plump curves beneath a loose jacket and a flowing scarf, chunky jewelry on her wrists and fingers, his mother looked sturdy and unfashionable in a flowered print dress, her hands bare of ornamentation, and no makeup.

"I'm glad to meet Jonathan's American friends," she said, leading them around the house to where a mopane tree shaded an area with wooden-slat lawn furniture in a backyard screen house. Reggae music came from a radio in the house next door. Behind the house on the other side, two children played in the dirt near the back door.

"Cooler out here," Jonathan's mother said, offering bottles of orange soda that rested in a tub of ice. When only Sela and Nefari accepted, she said, "Maybe Mr. Clay would like a beer."

"Sounds good," he said. "Never pass up a beer."

Mrs. Clay shook her head. "He makes it sound as if he drinks all the time. It's not so, Mrs. Mokane. But you know, beer does sound good. It's so hot." She glanced at Mrs. Mokane. "If that's all right?"

"I think it's a good idea," she said. "How about you, Grandma Minnie, if I may call you that?"

"I'm Grandma Minnie to everybody and, long as it's cold, that soda sounds good to me."

Soon they were all sipping and talking, mannerly, distant.

The skin around Sela's mouth stretched tight. Jonathan wanted to kiss the tension away, apologize for suggesting she bring her family to Zimbabwe.

"You suppose we're really Shona?" Nefari asked, going into the yard to examine the sculptures, large soapstone and granite carvings sitting among fan palms and aloe and bird of paradise plants. The carvings were some of the best outside museums, and his mother was rightfully proud of her collection. But no one remarked upon them.

"Are we Shona? I suppose it's a possibility," Mrs. Clay said.

Mrs. Mokane said, "Maybe your original people were N'debele. They came here after us, after we Shonas."

"Oh, I suppose that's possible, too," Mrs. Clay said.

The two women smiled at one another as if happy to find something to agree upon.

"Or maybe neither," Nefari said coming back into the screen shelter. "How about Zulu instead?"

Mr. Clay looked confused. "Zulu?"

"Actually," Nefari said, "Americans got so much white in them, I wonder if we really belong anywhere in Africa." She darted a look at each one.

Trying not to scowl, Jonathan glanced at Sela, saw her sit up straighter, look toward his mother. The music from next door changed, to a mock tribal beat and the radio announcer said that Zimbabwe Cola beat Coke two to one.

Mr. Clay crossed his legs. "Don't mind Nefari and forgive her rudeness."

"I think it's her age," Mrs. Clay said.

Sela leaned forward, the sun striking her full in the face, bathing it with light. "What do you think, Mrs. Mokane?" she asked. In the sudden brightness Sela's brown face seemed lighter, and she looked as exotic and foreign as the almost extinct rhinos.

"What do you mean, Miss Clay?" His mother's smile began to retreat, and Jonathan wished he had spoken to her first, explained how it was.

Sela leaned even more into the light. "Do you think African-Americans are almost as pale as the sands of the Kalahari desert?"

"But aren't you?" Mrs. Mokane asked, her lilting voice suddenly sounding very British.

For a while, no one said anything, and Jonathan berated himself for suggesting that Sela bring her family to Africa. He had opened her up to being hurt. He rose, ready to rescue her, run off, leave them all to their stupid prejudices. The kids in the yard next door were watching as if they knew something strange was happening.

Grandma Minnie fixed her gaze on Sela. "I ain't seen that Kalahari desert. But I seen sand before, and sometimes you favor one grain, and sometimes another," she said, lifting her chin at her.

"Grandma!"

"Don't argue with me." Her chin went higher. "You neither." She fixed her gaze on Mrs. Mokane. "You're maybe thinking we're not as good as you all cause we kinda got bleached through the years. Well, I'm saying it makes no difference. The important fact is we all come from the same stock and place. And we all got things to overcome."

Jonathan eased back into his chair. "I know it."

His mother nodded. "We know it very well here."

"See, what did I tell you?" Grandma Minnie said. "Maybe we don't hold with bride price and all that, but we recognize quality. Like those statues in the yard. And we sure like our rhymes." She grinned at Jonathan. "Ain't that what you supposed to do, give us some poetry 'bout Sela if you want her for your wife?"

He nodded, surprised and hopeful.

Grandma Minnie tapped him on the hand. "I heard you drink beer and sing her praises. Sounds like a mighty good thing to do."

"You know about that custom of ours?" his mother asked, looking as surprised as Sela had earlier.

Grandma Minnie nodded.

"And you know about my son's intentions before I do?"

"I think you know."

"Yes." She regarded Jonathan thoughtfully.

He wanted to say, "I'm sorry, Mama," but now was not the time for it. Sela was looking at him with questioning eyes, and then looking away before he could signal his love for her.

"Grandma, how come you never told us you knew about the rites for a proposal?" Mrs. Clay asked.

"I don't tell everyone all I know," Grandma Minnie said with a laugh.

Jonathan felt the tension begin to evaporate. "Maybe we need another beer," he said, thinking about the first of the poems he would recite in Sela's honor. *It would be all right now,* he thought, beginning with words they'd all know, catching everyone while they were smiling. The differences between the families would be ironed out in talk, in song and laughter, and the poems and praise he would dedicate to Sela. Anything else would happen when he and Sela were alone, and it would be good.

"I think I'd like to recite the first of the poems dedicated to the woman I love—Sela Clay."

She stalked the far reaches of Lobengula
matching steps with shumba, lion proud

His poem, fashioning itself as he spoke, began to rumble, the rhythm grow, and he knew a keen sense of rightness for this blend of the old and new.

The band in the Livingston Room at the Victoria Falls Hotel played a slow, dreamy piece, and Sela floated through it in a trance, her feet winged, her soul on fire. Jonathan's white linen, her burgundy chiffon, cried glamor, romance, and she should be content, but despite the long, warm, convivial afternoon with family, still Jonathan had said nothing to her. Frustrated, she followed him around the floor, whirling, his strong lead making them the center of all eyes. The tables with their white tablecloths and the white-faced tourists and white-jacketed black waiters blurred by. Sela had laughed with delight when a woman from Michigan had asked for her autograph and a man from New Hampshire had asked, "Aren't you that woman from television?" Jonathan had beamed proudly but, despite his obvious pride, and his almost talk of marriage that afternoon, he had said nothing to her personally.

Unwinding from his arm, she pirouetted and executing a quick step, she smiled when his arm tightened around her. She murmured, "You're Fred Astaire, I'm Ginger Rogers, and we're going to dazzle the crowd."

He shook his head. "You've got it wrong. We're ourselves, the not-so-famous Jonathan Mokane and the delightfully talented and terrifically important Sela Clay."

She smiled. "Hyperbole will get you everywhere. Actually, I'm the woman who shot a lion."

"The woman who shot a lion and is making a movie."

"Josh wants to sign me on full time." She swung out, came back, followed Jonathan into a dip.

"Meaning?" He leaned over her.

"Work." She faced him. "He wants me to commit to another picture. As for the other, he's given up on me romantically. Anyway, I don't think he was ever really serious. I was a habit."

"I'm not so sure about the first, but I can understand the second. You're a habit I don't want to break." He hooked his hands together at the small of her back, turned her slowly, his torso firm against hers. "I want you around forever."

The fire racing through her became localized. "So

how are we going to work that?" She was still reeling from the day, his mother, hers, Grandma Minnie. The awkward talk and laughter that had finally become easy and relaxed.

"You sign on with me instead of Josh."

She pushed slightly away, glanced over his shoulder. The Impala Diane she'd eaten began to feel like lead in her stomach. "I work for you?" She'd expected him to talk marriage. Wasn't that what the poem was about?

"Work *with* me. If anyone is going to do documentaries, I think it should be us."

"You mean you're going to give up the safari camp, forget the tourists?"

"No, I'm going to do that during the high season, and then film during the shoulder seasons."

"Spring and fall. What about the rest of the time?"

"I can see us spending the rest of the time in the U.S. promoting the whole thing."

"Us?"

"You and me, of course."

"Of course," she murmured. So poetry was only a means of pleasing the old folks, not a commitment to marriage. She pulled away slightly.

"It would be a natural. Wildlife Safari films, with the noted American talk show host, Sela Clay."

Had she missed a beat in the music, notes played that she'd ignored? She frowned, looked over his shoulder to the people watching from their dinner tables. Why wasn't he talking marriage now? That had been in the plans. She followed him through a flashy finale, her feet and legs moving in a forced pattern, but nothing said she had to conform to his ideas of love, she thought, forcing a smile that skimmed over him. Her mind was nagging at her and, before the band began the next song, she walked off the floor.

He followed her to the table, held her chair, sat close to her.

"I expect you have the work contracts drawn up," she said, toying with her wineglass, the liquid ruby red and fine tasting but suddenly turning to rust in her mouth. The wine steward jumped forward, poured the rest of the bottle, the best of the local vineyards.

"Not yet." Jonathan clicked his glass against hers. "That depends upon you. If I have to learn American slang, I'll expect you to say bloody at the proper times."

"It sounds as if you have it all worked out."

"Yes, I want to spend the rest of my life with you. It doesn't matter what the differences are between us, we'll work them out."

She forced a laugh. "You make it sound simple."

He chuckled and then he said, "Let's get out of here. I want to kiss you, and I expect all the people watching would be shocked."

"All those proper British people would be, but the Americans would probably applaud," she said, her voice so crisp that he raised his eyebrows, and the thought zipped through her that she wanted to be kissed so much that it was like a mantra repeating in her mind: But did Jonathan really want to marry her? Despite everything she'd said and done, she was an old-fashioned girl, ready for that ring on her finger.

He led her out to the hall and through the glorious white and green lobby, to the grounds where Zimbabwe's sky flashed a million stars. A midnight sky. "Your father said if I tried to pay a bride price he'd deck me. I take it that means knock me down." He held out his arm.

She took it and suppressed the urge to pinch it. "If I didn't first." So he wanted a full-time, live-in partner, one who would help him succeed in a world that she knew more about than he did. Well, he certainly had another thing coming, she thought.

Then he turned her into his arms and kissed her.

A couple sitting on the verandah smiled.

Rapidly, he led her down into the gardens. The sweet scent of hundreds of unseen blooms shed their perfume to the air. Letting him snuggle her closer into his arms, she muttered, "Tell me more about this wonderful partnership. Do I keep my American citizenship."

"Yes, and I keep mine in Zimbabwe. The only thing I've been wondering about, do you want to get married, while your family is here?"

"Marry?" she cried.

"Of course, what else did you think this all means?"

His kiss traveled from her ear down her neck.

"Nothing, nothing at all," she muttered. "A wedding here is a marvelous idea," she added, all doubts fleeing like scavengers when a predator approached. "A melding of the old and the new."

"Yes." His lips found hers. She let her own emotions answer him in a quivering crescendo of hugs and kisses. "We could get married here on the lawn." The ceremony played in her mind.

"Native dancers and you in a long white American gown. Flower girls and Shona traditions. I was impressed with your grandmother's knowledge about the beer and poetry."

Sela grinned. "You know, I was afraid you were backing out, that you weren't thinking of marriage, with all that talk about working together. So when my folks arrived, I decided to hedge my bets."

"What do you mean?"

"I told Grandma Minnie about the beer and poetry and she took it from there."

Jonathan looked startled and then, slowly, he began to laugh.

Sela joined him, fastening her arms around his neck as if she would never let go, knowing the rainbow they'd found was far-reaching enough to span an ocean, make little of problems. Anyway, the magic of the midnight sky would shed light on their lives forever.

About The Author

Crystal Barouche is the pseudonym for a multipublished writer. Born in Ohio, the world traveler has also been a creative writing teacher as well as newspaper feature writer and a magazine columnist. She lives in Roseville, California with her family.

Look for these upcoming Arabesque titles:

January 1998
WITH THIS KISS by Candice Poarch
NIGHT SECRETS by Doris Johnson
SIMPLY IRRESISTIBLE by Geri Guillaume
NIGHT TO REMEMBER by Niqui Stanhope

February 1998
HEART OF THE FALCON by Francis Ray
A PRIVATE AFFAIR by Donna Hill
RENDEZVOUS by Bridget Anderson
I DO! A Valentine's Day Collection

March 1998
KEEPING SECRETS by Carmen Green
SILVER LOVE by Layle Giusto
PRIVATE LIES by Robyn Amos
SWEET SURRENDER by Angela Winters

SENSUAL AND HEARTWARMING ARABESQUE ROMANCES FEATURE AFRICAN-AMERICAN CHARACTERS!

BEGUILED (0046, $4.99)
by Eboni Snoe
After Raquel agrees to impersonate a missing heiress for just one night, a daring abduction makes her the captive of seductive Nate Bowman. Across the exotic Caribbean seas to the perilous wilds of Central America . . . and into the savage heart of desire, Nate and Raquel play a dangerous game. But soon the masquerade will be over. And will they then lose the one thing that matters most . . . their love?

WHISPERS OF LOVE (0055, $4.99)
by Shirley Hailstock
Robyn Richards had to fake her own death, change her identity, and forever forsake her husband, Grant, after testifying against a crime syndicate. But, five years later, the daughter born after her disappearance is in need of help only Grant can give. Can Robyn maintain her disguise from the ever present threat of the syndicate—and can she keep herself from falling in love all over again?

HAPPILY EVER AFTER (0064, $4.99)
by Rochelle Alers
In a week's time, Lauren Taylor fell madly in love with famed author Cal Samuels and impulsively agreed to be his wife. But when she abruptly left him, it was for reasons she dared not express. Five years later, Cal is back, and the flames of desire are as hot as ever, but, can they start over again and make it work this time?

Available wherever paperbacks are sold, or order direct from the Publisher. Send cover price plus 50¢ per copy for mailing and handling to Penguin USA, P.O. Box 999, c/o Dept. 17109, Bergenfield, NJ 07621. Residents of New York and Tennessee must include sales tax. DO NOT SEND CASH.